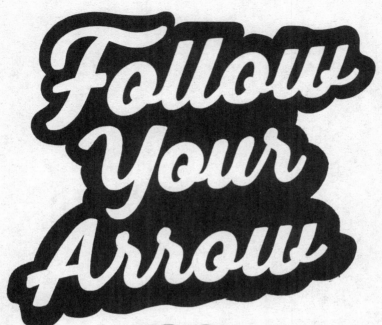

ALSO BY JESSICA VERDI

And She Was

What You Left Behind

The Summer I Wasn't Me

My Life After Now

I'm Not a Girl
(co-written with Maddox Lyons;
illustrated by Dana Simpson)

Follow Your Arrow

JESSICA VERDI

Scholastic Press

New York

Library of Congress Cataloging-in-Publication Data available

ISBN 978-1-338-64046-5

1 2020

Printed in the U.S.A. 23

First edition, March 2021

Book design by Maeve Norton

FOR MARKÉTA SUSAN

@Hi_Im_CeCeRoss: Happy first day of spring!! 🚀 Watch this space at 1 p.m. Eastern TODAY. @SilviaCasRam and I will be going #live with a brand-new, REAL-TIME #unboxing vid! PLUS!!! We have some VERY exciting news to share. Hint: #pride. 🤍 🏳️‍🌈 😄

CHAPTER 1

I study the app post like it's a Renaissance painting, dissecting and analyzing each detail before tapping the button that will send it out to the world. It took me ten minutes of crafting and deleting and rewriting to land on this combination of words and images and emphasis, but I'm still not sure about it.

Do the all-caps and exclamation points convey the right level of enthusiasm, or does the tone tip over into annoying? And I purposely limited the hashtags to three, because too many and people will just scroll right by instead of putting in the effort to read, but maybe I should have hashtagged #spring and #news too? For discoverability? And the emojis . . . I love emojis, but sometimes I wonder if everyone else in the world is over them and I'm showing how out of touch I am when I use them too much. Not that anyone's said, "Hey, CeCe, you might want to rethink how many emojis you use" or anything. I just . . . I don't know. I worry.

"Does this look okay?" I ask Silvie, holding the screen out. We're lying on the floor in her room—our usual hangout spot. My leg is draped over hers, and we're both scrolling on our phones—our usual position.

Silvie's room is spacious, artfully designed, and looks like an

#ad. Lots of white furniture, framed photography, and intentional pops of color. We spend most of our time at Silvie's house, especially on weekends when my mom's working long hours, or when we have a video to record or a livestream to do, like today. The sleek lines and bright light of her bedroom make for a way more professional backdrop than the chaos of mine.

Silvie skims my post draft in one point five seconds, then glances back at me. "Looks good. Why haven't you posted it yet?"

"I needed to get it right."

She rolls her eyes. "Ceece, we go live in"—she checks the time on her own phone—"ten minutes. Just post it; it doesn't need to be perfect."

She doesn't get it. She could post *Hey. Live video at 1. Watch it.* and get fifty thousand likes and a hundred new followers within minutes. Everyone loves Silvia Castillo Ramírez.

I, on the other hand, have had to work incredibly hard to get people to like me and care about what I have to say.

I hold my breath and tap POST. "Okay. Done."

Silvie goes back to scrolling.

When I first joined social media in seventh grade, @Hi_Im_CeCeRoss was a lot different than it is now. Not only my follower count and reach, but the content itself. The few people who actually read my posts probably got a kick out of the twelve-year-old white girl in the Midwest going on epic rants about #gerrymandering and #prisonreform and #healthcarepolicies. But I'd been fighting against my father's conservative beliefs pretty much since I was old enough to speak.

It was not only all I knew; it was *who I was*. And at first, the app felt like a natural extension of that: a chance to express my views without my dad telling me I was wrong, or that I'd understand when I was older, or that I was embarrassing myself. I didn't edit, didn't self-censor, didn't obsess. I posted whatever was on my mind.

But then my father left.

And everything changed.

Suddenly I didn't want to be The Girl with All the Opinions anymore, the girl who was so strong-willed, so defiant, it had torn her family apart. I just wanted to be happy, for once. I wanted—needed—a chance to breathe.

When Silvie and I met, she already had a following online— people actually *listened* to her, looked to her for her thoughts and perspective. Sure, her feed was mainly about stuff like #fashion and #style, but still. She was happy.

So I followed her lead.

For over two years now, I've done everything I can to make it look like my life is as shiny and special as Silvie's. And that's the thing about social media: You get to decide how people see you. You *can* become a casual, confident, carefree girl with more friends than she can keep track of and not a single problem to be seen. Every post, each comment, is another stitch in the tapestry of my online world. A heavily filtered selfie here, a post with a potentially controversial opinion edited out before being posted there, and about a zillion tongue-biting, sugary-sweet replies to haters. And honestly, even the haters are tolerable, because #lifestyle influencing might invite eye rolls, but it rarely invites the vitriol that fighting over immigration policies does. It certainly doesn't lead to shouting matches so intense they make the walls of your house shake. It doesn't stretch the limits of family, and it doesn't result in divorce.

"You really need to stop overanalyzing everything," Silvie says, clicking her phone off, untangling her leg from mine, and standing to stretch. It's an unseasonably warm day for late March in Cincinnati, but the loss of skin-to-skin contact sends an instant shiver over me. "It's not good for you."

That's where she's wrong.

Overanalyzing—though I prefer to call it *curating*—has *worked*. Silvie may have 1,200,000 followers, but I have 985,000. She might have six sponsorships at the moment, but I have four. We're both continually featured on Famous Birthdays's "trending influencers" list.

Life isn't perfect, the *world* isn't perfect, but the time I spend on the app is as close to perfect as I've found. It's my loophole. And I'd like to keep it.

Speaking of, I need to retouch my makeup before we go live. I sit at Silvie's vanity and uncap the eyeliner I keep at her house, while she comes up behind me and grabs her brush. People often do double takes when they meet my girlfriend in person for the first time, because her combination of blue-green eyes, dark hair, and olive skin is unexpected. But those same people invariably go back for a third and fourth glance. Silvie is truly one of the most beautiful people most of us have ever seen, even online.

I, along with most of the world, am a little more ordinary-looking than Silvie. But in moments like this, studying our side-by-side reflections, it's not hard to see what our fans see: Silvie and I don't only look good together; we look like we *go* together. Our hair is almost the same shade of dark brown— Silvie's long, mine falling in a blunt bob to just above my chin. And even though Silvie's seven inches taller than me, we *fit*. My skin is pale, and my eyes are a basic brown, but I think I have nice eyebrows and shoulders, and my earlobes are just the right shape for earrings. The ones I'm wearing right now are little yellow dangly houses; they were a birthday gift from Silvie last year. Silvie's wearing the LESBIAN LIKE WHOA T-shirt she got at a thrift store.

She finishes fixing her loose side pony, and I wordlessly hand her a bottle of hand lotion. Whenever she brushes her hair, she likes to rub a tiny bit of lotion into her hands, then gently tamp down the frizzies on the top of her head. After being together for over two years, we know each other's quirks like they're our own.

"This stuff is the best, isn't it?" she says as she squeezes a small amount of lotion into her palm and massages her hands together.

"What, the hand cream?" I lean closer to the mirror and dab some of Silvie's coral-tinted lip gloss onto my lips.

"Yeah, all the Dana & Leslie stuff. It's insane that they're not more mainstream."

"Well, that's what they have you for." I give her a smile, then quickly devote my attention to applying a pointless second layer of lip gloss.

Dana & Leslie is the gender-inclusive, organic, cruelty-free skincare brand Silvie's an ambassador for. I fully support their mission, and the partnership has been great for Silvie, but if I'm being honest, I can't stand the cloying smell of that lotion. And the face wash dried my skin out.

I've been avoiding sharing my opinions on Dana & Leslie with Silvie, because she's really proud of her collaboration with them, and I don't want to start a fight or come across as unsupportive. I even purposely left all the products she gave me out in plain view on my bedside table at home just so she would see them when she came over.

But I guess I don't have her fooled. She's staring at me, unblinking, in the mirror, clearly waiting for a more emphatic agreement that Dana & Leslie products are, in fact, "the best."

Sigh.

Silvie and I mastered the art of the face-off long ago, and I have no choice but to allow myself to stare back. I know what she's thinking, she knows what I'm thinking, and we both know we're on a moving bus, just a stop or two away from The Argument of the Day.

But we're only four minutes out from one p.m., so Silvie returns the Dana & Leslie lotion to its home on the vanity and wordlessly finishes her hair.

"Looks nice," I say gently, an attempt at keeping the atmosphere light.

Silvie and I have always bickered. It used to be a point of pride for me. It proved, I thought, that you can be in a committed, long-term relationship with another person but still have your own thoughts and opinions, likes and dislikes. Like this painting I saw once at a museum of two people forehead to forehead, balancing on a board placed on top of a ball. I remember thinking that, apart from it being a man and a woman in the painting, the depiction could have been me and Silvie. Two individuals, each unique and strong-willed, yet when they're together, perfectly balanced. Not halves of a whole, but two wholes who do better together than apart.

Lately, though, the board has tipped, and our balance is off. It seems every little thing I've said or done these last few days has annoyed Silvie. She hasn't been smiling as much, hasn't been finding excuses to touch or hug or kiss me all the time like she used to. The bickering has turned into arguing, and the arguments are taking longer and longer to rebound from.

I know she's stressed about the prom planning. It's part of her responsibilities as president of our school's Gender and Sexuality Alliance (I'm vice president—our dynamic is nothing if not consistent). Silvie and I had planned to spend this afternoon brainstorming not-cheesy prom theme ideas to bring to our next GSA meeting. We also wanted to put out feelers to @DJRio, a Chicago-based DJ who follows us both on the app, to see if he'd consider DJing our prom. But I can't help but feel like there's something else going on with her.

"Just don't post about it," she says finally, her tone clipped.

"Post about what?"

"That you don't like the Dana & Leslie products. It was really nice of them to send extra freebies for you."

In one second flat, the air in the room goes stale.

"Are you kidding me?" I splutter.

"What?"

"Since when do I post about stuff like that?"

This makes no sense. I don't post *anything* without double- and triple-checking it. I would never do anything to jeopardize Silvie's career, or the work we both do, or *our freaking relationship*.

She knows that. But all she says is "Just saying."

"Right, okay." I mimic the action of typing on my phone and pretend to read aloud. "Hey, just thought you'd all like to know that Dana & Leslie, the company my girlfriend, Silvia Castillo Ramírez, is an ambassador for, is overpriced garbage and I don't know why anyone would ever want to use the stuff. 'K' byeeee!"

I wait for her to apologize. Laugh at the ridiculousness of it. She doesn't. She simply picks up her phone again and asks, her voice flat, "Ready to go live?"

NO, I'm not ready to go live, I want to retort. *You're being a brat and really unfair and we need to talk about this.*

But it's one o'clock. We have work to do.

I check my teeth in the reflective, silvery material of my phone case, and nod. Without further discussion, we sit on Silvie's bed. Our bodies inch closer together and our smiles appear. Silvie hits the GO LIVE button.

"Hey, everyone!" I say, giving a little wave as the screen projects our images back to us.

"Happy Saturday!" Silvie says.

"And happy spring!" I add. Today is March 20, the official

first day of spring. I *love* spring. The hours of sunlight stretch longer, you can wear dresses without tights underneath, and avocados are in season again.

"Oh yeah! Spring break is only three weeks away!" Silvie says. "I'm going to Mexico to visit my grandparents, and we have plans to spend a few days at the beach. I cannot *wait*."

"Bring me back a seashell?" I squeeze her hand, and she laughs.

"I'll bring you a hundred seashells, babe." She looks at me with hearts in her eyes, and I take my first real breath since the lotion debacle. *We're back at equilibrium*, I think with no small measure of relief. *It was just bickering, not fighting. She's not mad at me. Everything's fine.*

"We have lots to share today, so let's get to it, shall we?" Silvie says.

"Yes, let's!" I slide a sealed brown box across the bed into the camera frame and grab scissors from Silvie's nightstand. "This package just arrived this morning from an awesome new company called Benevolence." Silvie holds the camera steady as I slice the packing tape open. Our followers *love* a good #unboxing vid, and I have to admit, I do too. There's something inherently relatable about the feeling you get when a new package arrives on your doorstep, the little thrill that zips through you as you open it up, eager for its secrets to be revealed. Will the item inside match your expectations? Will it fit? Will it be the right color? Or maybe it's a gift from someone, and you have no idea what you'll find beneath the cardboard box flaps.

Silvie and I don't have an official commission-based or pay-for-posts arrangement with Benevolence, but companies often send us free stuff in the hopes that we'll share the products on our app accounts. We almost always do. Once or twice we decided not to because the company that sent the stuff was well-known for supporting politicians whose values didn't align with our own, but that doesn't happen often.

I remove the packing materials and extract the pieces of clothing one by one, holding them up for the camera. Scrunchy blue socks. A soft tank top in a red-and-white geometric pattern. A forest-green cropped-length hoodie. A pair of mustard-yellow short-shorts with white polka dots.

"Oooh, give me those!" Silvie says, propping the phone up on her nightstand so she's free to duck out of frame and try the shorts on.

I keep talking, keep describing the clothes to our over 70,000 real-time viewers. "This stuff is super cute," I say honestly. "And the best part is it's all eco-friendly." I take the little information card out of the box and read aloud. "Benevolence clothing is made from one hundred percent hemp, which requires fewer chemicals and much less water than cotton to produce."

I have a captive audience—I could totally take this opportunity to talk more about the importance of choosing carbon-neutral and sustainable products when buying new, but I don't. Environmental efforts are considered political, and I make sure to keep politics far away from my content.

"Everything is so *soft*!" I say instead, sliding the fabric of the tank top between my thumb and pointer finger. "I bet this would look great under a pair of overalls."

Silvie pops back into the shot, doing a spin and showing off the shorts, which fit her perfectly, surprising literally no one. Her legs are so long that shorts *always* look good on her. The girl is like a freaking mannequin.

"These shorts are mine now, thank youuu," she says with an adorable gleam in her eye.

"You look amazing, babe," I tell her, and she grins.

She picks up the phone again and leaps onto the bed beside me, bouncing us both. "Okay! Ready for the other big news?"

"Yes!" I say eagerly, though of course I already know what she's about to say.

"June is a little over two months away, and you know what June is?" She grins at me.

"June is Pride month!" I reply.

"Yup! Each year, throughout the month of June, Pride parades and celebrations are held in cities across the world." Silvie's facing the camera again. "And . . ."

She pauses for dramatic effect, and I do a little drumroll sound.

"CeCe and I have been asked to *lead* this year's march on Cincinnati! We're going to be the grand marshals at our hometown Pride parade on June fifth!" She sends up a confetti filter over our faces.

"Not only that," I add, "but we've been asked to give a speech at the pre-march rally!"

Talk about #goals. By its nature, this event will be slightly more political than our usual thing, which is a little scary. But I've worked so hard to get people to like me, and this invite is proof that I've made it. People want to hear me and Silvie speak. They care what we have to say. Even just the *idea* of that is a dream for me. How could I say no? And besides, Silvie and I will be doing it together, standing side by side, addressing a crowd full of allies with a speech we both wrote.

Silvie gives our now 78,000 real-time viewers a few more details and sets a countdown clock on her app profile. "We still have some time before the event, obviously," she says, "but mark your calendars if you live in the Cincinnati area! We want to meet as many of you as we can!"

We end the live session the same way we always do: I throw an arm around her and kiss her on the cheek. Sometimes Silvie kisses me in these moments, and sometimes I kiss her. But it's always on the cheek, and always right before we sign off.

The feed stops.

"Hey, I'm sorry about earlier . . ." I begin lightly, riding the high from our announcement, but Silvie pulls away.

And just like that, the energy bleeds from the room, seeping under the door and through the air conditioner vents.

She'd only been pretending everything was normal during the live feed; I see that now. I should have seen it earlier, but I wanted everything to be fine so badly that I chose to pretend her way-too-fast mood shift was real.

Silently, Silvie adds the video to her stories stream and tags me, then starts scrolling mindlessly, her eyes affixed to the screen.

"What's wrong?" I ask after a moment. It comes out whinier than I'd planned. I want to add, *Don't make me guess. Just talk to me—we'll figure it out. I love you.* But I don't say anything more.

She shakes her head. "Forget it."

"Forget what?" I honestly don't even know what we're talking about anymore.

"Nothing. I don't want to talk about it."

"But I *do* want to talk about it." I need answers. Clarity.

Silvie doesn't say anything. She's still looking down at her phone, scrolling so quickly I know she's not actually absorbing the posts.

"I'm sorry I don't like the Dana & Leslie stuff, okay?" I continue. "But is that a requirement? That we have to like all the same things?"

"Of course not."

"So what, then?"

"I don't know," she mumbles after a beat. Still not looking at me. Still avoiding me.

"You *do* know," I press, starting to feel like I'm *asking* for her to yell at me. "Something is on your mind, Silvie. Just tell me."

"I don't want to!" she finally blurts, clicking her phone off and dropping it onto her bedspread. "Stop pushing me!"

I gape at her. "Pushing you? I'm not *pushing* you! I'm trying to catch up to wherever it is *you* are. You keep snapping at me. I just want to know what I did to make you so mad at me."

"I'm *not* mad at you," she says. "I already said I wasn't mad at you. Jeez, CeCe."

"Well, you didn't say that, actually," I half shout. "But how about *I'm* mad at *you* now?"

She has the audacity to look shocked at that. "For what?"

"Silvie, you just accused me of planning to trash-talk both you and an entire company online. For literally *zero* reason. Don't you know me at *all*?"

"I didn't mean that, all right?" Her chest rises and falls with a shuddering breath. "Can you just let it go? Please?"

Let it go. I've gotten really good at letting things go over the years. I know how to put my feelings aside for the sake of keeping the peace. I know how to shut up and smile when all I want to do is scream. I just didn't think Silvie would ever request that of me.

"No." My voice comes out on a strange waver, as if I'm battling to stay upright on a tightrope. "I think I deserve an explanation."

The seconds pass.

Eventually she nods, like she's decided to give in.

I wait, anticipating some semblance of an explanation.

But that's not what I get. Out of nowhere, Silvie pitches forward and kisses me. It's not what I was expecting, but, hey, I can roll with this. I immediately slide closer, kissing her back. We've done this countless times; I know the give of her lips, the curves of her face, the taste of her lavender tea obsession so well they've become a part of me.

But this kiss . . .

It's different.

Oddly, it reminds me of our very first one, when we were

younger and pent up with not only those unbearable, impossible-to-articulate feelings of unexplored need, but also that added layer that all queer kids have to deal with. That feeling of something akin to delicious danger. Of everything feeling so freaking *right* for once, even with all the people telling you it's wrong.

This kiss isn't that, exactly. But it is just as loaded.

And it stops as suddenly as it began.

Silvie pulls back, putting her palms out to carve some distance between us.

"We need to talk, Ceece," she whispers, picking at the stitching of the bedspread. Her lips are still pink and the tiniest bit swollen from our kiss.

"That's what I've been trying to do," I insist.

"I really wasn't planning on doing this today," she continues, almost to herself.

My stomach grows cold. "Doing what?"

She turns her phone over, so the screen is facedown, and she finally, *finally* looks at me fully. Her meaning is crystal clear in her eyes.

Need to talk. Wasn't planning on doing this.

I suddenly feel woozy, like I've been pitched headfirst over a precipice. I leap off the bed just to feel the sturdy floor beneath my feet.

"No." Only after the word is out there in the room do I realize I'm the one who whispered it.

@happyfaceJen: Looove that tank top. 👆 For sure going to check out #benevolence's stuff!

@TaylorMarie_1: #Cevie is my #OTP

@mac_0_0: Where's my #straightpride parade???

@SoussssChef: I live in Columbus but I will DEFINITELY be at Cincinnati Pride this year!!!! Best news ever!!

@Monica1864: You ladies are TOO CUTE I can't stand it! 💗🖤💗💗💗

@glamupanddown: Love your earrings, CeCe!

@XmasElf1225: Happy spring, CeCe and Silvie!

CHAPTER 2

Silvie blinks. "No?" she echoes.

"No," I say again, louder this time. "I mean—" I toss my phone onto the bed and push my hair off my face. *"NO."*

Silvie and I met two and a half years ago, on the second day of freshman year, at the inaugural meeting of Neil Armstrong High School's brand-new Gender and Sexuality Alliance. Silvie wasn't out yet, and I was only out to my mom. It was like we'd been waiting to find each other. Because after we met, everything fell into place.

Our hands linked. Just like that, almost on their own. No discussion, no putting out feelers with our friends to see if she'd told anyone she liked me. I'm not sure who reached out first, but there it was—Silvie's fingers weaved through mine, warm and soft and gripping tightly, at GSA meetings, in the halls between classes, during lunch. Not long after our hands linked, we kissed. And kissed and kissed and kissed. And then we went public—first to our families, and then online.

At the time, Silvie's followers numbered at around three thousand. Mine were in the hundreds, mostly friends from school. Cut to a couple years later, and the world knows us as "Cevie," one of the internet's most beloved #OTPs.

It can't be over. *We* can't be. We still love each other. There's still so much more to do. More world to conquer.

"CeCe . . ." Silvie's saying. "I think . . ."

I step away from her and begin to pace, treading invisible patterns into the teal rug she bought for selfie-taking purposes. The color almost exactly matches her eyes. *Don't say it, Silvie. Please.*

But apparently she's made her decision. She brings the knife down so easily it's like she's cutting through water. "I think we need to break up."

A gasp leaves my body, and it sounds a little like *"Why?"*

Silvie keeps picking at the bedspread. I want to tell her to stop, that she'll ruin it. "I really hadn't planned on . . . But you pushed . . ."

"I didn't push." My voice is as weak as I feel.

"Okay, you *asked*. Better?"

"Not really."

She ignores that. "Lately things between us have been . . ." She searches for a moment. "Work."

"Work?" I repeat, feeling like I've been punched. That's not what I expected her to say. *Different*, maybe. Or *harder*. But *work*? That's just mean.

My heart, so full since the day Silvie and I met, springs a slow, painful leak.

"You haven't felt it?" she asks again, clearly still hoping for backup.

"No," I say. "Not that." The truth is that even with the shifts,

18

the tilted balance, Silvie has always remained a "want to," never a "have to" for me. I take a breath and try to keep my emotions in check.

"Oh, Ceece." Her voice cracks, and I risk a glance at her. She's gazing at me with shattered-window eyes. "You know we've always fought."

"Bickered," I correct. "But we've had fun too, haven't we?"

"*So* much fun," Silvie agrees quickly. Reaching for my hands, her still sitting, me still standing, she threads our fingers together. These hands have grasped each other countless times, through romance and exploration, joy and laughter, anger and fear and disappointment. I want to pull away. Or more like, I want to *want* to pull away. I hate that I cling to her tighter, even as she's in the process of breaking my heart. "When was the last time we laughed, though? Like *really* laughed, not for the camera."

At first, I assume it's a rhetorical question, so I just nod to let her know I'm following, but she's searching my face, expecting an answer.

"Oh." I think back. "I can't remember, actually." Silvie and I used to laugh constantly. About all kinds of stuff, whether it was truly funny or not—we were just so *giddy* all the time. I know that doesn't happen as much anymore, but . . .

"Something's missing, babe," she says, her broken-glass eyes shimmering.

"What is it?"

"What?"

"The thing that's missing. What is it?" I know I sound frantic. But maybe if she names it, I can find it and bring it back. "It's not attraction. Or admiration. Or love. Those things are all still there—for me, at least." I clear my throat.

"I don't know," she says, neither confirming nor denying that those things are, in fact, still there for her.

"Was it something I did? Or didn't do?" I ask. She said it was "work." But did she really mean *I* was work? Was I too difficult, too opinionated? Did she decide I wasn't worth the effort, just like my dad did?

"No. CeCe, of course not. It's just . . . a feeling." An unnamed feeling that's about to change our lives. "I really wish you were feeling it too," she says quietly.

"Well, I'm not." The words come out clipped. Part of me wants to be nicer, to recognize that this is hard for her. But why should I?

Silvie brushes her thumbs back and forth across my hands, leaving light tingles in their path. One of us needs to let go. Neither of us does.

Could this really be the last time I'll be allowed to touch her like this?

When did everything change?

Her fingers are longer than mine, her nails short and bare, as always. But she wears rings on almost every finger, the same ones every day; I can identify each one just by touch. "How long have you been feeling this way?" I ask, needing the answer but not wanting it.

20

She shrugs. The obvious effort it takes adds to the air of exhaustion surrounding her. "I don't know. Three months, maybe?"

I suck in a breath. *Three months?*

Stark reality spreads from my heart through the rest of me, up my throat and behind my eyes.

Three months ago, my mom and I spent Christmas Day at Silvie's house, with her family. Three months ago, Silvie and I were researching which colleges would be right for both of us, because we didn't want to have to spend four whole years living apart.

Two months ago, we went to New York to visit her brother at school. In the light of the setting sun on the Brooklyn Bridge, we attached a padlock to the railing. CECILIA + SILVIA FOREVER, it proclaimed in pink nail polish. We threw the key over the side and watched as it vanished into the river—I told myself that for one time only, romance conquered littering. We held each other and kissed and marveled at how perfect the moment was, as snowflakes twirled in the air around us.

One month ago, a famous fashion designer asked me and Silvie to model for his #LoveIsLove collection. We had a blast, standing side by side in front of the pristine white backdrop, dressed in expensive, tailored clothes and shiny platform shoes, our fingers intertwined, laughing and goofing around for the camera. I got one of the prints framed and gave it to Silvie for her birthday. She hung it right next to her vanity, and said it was so she wouldn't go a day without looking at it.

And while all of this was happening, she already knew she didn't want to be with me anymore?

I look at Silvie's vanity now, where the photo still hangs. It goes blurry as my eyes flood.

Here I was, thinking I was all savvy and perceptive, that I was so in tune with Silvie that I noticed the moment her feelings started to change. But apparently she's had the wool pulled over my eyes for a long time.

"Why didn't you say anything before now?"

"How was I supposed to?" Her voice trembles as it rises in volume. "It's not just us in this relationship, CeCe. Cevie is so much bigger than you and me."

She untwines our hands and stands, reaching out to cup my face now. I step back. "So you stayed with me, even though you didn't want to, because of our *fans*?" It's such a punch to the gut.

"Honestly? I was hoping things would get better between us and I wouldn't have to say anything." She sounds tired.

Of course she's tired. That's what happens when you keep your feelings secret for so long—it wears you down. After the countless DMs I've exchanged with teens who are terrified to come out of the closet, who are certain that if their parents find out their truth, they'll lose everything, I know that better than anyone.

The tears begin to fall freely, dripping off my chin and landing on my shirt, as if trying to feed life into the pile of dust that was once my heart.

I want to protest, fight back; it's what I'm best at.

I wish I could kiss her again. But somehow, somewhere in the span of the last few minutes, I lost that privilege.

Things are changing so fast. Too fast.

"It's really hard sometimes, you know?" she whispers. "Everything is always about Cevie. I've been out for over two years, and we've been Cevie that whole time. I don't know who I am without you. Without us. I think I need to figure that out."

So that's the "feeling." She did know how to name it after all.

"I understand," I say flatly.

She pulls me to her, not for a kiss, but a hug. I give in and squeeze her back; how can I not? I'll always give her anything she wants. Even this.

Her body shudders in gratitude, and she sniffles against the top of my head. Apparently we've run out of words, because we lapse into silence. A long, important silence. I grip her even more tightly. She clings back.

Sometime later, we untwine ourselves, wipe our tears away, and walk down the quiet hall.

"Headed home, CeCe?" Silvie's mom calls from her home office as we pass her door.

I glance at Silvie. She gives a slight shake of her head, a reassurance that we don't have to tell her mom right now. She'll deal with it later.

"Yup," I say not quite normally, stepping back into the office doorway and giving Verónica a quick wave. "Thanks for having me."

"Anytime." She swivels around in her desk chair to face me

more fully. "You haven't changed your mind about coming with us, have you? You know the invitation still stands."

She's talking about their family's spring break trip to Mexico; they'd invited me to come with them a couple months ago but I felt bad about the idea of leaving Mom alone for a week. Apart from the weekend in New York with Silvie this past winter, I haven't done much traveling at all. Not since the Disney World trip with my parents when I was seven. They fought the entire time; Dad blamed Mom for booking a trip they couldn't afford, and Mom blamed Dad for not putting even a penny's worth of value on our family's happiness. It was a blast, let me tell you.

"Thank you so much. Maybe, um, next year." Shivers prickle across my skin with the lie.

Verónica smiles, all warm and unassuming. "Of course. Bye, honey, see you soon." She swivels back to her computer.

But I won't be back here anytime, and I *won't* see her soon. The stark finality of the ordinary words is too much. Tears spring to my eyes and I make a beeline for the front door but stop short on the little foyer mat, staring at a doorknob I have no interest in turning.

Silvie reaches around me. Unlocks the lock. Opens the door. She opens her mouth too, but doesn't speak.

I don't know what to say either. We're in no-person's-land, hovering here by this doorway. Like we're on a layover at an airport in a foreign country but because we haven't gone through customs, we're not *actually* in the country. Until I cross this threshold, we're not broken up yet. We're still here, together, on

24

the ground but without the passport stamp that makes it official.

But I should leave before any of Silvie's other family members have the chance to interrupt. This goodbye needs to be just us.

I reach out to twirl the end of her ponytail around my fingers, trying to memorize the feel of it. Forcing a little smile, I say, "See you online?"

She smiles back. "See you online."

I step outside and, with a gentle click, the door closes behind me.

@AussieMackenzie: Happy #autumn, my southern hemisphere lovelies! In honour of our remarkable planet, which continues to provide so generously, despite humanity's lack of mutual respect, I got up early to meditate and watch the sun rise at #BronteBeach. How do you plan to spend your day? Let me know in the comments! Peace and love!

CHAPTER 3

Silvie and I broke up.

I one-thumb-type the text to Mackenzie as I walk slowly home from Silvie's house. For once, I'm not in the mood for emojis.

Normally Mack would still be asleep at this time of day—she lives in Sydney, so she's perpetually fifteen hours ahead of me (and sixteen during daylight saving time), and she's *very* stringent about her sleep. But she posted on the app seventeen minutes ago, so I know she's up.

At nineteen, Mackenzie is one of the most famous influencers in the world. Her brand is very New Agey; she's always posting pictures of herself doing arabesques on literal mountaintops, or filling homemade tea satchels, or creating crystal grids. And she's beyond gorgeous too: strong and tall with lots of curves, sun-kissed skin, long eyelashes, and shiny hair.

I only started following her because that's what you do in this business—you follow each other, pick up posting trends from each other, repost each other's stuff as if there's no competition between you at all.

But one day, after a mass shooting in Maine, Mackenzie went live on the app and let loose a profanity-riddled rant about Americans having an obligation to put more rigid firearm restrictions into place, like Australia did. The call to action was fierce, compelling, and totally off brand for her. I immediately DM'd her to let her know how much I loved it. How I felt the exact same way, even if I didn't say so publicly.

We've been best friends ever since.

Her typing bubble activates and I exhale in relief.

What?!?! she's written. OMG WHY. HOW. WHEN!?!

Like a half hour ago. She said she wasn't planning to do it today, but we got into a stupid fight and it all came out. She said she'd been thinking about it for a while and she wants to find out who she is away from Cevie. I don't answer the "why." I'm still trying to figure that one out for myself.

Oh CeCe I'm so sorry. 😭 💔 Are you ok??

I don't know. I think I'm still in shock. And then I say the thing I haven't been able to stop thinking since leaving Silvie's house: She could still change her mind, right? That's not totally impossible?

Change her mind about breaking up? Mack replies.

Yeah, I mean, maybe she THOUGHT she wanted to break up, but now that it's real she's second-guessing herself?

I checked Silvie's app page just before texting Mack. She hasn't posted about the breakup yet—and maybe that's what's given me hope. She's not sure about it anymore.

After a pause, Mack writes, You and Silvie have always been so simpatico.

I sniffle. Like 🐾 🐾

Mack sends back a smiley. Exactly. So don't you think you should...trust her?

What do you mean? Trust that she'll come back to me?

No, I mean...trust that if she said she wanted to break up, she probably meant it. 😞

Why do I like Mackenzie again?

But deep down I know she's right. Silvie isn't coming back. I wouldn't be feeling this way otherwise.

Yeah. Ok, I text back.

After a moment, Mack asks, So...are you going to post about it?

I guess I'll have to eventually. Dreading it. I wish Silvie would post about it first.

Maybe it would all feel more real then, and I'd have a better idea of what to say.

Take your time, babes. I'm here for you when you're ready. 🖤

I push open the front door of my house, and our scruffy mess of a mutt, Abraham, comes trotting over, tail wagging as if everything in the world is just *the best ever*. I bend down to scoop him up and nuzzle my nose in his neck fur as we make our way upstairs to my room. Abe is the best cuddler on earth, and I can't think of a better salve right now.

We curl up together on top of my royal-purple duvet cover with the giant image of Captain Marvel on it. I check Silvie's app page again. Her most recent post is still the no-longer-live session we did earlier. I share the video to my own page, more out of habit than anything else, and shove the phone under my pillow.

My room is the only space in my life, online or off, that

reflects the person I used to be. I should really change it, but I haven't been able to bring myself to.

Rainbows are everywhere, including the ceiling, which is draped with oversized Pride flags. (To be fair, I loved rainbows even before I realized I was bisexual. I've always gravitated toward bright colors, and rainbows are so happy-making.) My closet door is perpetually open, and the rack inside bursts with color and tulle and sparkle. Shoes are everywhere too—in the shoe cubbies but also in heaps on the floor, lined up on the windowsill, sticking out from under the bed.

On the top shelf of my bookcase sits a shrine made up of six prayer candles, each with a different idol's image: Michelle Obama, Malala Yousafzai, Ruth Bader Ginsburg, Janet Mock, Jonathan Van Ness, and Elizabeth Warren.

The biggest wall is covered from corner to corner with protest signs from marches I participated in before I got internet famous. GIRLS JUST WANT TO HAVE FUN(DAMENTAL RIGHTS)! HUMAN BEINGS ARE NOT ILLEGAL! WE'RE HERE, WE'RE GENDER- AND SEXUALITY-VARIANT, GET USED TO IT! THERE IS NO PLANET B! THIS IS WHAT DEMOCRACY LOOKS LIKE!

If you searched for "liberal agenda" on a stock photo website and an image of my room came up, you wouldn't think twice. There are plenty of people out there who'd call me cliché, or a lot worse, if they knew this part of me. But they won't get the chance to. They're not going to see my room, and they're never going to know just how hot my blood can get.

When I was ten months old, I said my first words. Not *Mama* or *Dada* or *bye-bye* or *Elmo*. Nope, according to my mom, the first English out of my little toothless mouth was a full-on phrase: "Hey, you!" immediately followed by "No!" Clear, with gusto, and directed at a kid on the playground whom I'd just watched steal a ball from a littler kid. It was like I'd spent enough time watching the world around me; I was done being an observer. I couldn't walk yet, but I had a voice, and I was going to use it for justice, dammit!

The kid gave the ball back.

Even though I don't remember it, I'm pretty sure that moment set my course. Solidified my obsession with setting things right, or at least trying to.

My dad would go on a tirade about why the United States needed a wall along our southern border, and I would fire back about how his "beliefs" were pieced together out of ignorance, racism, and white-man talk radio.

A teacher would send a female student to the office for wearing a tank top that revealed her bra straps, and I'd walk out of class too and demand a meeting with the principal to discuss the school's sexist dress code.

A conservative politician would suddenly start supporting marriage equality after one of his own children came out as gay, and I'd email him, shouting in all caps that it was his job to have a conscience *all* the time, and represent *all* his constituents, not to only be a decent human being when it affected his own family.

I've shouted until my throat was raw, dug my heels in, trying to get the other person to just have some *compassion* already, more times than I can count.

All it got me was after-school detention about six million times, a reputation for being difficult, and a messed-up home life. I know, deep in the core of my bones, that it was my personality, pitted against my father's, that directly contributed to my parents' fracturing. I'm not saying that from an "it's my fault Mom and Dad broke up" kid perspective. It was more than that. Mom didn't love the person Dad had become either, but she was better able to ignore his politics than I was. She could leave a room more easily than I could, knew how to put on her headphones to drown out the sound of the conservative news pundits. I didn't.

So of *course* it was our animosity—his and mine—that lit the flame that blew the family up. I was the instigator of the constant fights, and I was the reason Mom was driven to make a choice. She chose me. He didn't.

After that, I learned my lesson: no more politics, no more divisiveness. Because no matter how many families this stuff breaks up, how many kids on the playground who make sure the other kids know not to make friends with you, how many stomachaches and sleepless nights it gives you, *it never ends.* You never stop being certain that you're right, or hoping that if you stated your case just *one more time,* you'd change the other person's mind.

But you can't. You really, really can't. So what's the point? Why *shouldn't* you take the path of least resistance instead? The path that's wide enough for everyone, as long as they leave their baggage at home. The path that doesn't drive the people in your life away.

Then again, apparently you're never totally safe from being left.

"I'm home, CeCe!" Mom's voice carries up the stairs and through my open bedroom door. "Dinner?"

With a sigh, I sit up and place Abe on the floor. Time to tell Mom about the breakup.

• • •

"Pizza or burritos?" Mom asks from the other end of the couch. She holds up her phone, indicating the food delivery app. I know what she's doing.

A few years ago, during and after the divorce, Mom was so busy with work, and legal stuff, and even more bills than usual, and household upkeep. So, in an effort to help Mom and be useful around the house, even though I was only thirteen and didn't have a driver's license or money of my own yet, I came up with a system. When there were small decisions to be made, daily-minutia type things—the things that, when they add up, can drive you crazy even though they shouldn't—I'd step in and give Mom a choice between two options. Just two. Two is easy. *Cereal or toast? Orange nail polish or blue? Stephen Colbert or Samantha Bee?*

Ever since, the two-choice system has been our go-to whenever the other person is going through a challenging life moment.

"Pizza or burritos?" she asks again, wiggling her feet under the giant comforter we're sharing. The temperature outside dropped again, and we're bundled up in sweats and socks.

Abraham is sprawled out between us, across both of our legs.

He doesn't care what temperature it is, as long as snuggles are involved.

"Not hungry," I mumble into a throw pillow, knowing full well that's not how the two-choice system works. You *have* to pick one.

"CeCe." Mom's voice is soft. With some effort, I peel my tearstained cheek from the couch pillow and glance her way. My heart might be the broken one, but Mom is sad too. She loves Silvie. Loved, I mean. "It sucks," she says. "Believe me, I know. And we *are* going to wallow. But you also need to eat." She waves her phone my way again.

Mom can be such a *mom* sometimes. "Burritos, I guess. Vegan one." I'm not always vegan, but a bunch of cheese and sour cream wouldn't feel great sitting in my gut right now.

A few taps of her screen later, she says, "Done. It'll be here in thirty. Now for the next decision: *Killing Eve* or *The Office*?"

Normally I'd ask which *Office* she's thinking—British or American—but I'm not in the mood for a comedy, either way. And a bloody, murderous, pseudo-lesbian obsession sounds perfect right about now.

"*Killing Eve*. Definitely *Killing Eve*."

Mom hums to herself as she clicks through the streaming app on the TV and selects the show. Mom is *always* singing or humming. Most of the time she doesn't even realize she's doing it. She'll often be humming something, and the tune will inevitably get stuck in my head, and then I'll start singing it, and she'll look up at me, surprised, and say, "That's so funny, that song was in my head too!" As if she had no idea *she's* the one who got it into mine.

Mom and I are both usually all about the pop music. (She even almost named me Britney, as in Spears, but my dad convinced her Cecilia—the name of their favorite Simon and Garfunkel song—was better. That's one thing I can thank him for, I guess.) But right now she's humming something I don't recognize.

"What is that song?" I ask.

"Hmm?" Mom stops scrolling and looks back at me. "What song?"

"The one you're humming. It sounds, like, square-dancey."

"Oh!" She brightens up. "Didn't realize I was humming!" I'd laugh if I could manage it. "It's an old Patsy Cline song. My mother listened to Patsy a lot when I was growing up. I hadn't heard it in years, and then today a young man was playing it on the violin outside the Trader Joe's." She retrieves her bag from the hook by the front door and digs through it. "He had a CD for sale." She holds up the plastic square case.

That's random. "Do we even have a CD player anymore?"

"There's one in my car. Yours too."

"There is?" My car is less than a year old. It's a hybrid because, hello, the environment, but it's not fancy. As soon as I got my driver's license, I bought it with some of the money I'd made from sponsored posts. I literally had no idea it had a CD player. Why would anyone need one?

Mom rolls her eyes. "Yes, Cecilia. Not *everything* has to be done on the internet, you know. You want to borrow the CD? He's really very talented."

She hands the case to me. The cover is a grainy black-and-white photo of a young, dark-haired white guy playing the violin. His right arm—lifted, bow in hand—is partially blocking his face. *Joshua Haim, Violin* is written in nearly illegible cursive font along the top. The whole package needs a redo. No, actually, the whole package needs to be tossed into the garbage. I don't care how talented this guy is—if he expects to reach any degree of success, he needs to get out of the 1990s and put his stuff online.

I shake my head and give the CD back. "I don't like country music."

"It's not all country," Mom says. "There's some classical pieces on there too. But suit yourself." She tucks the disc into her bag and presses PLAY on the TV remote.

It isn't until the doorbell rings sometime later that I realize I've been staring at the shapes on the TV without really seeing them. If things were how they used to be, I would have been texting Silvie Jodie Comer GIFs throughout the episode, and she'd be texting back the fire and drool emojis and her cartoon avatar swooning, and I'd be giggling at my phone, and Mom would tell me to pay attention to the show, and I'd tell her I'm good at multitasking. And then I'd snap a picture of the TV screen, where Sandra and Jodie are the midst of a tension-thick scene, and hashtag it #payattentionMom #itsgettinggood, and thousands of likes would pour in, and everything would be fun.

Then again, if things were how they used to be, we probably would have been watching *The Office.*

Mom and I eat in front of the TV. I try to pay better attention, but my thoughts keep drifting. Spiraling.

I dig my phone out from under the pillow and check the app again. Silvie still hasn't posted.

I scroll over to my own feed, and my heartbeat begins to tumble. Apart from the Pride announcement, which was just a repost, my last original post, the one Silvie had to convince me was okay enough to send out, was *seven hours* ago. That's a whole workday for some people. A decent night's sleep. A season of *Killing Eve.*

I can't remember the last time I went seven waking hours without posting, or the last time my app story was inactive like it is now. There's always Wi-Fi, and always something to share, even on long flights and in dentist office waiting rooms and in the lunchroom at school.

A film of sweat pricks at the back of my neck, despite the low temperature of the room. I need to post something. It's non-negotiable. My followers expect it.

Quickly, I snap a photo of my picked-at burrito. My thumbs fly over the screen as I adjust it with filters and add a couple hashtags. #takeout #momtime #vegan

I mean to click POST, but I stop myself.

What am I doing?

This post is stupid. Nobody follows me for freaking *food* pictures. I delete the draft, and regroup.

"Hey, Mom? Can I post a picture of you?" She's going to say no. She always says no.

She pauses the show and raises one eyebrow. "Why?"

"My story is dark, and I need to get something up there. But I'm not ready to go public with the Silvie stuff yet."

Mom sighs. "CeCe . . ."

"If I post about *Killing Eve,* then people will be expecting Silvie to respond because everyone knows she has heart eyes for Jodie Comer, and then—"

"CeCe." Her tone is equal parts gentle and stern. It's enough to screech my next words to a halt.

I look at her.

"Please be nice to yourself," she says.

"What do you mean?"

She eyes my thumbs, which are still poised midair over the keyboard. "Your photo feed is the last thing you should be worrying about right now."

I wait a moment, hoping her meaning will sift into my brain. She sighs. "You're going through your first major heartbreak, kiddo. That's not a small thing. I think it might be worthwhile to put your own comfort and well-being first for once, instead of worrying about what your followers expect."

I appreciate her taking my heartbreak seriously. I do. Lots of parents would dismiss what I'm feeling right now as puppy love, and tell me to get over it. Mom is the closest person in my life, my only real family, my biggest ally. But even she doesn't entirely get me. She barely even logs on to the app; she doesn't understand that social media *never stops*. That there are always people, in every stretch of the planet, in every time zone, who are scrolling. If you're not visible, you're forgotten. You don't get to just take a break.

I shake my head. "Your job doesn't let you call out 'heartsick.' Neither does mine."

"I'm an adult. You're sixteen. I have a mortgage to pay. A child to feed. You don't."

I decide not to bring up the fact that I pay for my own phone plan and car insurance and clothes and haircuts. Or that I intercept the electric and water bills from the mailbox as often as I can, and pay them before she has a chance to.

When Silvie and I started making real money, my mom and Silvie's parents teamed up and sat us down for a long talk about "responsible finances." After a lot of thought, and a lot of discussion with Silvie and Mom, I came to some decisions about what I wanted to do with my earnings. Half of my checks immediately get donated to causes I deem worthy of support: human, women's, environmental, and animal rights orgs. No one understood why I'd want to give away half of everything I made—Silvie donates too, but not nearly as much as I do. She insists I give away so much because I feel guilty. That I'm trying to make up for not using my platform to fight for social justice issues. I don't know, maybe she's right.

The remaining half is split—25 percent goes to savings (for college), and 25 percent is the Whatever Fund. Sometimes this means helping Mom with expenses, and, okay, fine, sometimes it means going on a shopping spree or buying myself a car. Sue me.

"And," Mom continues, as if sensing what I'm thinking, "you're your own boss. If I worked for myself, you bet your butt I'd call out heartsick if I needed to."

"Yeah," I counter, "but there will always be pets who need vaccines and X-rays." Mom is a vet tech. She wanted to be a veterinarian, but couldn't afford the schooling. And then, when she and Dad split, she had to start working at the animal hospital more, so the timing has never been right. "Your customers will still be there, waiting for you. If I'm not posting and tagging, I'm replaced."

She sighs, eyeing me. "Do we need to have the talk again?"

She's not talking about The Talk that most teens dread having with their parents. Those conversations have always come relatively easily to us. She's talking about our version of the talk: the "the internet is scary and are you *sure* you know what you're doing?" talk.

"No, Mom," I assure her. "We do not have to have the talk again."

Mom lets out a long sigh, then barrels ahead anyway. "I don't love how much personal stuff you share on there."

"Sharing personal stuff is kind of the point." I resist the impulse to roll my eyes. "And there's a lot I *don't* share, you know."

"I realize that. But your last name is public information, and you talk a lot about living in Cincinnati . . ."

"Literally hundreds of thousands of people live in Cincinnati,"

I counter. "The odds of accidentally running into, like, a murderer who also follows me on social are low—"

"Low but not nonexistent."

"And," I keep going, "I never tag my location in posts, unless it's after the fact."

"Even so." Her expression becomes more contemplative and she glances at the way I'm clinging on to the phone. Consciously, I relax my grip. "It's an addiction."

Maybe it is, I admit only to myself. But not all addictions are bad, are they? What about Mackenzie's addiction to outdoor yoga?

But if I want to get Mom off my back, bringing up Mackenzie, with her five million app followers and line of designer juice cleanses, isn't the way.

"You can trust me," I assure her. "I know my limits."

She nods. "I do trust you."

I make a show of clicking my phone screen off and placing it on the coffee table, a little out of arm's reach. "Can we finish the episode now?"

Mom picks up the TV remote, but before she presses PLAY, she eyes me. "You're just going to be thinking about your phone, aren't you?"

"Of course," I admit with as close to a laugh as I've been able to achieve since leaving Silvie's house earlier.

Mom smiles. "All right. Why don't you post a photo of Abe? Don't those posts always get a lot of likes?"

She's not wrong. I snap a few shots of sleepy Abraham, edit

them, and upload a collage. The caption I type is, admittedly, tinged with snark and self-pity, but I let myself have that.

> @Hi_Im_CeCeRoss: This is what unconditional love looks like. 🐻 🤍
>
> #honestAbe #rescuedog #scruffypup #bestfriend

The relief upon tapping POST is instantaneous, if not complete. I'll still have to address the Silvie stuff more directly. But I have some time to work with now.

Later, after the food has been eaten, the dishes put away, episode four of *Killing Eve* queued up for another day, I give Mom a big hug and head up to my room. The overhead light is harsh on my cried-out eyes, so I make do with my little desk lamp.

Today has been an eternity. Was it really just this afternoon that I was kissing Silvie? My heart feels like a stomach after going too long without food—empty and sore and eating away at itself. Silvie was my nourishment.

But it isn't until I catch a glimpse of myself in the mirror that I understand why Mom was so worried. I look horrible.

Dark circles under my eyes, emphasized by the eerie light of the room. Makeup cried off and rubbed away. Lips pale and dry. One of my little yellow houses is gone; it's probably in the couch somewhere. And how appropriate, because that's exactly the look I'm rocking: a girl lost and without a home.

For a whisper of a second, I consider posting a selfie.

Unfiltered, unedited, showing the whole of the internet what I really look like—what I'm really *feeling*. Social media has lately been veering away from the airbrushed, professionally lit, high-def #plandids of the past in favor of more authentic, light-or-no-makeup, shot-on-your-phone candids. If I posted this selfie, it would be a *huge* departure for me, but not necessarily unheard of for social media as a whole . . .

I wish I could do it.

I wish I were brave enough.

I wish I didn't care what they think.

But I do care. And Mom was right when she said life online is dangerous, though not in the ways she thinks. Social media has given me more than I could have ever imagined, but I'd be lying if I said it wasn't also completely terrifying, having people monitor your every step. Cancel culture is rampant, and the world will turn on you so quickly. I've seen it happen—the wrong wording or visual at the wrong moment, and the person loses everything.

There's no way I'm going to risk it. I've lost enough for one day.

I turn out the light, crawl into bed, and click the phone off, sending what remained of my world into total darkness.

@SilviaCasRam: Hi, friends. I have some news to share.

As of today, @Hi_Im_CeCeRoss and I are no longer a couple. I want you all to know that CeCe and I have nothing but love and respect for one another, and we will be friends forever. This was not her fault—it was no one's fault. Sometimes things just change, as much as we wish they wouldn't.

I also want to thank each and every one of you for your support of #Cevie over the past two and a half years. You have given us so much, and it's changed our lives. I can only hope we've done the same for you in return.

#heartbroken

CHAPTER 4

I wake early the next morning. It's not like in the movies when it takes the person a minute to remember all the terrible things that happened the day before—the loss of Silvie was with me in my dreams all night, and it's the first thing on my mind this morning.

Eyes still half-closed, I root around in the blankets until I find my phone. A long list of app notifications clogs up the home screen, but I pay them no mind, because there are two new texts waiting for me.

Has Silvie changed her mind? Could she have woken up this morning and realized what a huge mistake she's made?

No. Of course not. The texts are from Mackenzie.

How are you holding up? 💙

And then: (PS Does Silvie not own eye cream?? Sheesh.)

I have no idea what that second text means, but the app notifications keep popping up, so I send her a quick heart emoji back and swipe over to the app. Mackenzie's for sure asleep by now, so I won't get an answer until later anyway.

My Abraham post has over a thousand comments, and there are another couple hundred direct messages in my app inbox, which is way more than normal.

Anxiety popping like firecrackers in my bloodstream, I dive into the pool of messages. Sharks are always circling there, even on a good day.

@Peppy_Pippa_4: Sending you love and healing, CeCe! 🖤 🖤 🖤

@MsGymBunnie: I live in Cincinnati too, and my bf just dumped me. Want to meet up to commiserate?

@Meena1717: I'm single, @Hi_Im_CeCeRoss! Date me! I'm cool, I promise!

@yourmom420: Oh please. You girls are sixteen. Stop acting like the world has ended.

@Cevie_4_Everrr: NOOOOOOOO. 😭 You and Silvia were #relationshipgoals. 💔 💔 💔 💔 💔 💔 💔

@MyNameIsAmes: WHAT HAPPENED?????

@SoccerFootballFan: RIP, #Cevie.

@sgerrin1981: You'll get through this, CeCe! We love you!

@Mac_0_0: Good. Now go date a MAN. There's still time to turn your life around.

Sleep hasn't entirely left me yet, and at first I don't understand how they know. I didn't post something in a dream haze last night, did I? But then I swipe over to Silvie's page.

She's posted two photos, side by side, so early this morning it was still the middle of the night. The first picture is of her and me at last year's Cincinnati Pride, rainbows painted on our cheeks, streamers in our hair, and our hands clasped tightly together. She's captioned it: *#tbt*. Today is Sunday, not Throwback Thursday, but she's never let that kind of thing stop her.

The second photo is a selfie, apparently taken last night because she's still wearing her LESBIAN LIKE WHOA shirt. It's the worst picture I've ever seen of her. I mean, she still looks pretty, because I think it's physically impossible for her to *not* look pretty, but she's got no makeup on, and you can see bags under her eyes, sallow cheeks, veiny eyelids. The lighting is unflattering, the picture itself is even a little blurry. Now I get why Mack mentioned eye cream.

I read her caption announcing our breakup. It isn't long, but it manages to get under my skin anyway. *No one's fault??? #heartbroken???*

She did *exactly* what I wanted to do but was too scared to. And look at the response—she has more comments than I do, more likes, more words of support and virtual hugs. She's even *gained* followers since yesterday.

I leap out of bed and pace my room, rage and jealousy heating my skin and numbing my extremities as I scroll.

@SoussssChef: You're an amazing human being, Silvie! You'll find someone better in no time.

@QueenofMexicoCity: ¡Te amo, Silvia!

@JanellesDad: Oh, Silvie, I'm so sorry. I know what it's like. Please know you WILL be ok! 💜 🧹

@IdahoFarmGirl: I can't believe CeCe left you. What an idiot. 🎱

This is so. Not. Okay. I did *not* leave her! Silvie doesn't get to be the "heartbroken" one. *I'm* the heartbroken one. She's the *heartbreaker*. Any sadness she feels she brought on herself. She doesn't get to take this from me too.

I tap the COMMENT button and begin to say as much.

But, as always, just before I click POST, something stops me. A built-in self-preservation system that trips me up every time, asking, *Are you* sure *you want to post this?* like those spiky things that stick up out of the ground in places you're not allowed to drive your car into.

And no. Of course I'm not sure. Of course I won't post this. It's not my brand.

Even if I clicked POST and then deleted the comment two seconds later, it will have been screenshotted. And that would make everything even worse—once something's out there, it's out there forever. Deleting only brings *more* attention to it.

Forcing myself to take a breath, I carefully and deliberately delete what I've written before any damage can be done. When the words are cleared from the screen, I exhale. Regroup.

Then, with a grip around my heart, I click COMMENT on Silvie's post once more.

#same

That's it. No *How dare you?!* or *SHE'S the one who did this, not me!*

Just *#same*. Diplomatic and safe, as always. Friends forever, we're totally in this together, it's no one's fault, blah blah blah.

Everyone will see it, but most importantly, Silvie will. I hope it makes her feel really freaking guilty.

I sit there for a minute on the edge of my bed, phone in hand. What I really want is to slink under the covers and go back to sleep. But no.

Silvie totally outshined me with her breakup post. The proof is right there on her feed. She's the star between the two of us, I always knew that. She's prettier than me, more confident than me, less worried about what other people think than I am. But I was okay with it, because she chose me. She loved *me*. How lucky was I!

Now, though . . .

I take in her post again. She knew exactly what she was doing when she posted this shockingly bad selfie. She knew how to come out looking like the hero, and make everyone forget—even me, for a second—that she's the villain here.

Silvie didn't only break my heart—she one-upped me.

I can't let her do it again.

I go to the bathroom and wash my face, then put on a little makeup. Just some concealer to mask the circles and mascara to brighten my cried-out eyes. Okay, and a little blush on my cheeks because rosy cheeks, even manufactured ones, say EVERYTHING IS FINE. Back in my room, I get dressed, tie a scarf around my unwashed hair, and hit RECORD on my phone.

"Hi, everyone. If you follow Silvie, you already know this, but you all are so important to me, so I wanted you to hear it from me as well. Silvie and I broke up yesterday." I flinch, and take a breath. I said the words to Mom yesterday, and texted them to Mackenzie, but they haven't dulled yet. "Thank you, from the bottom of my heart, to everyone who's reached out; your support has already helped me more than you know. Honestly, it's probably going to take me a little while to heal from this, but in the meantime, I'll be here, still posting, and I'll be watching your posts, soaking up inspiration from all you beautiful, amazing people." I kiss my pointer and middle finger, then throw them up in a peace sign.

I end the recording and upload it to my story.

There. Now *I* have the last word. And I didn't even have to ask for a second opinion first. It feels like a win.

Sitting back in bed, I scroll through my feed as the comments roll in. There are some more like the "oh please" and "go date a man" ones from @yourmom420 and @Mac_0_0, but remarkably, the vast majority of them are supportive and kind. My app friends seem to understand exactly what it's like to have your heart broken. My follower count does tick down by a couple dozen, but that happens sometimes, even when I haven't just made a life-changing announcement. There's a constant ebb and flow to follower counts—it's the nature of the app.

Silvie and I are tagged in a few online articles too, and those range from the matter-of-fact "latest influencer gossip" sort to the more vicious "further proof that LGBTQ+ people don't deserve love, anyway" variety. I skim only a few of them before settling back into my own feed.

I wish I could call or text Silvie or invite her over so that we could read all these comments together and respond to each person individually. Then again, if we're being technical, and you always should be when dealing with wishes, what I *really* wish is to be able to go back in time and stop her, somehow, from falling out of love with me.

The sun is fully up now, and as Abraham noses his way into my room, a new text comes through from Jasmine, one of my friends from school. It's a group text—Silvie's on the thread too.

You two broke up??? Jasmine has written. What is this going to mean for the GSA???

Jasmine is the GSA treasurer, and she takes her position very seriously. I don't blame her—the club is her main source of support, because her parents don't approve of her being trans. As if a person's identity is something anyone else gets to have an opinion on. It makes me so angry.

But also, Jasmine, girl, Silvie and I broke up less than twenty-four hours ago. Maybe give us a second to chill before roping us into a group text, yeah?

Nothing's changing, I text back. Don't worry.

Promise? 🙏 Jasmine responds.

Of course!

But guilt hits me when I remember that Silvie and I were supposed to discuss the prom yesterday and reach out to @DJRio. It's too late now; Silvie and I are no longer a united front, and I'd feel weird DM'ing the DJ on my own. Honestly, I don't want to think about the prom right now anyway. I was looking forward to the whole thing a lot more when I thought I'd be attending with my girlfriend.

Finally Silvie chimes in, and the notification with her name at the top makes my heart jump. Let's talk about it at school tomorrow.

Right. School. Tomorrow. I'd kind of forgotten.

I'll have to see Silvie. And talk to her about the GSA. And . . . be mature about it all.

Gonna be a blast.

@Hi_Im_CeCeRoss: I ♥ Cincinnati.

#MidwestGirl #parksofOhio #selfie #metime

CHAPTER 5

Though it's after noon by the time Abraham and I get to Smale Riverfront Park, the park people are sleepy, deep in their own Sundays. The joggers have earbuds in, and the dog owners are chatting with one another, coffee cups and leashes in hand.

I don't usually spend much time at the park, and especially not on Sundays. Sundays are for Silvie's house, and her dad's chilaquiles, and her two yappy Yorkies, and trying on clothes and taking selfies and making out in her room. Were, I mean. Sundays *were* for that.

But Mom's at work today, and hanging around the house alone all morning made me feel like I was just killing time before Doomsday School Day tomorrow. That wasn't helping my anxiety, so Abe and I decided we could do with some fresh air.

We select a bench, and he sits beside me, squinty-eyed smiling as the sun warms us.

I should post something, keep my story fresh and at the top of everyone's feeds. But what?

Until now, my app life and my Silvie life were braided so intricately together that they were nearly indistinguishable. For over two years, every photo or video either of us posted was rooted, sometimes directly, sometimes tangentially, in the soil of our relationship. People looked to us for style ideas and inspiration because we always gushed about how beautiful the other was, even when the corduroy shortie overalls (Silvie) or buzz cut (me) turned out to be missteps. Their likes and comments filled me, each one a boost to my confidence, a reinforcement of the perfect little world I'd built for myself on my phone.

I'm not sure I know how to be on the app without Silvie. I'm not sure I know how to *be* without Silvie.

But I've already lost her; if I lose my followers too, then I'll really have nothing left. I'll have to go back to being what I was: a girl mad at the world, with a messed-up family and more feelings and opinions than anyone has space or time for. No one wants that version of me.

Positivity. Fun. Lightness.

That's my #brand. I just need to find new things in that space to post about, separate from #Cevie. New ways to inject my shiny online world with even more glitter.

I snap a few photos of the park's landscape, taking care to frame them just so, then doctor them up a bit—the green grass labyrinth becomes greener, the blue of the sky bluer, the suspension bridge in the background a little more defined. I snap a selfie too, with my sunglasses on and a triangle of skin exposed between the strap of my tank top and my off-the-shoulder boatneck sweatshirt. I look cool and confident, like the whole world belongs to me. Not sad or bored or insecure at all.

I ♥ Cincinnati, I caption it, and add a couple hashtags for discoverability.

Almost immediately, the likes count starts ticking up up up, and for a moment, I can breathe again.

This is how I'll spend my time now. I'll pour everything I have into curating my profile even more, making it seem like I'm *totally fine*—no, totally *amazing*. And if it's true on the app, that's almost as good as it being true in reality. If there's one thing I've learned, it's that.

In a sudden burst of inspiration, I swipe the app closed, put my headphones on, and open a different app—the mindfulness one Mackenzie endorses. She gave me a code for a free membership a while back, but I haven't used it before today. Now seems like a good time, though. Fresh start, self-empowerment, all that.

I close my eyes and let the soft, disembodied British voice into my head. I can do this. I can be a person who meditates.

But as much as I try to stay focused on the breathing exercise and visualization, without the high distraction stimuli of the app, my mind keeps wandering. To school. To Silvie. Will she be friendly to me? Will we still walk to classes together and sit side by side at lunch? Or does this break mean a break from *everything*? Should I say hello first or wait for her to take the lead?

And then, as it always does in moments of quiet, my erratic brain hops to other things:

Climate change. Hurricanes. Australia on fire.

Puppy mills. Millions of dogs in shelters.

Police brutality. The conservative Supreme Court.

With each image, my heart rate climbs up a teetery staircase, to the top floor of the skyscraper where it used to reside, back before Dad left. Before I met Silvie. But somehow the meditation voice seems to know I'm having trouble concentrating, and keeps reminding me to note the distraction and then refocus on my breathing.

By the time the session ends ten minutes later, I do feel a smidge lighter. Mack would be proud. I send her a quick text to say thanks, then toss my headphones into my bag and help old man Abraham jump down from the bench.

"What should we do now?" I ask him. "Dog run?"

I take Abraham's wagging tail as a yes, and we set off in the direction of Fido Field. Abe doesn't usually do much at the dog park—he's always been more for cuddling and belly rubs than athletic activity—but he likes sniffing and watching the other pups, as if to check in with the rest of his species and make sure all is well. It's about a twenty-minute walk, but it's a beautiful day, sunny and not too hot, and it will be a good opportunity to post more photos from around the city.

I'm attaching my phone to my selfie stick at the new statue of civil rights icon Marian Spencer when I hear someone frantically calling my name.

"CeCe! CeCe!"

It's not a voice I recognize. I fold the stick back up in time to see two girls, maybe three or four years younger than me, half running, half speed-walking my way. Their faces are bright and flushed with excitement, as if they can't believe their luck.

They're both in floral sundresses and denim jackets, with sunglasses on their heads and bejeweled phones in their hands.

"It's really you!" one girl says.

"And, oh my god, that's Abraham!" the other one adds in delight as her eyes land on my dog, who's currently sniffing around for a good place to pee.

"Yup, that's Abe." I smile and give the girls a little wave. "I'm CeCe. It's nice to meet you." This happens sometimes, people recognizing me out in public. Not every day, not even every week, but every once in a while, a follower and I will end up in the same place at the same time. Usually Silvie is with me, and we can tackle the handshakes and pleasantries together. But I've been in this situation enough times to know how to handle myself. And these girls are clearly harmless.

"We know!" the first girl says. "We're your biggest fans."

"That's so nice," I say. "Thank you!"

"I can't believe we actually ran into you," the other says, bending down to take a picture of Abe. "We were literally *just* saying how cool it would be if we ran into you and Silvie someday, since we live in the same city." Her face flushes as she realizes what she said. "I mean, not that you and Silvie would be together—I just meant . . ." She trails off as she catches her friend's wide eyes and unsubtle head shake.

"It's okay," I say. "I know what you meant. And Silvie and I are still friends, so you never know. Maybe someday you will run into us both!" I'm trying to be airy and light, but from the girls' awkward expressions and the way they aren't holding my eye anymore, it's clear we all hear the strain in my voice. I straighten up and redirect, relying on my standby line: "Do you want to take a selfie?"

"Oh my god, really?" they squeal, almost in unison, and I try to hide my smile as they scurry over to flank me.

We take about ten shots in quick succession, and I open the app. "What are your handles? I'll tag you."

They blurt out their responses, talking over each other, and I have to ask them to repeat themselves a couple times as I search for them on the app. But in a minute or two, I've followed them both and uploaded our selfie to my story, with pretty flower stickers all over it to add to the garden ambiance.

We part with quick hugs, and this close, I catch a whiff of Dana & Leslie moisturizer. I'd recognize that scent anywhere; one of the girls is wearing it. Unexpected tears prick the corners of my eyes at the sensory assault, a cruel and unfair reminder of all the ways yesterday went wrong.

But it's not until Abe and I are out of the garden and the girls are out of sight that I let my smile fall. My face muscles are tight, and my hands are tingling with residual tension.

"You're okay," I whisper to myself, so softly I wouldn't know what I'd said if I weren't the one who'd said it. "You did it." My first in-person encounter with followers without Silvie: *check*.

I pick up Abe and walk along the river for a while with him nestled close.

As we pass the ballpark, music floats our way. A violin, I think. I'm so used to listening to podcasts or Spotify or audiobooks while I'm walking around the city that the ambient sound is a little disorienting. Disorienting, but not unpleasant.

I round the next curve, and spot the source. The violinist's eyes are closed, and he doesn't notice me approach. I stop to listen, because why not. I have no plans.

An open violin case rests on the ground, and some loose change—not even enough for a bus ride—glints against the blue crushed velvet. A handwritten placard is propped up against a small stack of CDs.

Joshua Haim, Violin. CD: $10.

I smile to myself. This city can be so small sometimes. Not that I'd ever admit that to Mom—she'd take it as confirmation that stalkers are indeed tracking my every move.

Joshua plays with confidence and clear joy. The song isn't one I've heard before, and I'm not the most musical person in the world, but even I can tell Mom was right: He's talented.

The piece ends with a long pull of his bow, and his left hand quavers a bit, giving the note some vibrato. The bow lifts off the strings, and for a suspended moment, everything is still, as if all movement and life around us has paused. Joshua's eyes remain closed, his instrument and bow still poised high.

As I start to retreat, he opens his eyes, and starts a little when he sees us.

"Sorry," I say quickly. "I was . . . uh, just leaving." I point my thumb in a random direction and take a step.

"No, it's okay," he says hastily, holding out his bow as if to keep me here. "I just didn't expect to see you." His face flushes.

"I mean, I didn't expect to see *anyone*. People don't really stop, you know?"

"My mom did," I say with a shrug.

Joshua's forehead creases. "What?"

I nod toward the pile of CDs. "My mom bought one of your CDs the other day," I explain. "Outside Trader Joe's."

His dark eyes dawn with recognition, and it's the first chance I've had to get a good look at his face, without it being half-hidden behind the instrument. He's not movie-star gorgeous or anything, but he's definitely more attractive than his stupid CD cover suggests. He's lanky and tall, with fair skin and lots of brownish-copperish hair. He's wearing faded, slim-cut black jeans and a soft-looking white T-shirt. Kind of dorky, kind of artsy, but kind of cute too. I'm sure there are people out there who'd be into his whole vibe. Even more reason for him to rethink his marketing strategy.

"Maggie is your mom?" he asks.

A laugh pushes its way out of me. Of course my mother is on a first-name basis with this kid. She makes friends everywhere. "Yep."

"She was really nice. That was the only CD I've sold all month." He puts his violin and bow down, on top of the coins, and extends his hand. "I'm Josh." His shirt, I realize now that the violin is out of the way, says I'LL BE BACH. I can't help but grin at the pun. It takes a very specific, low-key confident kind of person to unironically rock a graphic tee. Silvie is one of those people too. Me, not so much.

We shake. "CeCe."

"Nice to meet you, CeCe."

I brace myself, waiting for him to connect the name with my face, and the moment to turn into a repeat of the garden scene of a half hour ago. But he doesn't. I'm more relieved than I probably should be.

"And who is *this*?" Josh drops down to Abraham's level, where the dog has flopped onto his side, tail wagging so furiously it's almost blurry to the eye. This guy he's never met before could well be a dog-napper out for raw materials for the world's scrappiest fur coat, but if there's a belly rub involved, Abe is willing to take the risk.

"This is Abraham," I say with a laugh as Josh buries his face in Abe's neck scruff and whispers what a good dog he is. "He's my incompetent guard dog."

"I love you, Abraham," Josh says, scratching behind Abe's ears. The expression on Abe's face says the feeling is mutual.

"You like dogs, huh?" I say, amused, when Josh finally extracts himself from Abraham's charms and is standing upright again.

"I *love* dogs," he says. "We can't get one, though, because my sister's allergic."

"That sucks. I can't imagine life without my dog." The words come out genuine and simple, not at all colored by the fact that I used to be unable to imagine life without Silvie too.

"Tell me about it," Josh says. "It especially sucks for her, because she loves dogs too, and she'll never be able to have one.

My dad once tossed around the idea of getting one of those hypoallergenic breeds, but they're like a zillion dollars and that just feels wrong when there are all those dogs in shelters, you know?"

I blink, surprised. I was literally *just* thinking about shelter dogs, back when I should have been meditating. "Yeah. Abe was a shelter dog, and he's the best."

"We have a cat," Josh says. "His name is Ears."

"Ears?"

He laughs, his whole face lighting up, and again, I'm taken aback—no one smiles like that for someone they don't know, do they? All open and unfiltered.

"Yeah," Josh says. "Sometimes I forget how weird the name is. Gabby—that's my sister—named him when she was five. She said she was going to name him Whiskers, but he was a special cat who needed a special name. So she picked a different body part." He grins. "My dad and I had to agree it made a lot of sense. Ears *does* have cool ears—he's almost all black, but the tips of his ears are bright white."

He's positively beaming. I can count the people I smile like that for on two fingers. Well, one now: Mom. If I ever get to the point of being able to smile at Silvie again, she's getting the app smile. A little more staged, a little less unabashed.

I reach down to scratch Abraham's head, just to have somewhere to deflect my attention. "You know no one really listens to CDs anymore." I regret it the second it's out of my mouth. What is wrong with me? If we were corresponding online instead of in person, I would have been able to delete the words before sending and no one would have been the wiser.

Josh's cheerful demeanor deflates a little. "I know," he says, resigned. "I just like being able to hold a CD or record in my hands. It feels more . . . real? Complete? My dream is to be able to press some of my stuff onto vinyl, but CDs are a lot cheaper and easier. For now."

"I get that. Is your stuff also available on streaming, though?"

He shakes his head. "I've been meaning to do that, but I haven't gotten around to it yet."

I gesture to the handwritten card in his violin case. "I bet if you put out a sign with your social media handle, people would look you up. You'd build a following. And you could sell songs for download."

He toes a crack in the pavement where some grass has found its way through. "Yeah, I'm not really into that stuff."

"What stuff?" I ask. "The internet?"

He laughs. "I'm not *totally* analog—I listen to music online, and I'm really into podcasts. I just prefer not to be on my phone all the time."

"Are you on social media?"

He laughs again and shakes his head. "Nope. And have no desire to be."

I gape at him. This guy is the first person I've ever met who was born in this century who doesn't use the app. Literally—the first one. I'd say that explains why he didn't recognize me, but

I'm not sure he's the type of person to follow a #fashion influencer even if he was on social media.

I'm trying to come up with a response that won't sound too judgy when my phone vibrates. I glance down—one new direct message, from Kathleen Khan, one of the organizers of Cincinnati Pride. Sweat beads at the back of my neck.

"All okay?" Josh asks, yanking me out of the mental hole of panic I've started to slip down.

"Yeah." I rub my eyes, remembering too late that I have mascara on. "Sorry. I should be going, actually. It was nice to meet you."

"You too. Oh, hey, where do you go to school?"

"Neil Armstrong High. You?"

"Delilah Beasley. I'm a junior."

I nod. "Cool. I'm a junior too."

He hesitates, then crouches down to pet Abe again. "Actually, we just moved here from Florida, so I don't know that many people yet. Maybe . . . I'll see you around?"

Oh. That's random. I'm not used to making friends in any offline, non-school kind of way. But Josh seems sweet, and I already feel like a jerk from the CD thing, so I try to keep my answer friendly, if noncommittal. "Um . . . sure," I say. "Totally."

Giving him a little wave goodbye, I continue on my way, Abe trotting by my side. Unless Josh decides to follow me on the app, I'm pretty sure I'll never see him again.

Direct message
From: @Kathleen_A_Khan
To: @SilviaCasRam, @Hi_Im_CeCeRoss

Dear Silvia and CeCe,
The Cincinnati Pride team was shocked and saddened to hear the news of your breakup. We are sending you both all our best during this difficult time.

That said, we have widely publicized your attendance (see attached flyer and social media campaign) at Cincinnati Pride this June, and have received quite an enthusiastic response from prospective attendees, several of whom will be traveling from other states and who are hoping to meet you both in person.

We are hopeful that your commitment to being our parade grand marshals and speaking at the pre-march rally remains intact. With your help, we believe our event will make a splash on this very important day for our community and planet.

Please do let us know your plans at your earliest convenience.

Your sisters in Pride,
Kathleen, Indigo, and Xiomara
—2 attachments—

CHAPTER 6

I find an empty bench at the dog park and open my DMs. The second I read Kathleen's message, I'm gripped by guilt. I should have reached out to the march organizers immediately, to discuss the situation and weigh our options. I hate leaving people in the lurch.

And the timing of it all really makes me mad. Silvie broke up with me literally *minutes* after we made the announcement about the march. I know she said she hadn't planned on dumping me yesterday, but still . . . we could have avoided all of this! If she was having doubts about us, we shouldn't have even accepted the offer in the first place.

And now I have to text her—which I both really want to do and really, really don't want to do. But we need to figure this out.

Hey, I type. Did you see Kathleen's message?

A few seconds later, her response comes in. No, hang on.

I wait, not at all patiently.

Finally her typing bubble activates again. I stare at it with laser focus. *Hit send*, I plead silently. I hate that I'm so desperate to see her words on my screen. I hate that I have no idea what she's thinking.

When it came to Silvie, I used to know everything.

Hit send hit send hit send.

When her text comes through, it's barely two sentences. Not nearly lengthy enough to match the amount of time she took to write it, which probably means she censored herself as she wrote, typing, then deleting. She used to fire texts at me without even rereading, which resulted in some pretty epic autocorrect fails. Once, she invited me over because her mom had made a huge batch of queso dip, but her phone had made it "quest" dip. So naturally I showed up at her house with a sword and a cape.

Ugh, she's written now. What do you think we should do?

What I want to reply is: *You tell me!!!! This is YOUR fault.*

What I actually reply is: I mean, obviously the march will still happen if we aren't there…

Which is true. There are many other queers and allies in the world, and in Cincinnati, who will be marching for their own reasons and don't need us. And the event is two and a half months away—that's more than enough time for the organizers to find replacements for us.

That's not all I was going to say, but Silvie doesn't let me finish my thought. Her reply pops up while I'm still typing, and I'm suddenly even madder.

Yeah, she's said. Let's cancel.

I delete what I'd drafted, and instead send back, in all caps: NO.

My number one tenet of influencing is to always be grateful and remember how lucky I am. The income, the internet fame, the free stuff . . . it's all bonkers. I know that. I also know that if I don't take my commitments seriously, not only will a lot of people be disappointed and inconvenienced, I'll be replaced in less time than it takes to click UNFOLLOW.

I start to type all this out, but stop myself. Silvie knows. We've talked about it many, many times. Just because we're no longer girlfriends doesn't mean her memory of our time together has been wiped.

She also knows how excited I was to be invited to speak at the rally. How much it meant to me to be given this precious opportunity to express myself in an honest, unfiltered way.

Hoping to nudge her in the right direction, I write, They're counting on us being there.

No response. No typing bubble. Nothing.

Abraham finishes his investigative lap around the gravel and comes to sit at my feet, looking up at me with his cloudy brown eyes. I reach down to muss his scruffy head, but don't take my eyes off my phone.

I can't take it any longer. Silvie? I type. You there?

Yeah. Sorry, she writes back. Thinking.

What does she have to think about? I know she wants to go to the parade. So all she has to figure out is whether she can stand being there with *me*. Surely it's not *that* hard of a decision?

I'm not sure it's a good idea, she eventually texts.

Where's the punch-to-the-gut emoji? Because it would be my only honest response right now. Is the idea of being seen in public with me that offensive to her?

71

But you should definitely still do it, she continues. It always meant more to you anyway.

I shake my head as I type. I can't do it alone. It's the truth. I've always felt more confident with Silvie by my side, and despite how awkward it would inevitably be, that's a fact that remains true.

Of course you can.

She leaves it at that, and I stare at the text, trying to decipher her tone. Does she mean *Of course you can! You can do anything, CeCe! You're amazing!* Or does she mean *Come on, CeCe. We're not girlfriends anymore. You really need to stop being so dependent on me.*

Because I don't know what she meant, I don't know how to reply. So I don't. It feels weird to leave a text conversation with Silvie without an *xoxo* or 👄, but this is not the first weird thing about this weekend.

I clip Abe's leash back on, clap my headphones over my ears, and put my favorite song in the world—Mika's "Elle me dit"—on repeat on Spotify. It's in French, but I've read the translated lyrics so many times, they're practically stamped on my brain. In the song, a mother tells her gay son to get off the internet, get out of the house, and do something with his life. Ironic, I know. But she says it because she knows he's special. Because she knows that if he would just take some risks, he could live an incredible life.

By the time I get home, I've listened to Mika sing "Why are you wasting your life? Dance, dance, dance!" so many times it's become a mantra pulsing through my whole being.

I swipe over to my DMs and send the message before my self-preservation instinct inserts itself.

Direct message
From: @Hi_Im_CeCeRoss
To: @Kathleen_A_Khan

Hi Kathleen,
Thank you for your message. Slight change in plans: Silvie is no longer able to join in on the festivities in June, so I'll be attending the event alone. Otherwise everything else—speech, grand marshal, etc.—will remain as is. Hope this is okay?

CeCe

I watch the DELIVERED receipt turn to READ as Kathleen opens my message.

Channeling Mika and every strong queer singer I've ever listened to, I try to look at my response to Kathleen as me taking a step toward independence, putting myself first for once. Because this *is* what I want. Truly.

But I'm terrified.

And because it was Silvie who told me to do the event alone, a big part of me can't help but feel like I'm still letting her decide things.

Kathleen's reply comes back almost immediately.

Direct message
From: @Kathleen_A_Khan
To: @SilviaCasRam, @Hi_Im_CeCeRoss

Hi CeCe,
Thanks for the update. That works for us. I'll be in touch with further details as we get closer to the day. And let us know if you have any questions as you work on your speech.

Silvia, if you change your mind, the offer still stands.

Kathleen

@Hi_Im_CeCeRoss: Monday morning school vibes! Loving this #houndstooth pattern dress from #OneFourUnCouture. Don't wear dresses? That's cool! You can still rock the houndstooth trend—socks, shirts, shoes, neckties, whatever. Anything goes if you wear it with confidence!! ⭐

#selfie #trends #fashion

CHAPTER 7

I beep my car locked, and smooth the skirt of my dress as I walk into school.

It took me twice as long to get ready for school than normal. I wanted to look good—really good, the kind of good that makes your ex-girlfriend reconsider all her choices. I decided on my black-and-white houndstooth-print cinched-waist dress because Silvie likes it, but also because it's on trend right now and looks awesome in black-and-white-tinted photos, so it'll give me lots of good selfie fodder throughout the day. I dressed it down for school with chunky boots, a blue cardigan, and lots of rubber bracelets.

But as I make my way through the crowded halls, scanning the sea of heads for Silvie, I'm second-guessing the whole outfit. The thing about being with someone for such a long time is, they see through you. Silvie will take one look at me and *know* I put in extra effort today, and she'll know why, and that will be that—I'll have given her the upper hand. Again. Maybe I should have just said screw it, and gone with leggings and a baggy sweatshirt. But then I would look as heartbroken as I feel, and that would be a victory for Silvie too. #CantWin

Jasmine is waiting at my locker.

"What's the plan?" she demands. I suspect she's been wearing this same expression of concern since Saturday.

"Hi. I like your lipstick," I reply as I work the combination lock open. It's a too-obvious attempt to placate her, I know, but also I really do like her lipstick. Jasmine's style is preppy feminine—today she's wearing a white top with a peplum around the waist and eyelet detail at the neckline, baby-blue jeans, and ballet flats. Her pin-straight black hair just brushes the tops of her shoulders; I know she's been working hard to grow it out, and it looks really pretty. Her lipstick is the exact same shade of coral as her nails, and while I'm not one for matchy-matchy, I'd definitely give the lip color a try. "Where'd you get it?"

"Sephora. It's called Tiger Stripe." Then, without missing a beat: "Did you get in touch with DJ Rio?"

I sigh and lean back against my locker door, hugging my first-period books to my chest. "For prom, you mean?" Of course that's what she means; I have a broken heart, not a broken head. But I'm in avoidance mode.

Jasmine pins me with a flat glare.

"No." I sigh. "We didn't get in touch with him."

"Because he didn't write back, or because you didn't message him at all?"

My cheeks heat, and Jasmine sees it.

"I *knew* it." She groans. "The second I saw Silvie's post about your breakup, I knew this would happen. We have to get this thing planned, CeCe. And the president and vice president *need to be speaking to each other* if anything is going to get done."

Typically the student council is in charge of prom planning, and they usually have a whole school year to do it. But last year was a huge debacle—the student council president decided to implement an opposite-gender-dates-only policy. And he was a popular senior, one of those physically imposing, loudmouthed types, so apparently no one on the council was willing to argue with him about it, and the rest of the student body didn't even know about any of this until a couple of students showed up that night with same-sex dates and were told they weren't allowed in. It ended up being fine in the end—the chaperones found out what was going on, promptly banned that guy from manning the door, and instructed the other ticket takers to let in anyone with a ticket—but in the moment it was a mess and it ended up all over social media. Silvie shared a bunch of the posts on her page, and I really wanted to do the same, but I chickened out.

Anyway, after that, there was a lot of debate about whether a different club should take over prom duties, and by the time the administration decided on the GSA (in a clear effort to over-correct), it was February. And that's how we ended up scrambling to plan a formal event for over six hundred juniors and seniors in less than four months.

I open my mouth to say, *Of course we're speaking to each other*, but close it before the lie can come out. Jasmine picks up on my hesitation.

"What?"

I glance around to make sure no one can hear us, and lower my voice. "Silvie decided she doesn't want to do Cincinnati Pride with me. I'm going to do it alone." Anxiety twinges in my gut as I say it. *Don't think about that now*, I tell myself.

Jasmine's perfectly threaded brows go sky high.

"So . . . yeah, I don't actually know how the prom planning is going to shake out," I admit, defeated.

A beat passes, and then Jasmine takes out her phone and begins composing a group text. "I'm calling an emergency GSA meeting."

"We already have a meeting scheduled for tomorrow," I protest. "I was going to brainstorm theme ideas tonight."

"Lunchtime. Art room. See you then." Jasmine's still typing as she walks away. A few seconds later my phone vibrates with the message.

● ● ●

I make it through the first half of the day without bumping into Silvie, though I can't help being on watch for her everywhere I go. We don't have any classes together, which used to bum me out, but now it feels like a small mercy.

Seems like everyone else in the world is in my face today, though. Every five seconds it's:

"CeCe! Come *here*! You look like you need a hug!" (Followed by a giant hug from a person I've only spoken to maybe twice before in my life.)

or

"I couldn't believe it when I saw your post! You know I'm on your side, right?" (From someone I know for a fact shared Silvie's breakup post, but not mine, on her own page.)

or

"What even *happened*? I know you can't tell the whole story

online, but it's just us here—I promise I won't tell anybody."
(With a whisper and a wink.)

or

"It's better not to be tied down in high school anyway." (From
a teacher. A male one. Accompanied by an awkward shoulder pat.)

I keep my app smile on the whole time, and my responses gra-
cious and neutral. I don't have anyone at school I can truly
confide in. Jasmine and the other GSA members are my friends,
and they know what TV shows I like and what my favorite foods
are, but I don't open up to them about real stuff. Family stuff or
my grab bag of insecurities or anything like that. But I never
minded before. Apart from Mackenzie, whom I've never actually
met in real life, Silvie was my best friend. She, and my followers,
were my full-time everything.

Finally, at lunch, I spot Silvie at the back of the cafeteria line.
I grab a tray and silently get in line behind her. I can't dally—
Jasmine will have my head if I'm not at the art room with my
food in the next five minutes.

Silvie doesn't notice me at first, so I take the moment to drink
her in. Her hair is loose and falls in soft waves down her
back, her natural chestnut highlights shimmering under the
lunchroom fluorescents. She's wearing a cropped white T-shirt,
an open red flannel that she found for three bucks in the men's
department at the Goodwill, jeans, and high-tops—she looks
like the goddess of cool. Just as she'll know how long it took me
to get dressed this morning, I know without a shadow of a
doubt that she threw the outfit together effortlessly. Her rings

glint as she pushes her tray forward, and my fingers twitch to reach out and grasp her hand. I bet they're cold—her hands are always cold. I used to love how they felt on my skin.

As Silvie reaches for a cup of sweet potato fries, I say, "Can you grab me one too?"

She jumps a little at the sound of my voice, and I feel a smug sense of satisfaction at catching her off guard.

"Oh. Hey," she says after a second, setting the fries on my tray.

"Hey." We take a few steps forward, and I grab a veggie burger. A couple more steps. Silvie selects a fruit cup. The line is moving slowly, and I feel people's eyes on us, watching to see what kind of breakup this is going to be. "How are you doing?" I ask.

"Fine." She's not looking at me. "You?"

"Fine." Two more steps. "Heading to the art room now?"

"Yup."

"Jasmine's really worried about the GSA," I say.

Silvie approaches the register and pays for her lunch. "Jasmine worries about everything."

"Yeah."

"Well, see you there." And she walks away. Even though I'm only fifteen seconds behind her and we're going to the exact same place.

A lump forms in my throat as I stand there, staring at her back. She really couldn't wait for me? It's so small, all things considered, but it feels so mean.

"Here you go, sweetie." On a delay, I blink and reacclimate. Donna, the lunch cashier, is trying to hand me back my card.

In a daze, I take it. "Sorry. Thanks. Have a good day."

My mind is going haywire as I drift through the halls and up the stairwell to the art room. By the time I arrive, the seven other GSA members—Silvie, Jasmine, Deri, Ramsey, Peter, Ariel, and Manny—plus our adviser, Ms. Janet, are already seated around the big art table. We have a few freshman members too, but they don't have lunch this period. I take the seat closest to the door, my thoughts still racing.

"Okay," Jasmine jumps right in. "I called this meeting because we all know Silvie and CeCe broke up, and we're really sorry about that." She gives me and Silvie each a sympathetic look, and the other GSA members murmur their condolences. I've never felt so awkward, so *watched*. Not even in those moments before I tap POST. The spotlight only feels good when you walk into it voluntarily.

"I want you both to know you're going to be okay," Ms. Janet chimes in, with her usual gentle, art-teacher voice. "Sometimes, when relationships end, it can feel like the end of the world. But in time you'll be stronger than ever. And you'll both find love again, if you want it, I promise."

I know she's trying to be helpful, but whatever happened to teachers minding their business? I'm sick of everyone feeling like they own a piece of this.

"Thanks," I mumble, just as Silvie says, "I know."

"So, this is all a little awkward," Jasmine says, redirecting us back to business. "But it's only three months to prom and we have a *lot* of planning to do, and the GSA *cannot* fall apart."

"It's not going to," I insist.

Jasmine levels me with her gaze. "Didn't you say you two aren't really talking?"

I look down at my untouched lunch. "Yeah . . ."

"And you said you didn't mind using your connections to get us a baller DJ, but then you didn't even message him. *And*"— she pushes on before either of us can respond—"when I texted you both this weekend, *you* said things would be fine but all Silvie said was 'We'll talk about it at school.' Right?"

Out of the corner of my eye, I see Silvie nod.

"Which is really freaking ominous," Jasmine says. "At the very least, it's a sign that you two are on different wavelengths. And I'm sorry, but we can't risk a lack of communication messing everything up. This club is important to me. It's important to all of us."

Ramsey, Peter, and Ariel all nod their heads in profuse agreement. Their parents aren't any more supportive of their identities than Jasmine's are.

"It's important to me too," I mumble, but I'm not sure they hear me.

Back in middle school, most of my friends were swooning over the guys on the soccer and football teams. N o n s t o p. I rolled my eyes at them and went back to paying attention to things that I deemed more important.

Then, one summer, Rebecca H., one of the other day camp counselors-in-training, started flirting with me, and boom! I had those heart-racing, gooey-tummy feelings too. Me! Book smart, contrarian, the-sum-of-humanity-is-greater-than-its-parts me. The feelings were big, and they were intense. And they weren't limited to boys. In fact, boys were more of a supporting character in the whole production.

It threw me off balance. For so long, I'd been singularly focused on outward expression, and now this entirely inward thing was happening. Had I just become one of the people I was fighting for? I wasn't sure. I liked girls, but I liked boys too, at least in theory. What did that mean?

It took some time, and a lot of Googling, to get past the gay vs. straight binary and realize there was another option. Lots of other options, actually, one for each letter in the initialism. I was that little *B* tucked unassumingly between the *G* and *T*.

And then I met Silvie, and this small but mighty group of queer and questioning kids at school, and any lingering questions I had were either answered or disappeared completely. I interact with LGBTQIA+ people online all the time, but even now, years later, the people in this GSA remain the only ones I know in real life. I need this club too.

"Last year's prom was crap," Peter speaks up, his jaw set. "And I'm a senior now, so this is my last chance to get to dance with my boyfriend at the prom sans drama, and I really need it to happen, okay?"

Silvie nods. "I know. I've been thinking about this all weekend."

She has? I mush a fry between my fingers, curious to hear what she's going to come up with.

Silvie continues. "And I think it makes sense for me to step down as president." *What?* "Jasmine's right—we have a lot of work to do over these next couple of months, and it'll just be easier that way. Less tension."

"That's very generous and diplomatic of you, Silvia," Ms. Janet says, and chatter picks up again as people weigh in on Silvie's oh-so-giving martyrdom.

No, but seriously. *WHAT?*

All the feelings that have been tumbling around inside me since Silvie brushed me off in the cafeteria start to overflow. It's clear now that despite my hopes—and promises to our followers—of us remaining friends, that's not going to happen. And it's already started to affect the GSA and the prom. So, yes, one of us should probably step down from office. But why should Silvie get to decide? She is *not* the unilateral ruler of everyone's lives. And she definitely does not get to be the good guy again, when *she's* the one who is refusing to be civil. We're not in the app, we're not DM'ing with Kathleen; we're in a classroom in our school, phones put away, and I get to be me here.

"Actually," I say, loudly enough that everyone stops and turns to look at me. *"I'll* step down. Silvie's a more natural leader than me, anyway. And I've been trying really hard to be okay with everything, but . . ." I look Silvie in the eye now for the first time since Saturday. "I need some space." I clear my throat. "It'll be better this way. For all of us."

A stunned hush shrouds the art room. They're not used to me being the assertive one. They didn't know me before.

Peter is the one to finally break the silence. "I'm fine with whatever." He holds up his palms and rocks back on his chair.

I nod, thankful for that grain of permission. "Jasmine, would you like to be vice president?"

She's still speechless. But it doesn't take her long to nod.

"Okay. So Jasmine will be vice. Deri, you'd said you wanted to run for treasurer next year, right?"

Deri, a sophomore, nods, a little awkwardly.

"Does anyone else want to run, or is everyone okay with Deri taking over as treasurer?" I say.

I take the lack of response as an affirmative.

"Great. So Deri's treasurer now. We all good here?"

The air in the room is still tinged with bewilderment. But, slowly, everyone nods their agreement. Including Silvie.

I pop a cold sweet-potato fry into my mouth. The seconds tick by. Still, barely anyone moves. I sneak a glance at Silvie and feel a smug burst of satisfaction when her expression confirms she's just as caught off guard as everyone else.

Sitting back in my seat, I wave a hand around as if to emphasize the fact that I am no longer in charge of anything here. "Carry on."

Finally, Silvie sets her tablet on the table. "Well, since there's still twenty-five minutes left in the lunch period, let's go over some ideas for themes."

Everything reanimates as the other GSA members produce their own lists and begin calling out suggestions.

"Under the Sea!"

"Moulin Rouge!"

"Enchanted Forest!"

"Masquerade!"

I'm the only one with nothing.

It doesn't make sense, but right now, that feels surprisingly okay.

@Hi_Im_CeCeRoss: It's officially #springbreak! Really looking forward to a week of NOTHING to do but rest, have fun, and practice some much-needed self-care. 😎

One great and inexpensive way to pamper yourself is to pick up a new nail polish shade at your neighborhood drugstore. 💅 I just gave myself a mani today—with my favorite #GirlSquadNails gel polish, obvi. My color this week is Sunshine Yellow. What's yours?

#sponsored #ad

CHAPTER 8

In the weeks leading up to spring break, Silvie and I steadfastly avoid each other in the halls and at lunch. I've taken to eating in the library by myself, since our former lunch table was made up mostly of our GSA friends, and President Silvie got to claim them in our divorce settlement. It's not so bad; I have the library's Wi-Fi and the app and my followers to keep me company. And I still see the GSA people at our weekly meetings, though Silvie and I have an unspoken agreement to not make eye contact with each other in those moments. But I still peek at her sometimes, when she's not looking.

Prom planning is moving along steadily, apart from the fact that there's still no agreement on a theme. The deadline for ordering decorations is fast approaching, so consensus or not, we're really going to have to nail down a theme as soon as we return from break.

Our break doesn't officially start until Friday afternoon, but Silvie cuts out a little early and flies to Mexico Wednesday night. I know this not because she told me but because I can't stop stalking her profile.

She's posting a ton of vacation pics, and her feed and stories are, as always, effortlessly compelling—beach read recommendations, mouthwatering collages of her abuela's home-cooked meals, family photos.

There's one picture of her and her cousin playing soccer on the beach that I keep going back to. She's wearing a white bikini I haven't seen before, and she looks so amazing that every time I look at the photo, my heart starts racing and my fingertips tingle, remembering the way they used to lightly brush over her skin.

I have to stop tracking her every move online. I know I do. It's not healthy to resent her for being happy and strong. But her page is always just a tap or two away, and if she's posting these things publicly, that means she wants people to see them, right? And I'm a person. So really, what's so wrong about it?

I configured my settings in the app so that I would get sent an alert every time she viewed one of my posts. That probably wasn't the best move. I just . . . needed to know she hasn't completely forgotten me.

Not that I'd admit any of this on the app, though. As far as the world knows, I'm handling the #Cevie split like a champ. My selfie game has always been generally strong, but I've been leaning into it more lately, with more of a focus on "me" than "us."

You're right, Lizzo, I post on Saturday while on a lunch date with myself. *I AM my own soul mate. #tableforone*

Later that afternoon I'm sitting on my front porch with a glass of fizzy water and bag of gummies, favoriting Greta

Thunberg's posts en masse, when Mom turns onto the block, her sun roof open and music loud. It's Josh's CD again; Mom's been listening to it a lot. She says the violin-y classical/country mix is "enriching." Whatever that means.

She waves to me through the open window, and I wave back.

"Hey," I say as she lumbers up the porch steps. She's on her feet most of the day at work, and even her orthopedic clogs and the water bottle she's constantly refilling can't fully head off the daily exhaustion.

"Hi, honey. How are—" Her face falls before she can finish her sentence. "Crap."

"What?"

She shakes her head. "I'd meant to stop at Trader Joe's on the way home. Totally forgot. We don't have anything for dinner."

"Oh. Well, that's okay."

"Yeah, I guess we can order something and I'll deal with the shopping tomorrow. Burritos again?"

But I'm already on my feet. "Nah, I'll go to the store. I need something to do anyway. Text me your list."

• • •

As I walk across the Trader Joe's parking lot, a familiar sound greets my ears. It's the music from the park, and from the CD that Mom's been playing nonstop. Clear violin notes, like a needle through fabric, embroidering the wind and traffic.

Cincinnati isn't the hugest city in the world, but it's not exactly a small town either, and I don't often randomly run into people I know. But there Josh is, outside the store's entrance,

91

next to a huge row of shopping carts, playing his heart out like this is a totally normal place to hold an impromptu concert. This must be the spot where Mom first met him. His hair is messier today than that day at the park, shaking into his eyes as he pushes and pulls the bow fiercely across the strings. Today's T-shirt reads YOU CAN'T HANDEL THE TRUTH.

"You should livestream these public appearances," I say after the song curves and swoops to its finish.

Josh jolts, just like last time. I smile. Even here, in a hugely populated area, he's still surprised to see another person. I wonder what that's like, to not be constantly hyperaware of who's around and what they think about you.

He recovers quickly. "You're just full of advice, aren't you?" But he's grinning.

"Always." I smirk.

He brings the instrument to a ukulele-esque position and absently begins strumming the strings. "CeCe, right?"

"Good memory."

"No Abraham today?"

I shrug. "Grocery stores only allow service dogs inside. I tried to pass him off as an emotional support animal once, but they saw through it."

Josh laughs.

"That song you were playing was pretty," I say, and it was. Light and springy, like a butterfly landing on flower after flower.

He brightens. "You think so?"

I nod. "You know, I was serious about the livestreaming—you can do it from your phone, so more people get to hear you play. I know you're not on social media, but it would only take a couple minutes to get something set up." I almost offer to help, but stop myself.

"Maybe someday," Josh concedes. "For now I'm fine to just use busking as a way to practice playing in front of people. And I have about five hundred CDs to sell, so . . . yeah, that's kind of my focus right now."

"How *are* CD sales?" I nod to the stack of discs.

"Uh, I've sold six."

"Today?" That's not bad.

"No." His smile goes sheepish. "Since we moved here in January."

I laugh, and take that as a "case closed." But I'm not sure Josh realizes I'm the one who won.

"Well," I say, holding up my canvas shopping bags. "I'll let you get back to your playing. My mom's waiting for me to bring groceries home. Nice running into you again."

"Hey, CeCe?" he says quickly.

"Yeah?"

"Are you on spring break this week?"

"Yup. You?"

He nods, and shifts his weight awkwardly. "Would you maybe want to . . . do something? Hang out, I mean. With me."

"Oh. Um . . ." I freeze, racking my brain for the right thing to say.

If this were an online exchange, I could test out a few punctuation and emojis options before replying. Worst case, I'd just disappear, and then come back later after taking a long time to mull, and say *Sorry for delay, just saw this.* But I can't do that now.

It's not that I don't like talking to Josh—actually, I've really enjoyed both our conversations so far. I'm just so used to being cautious around new people, given the whole public persona thing . . .

Josh is already shaking his head and flipping through his sheet music. "Never mind. Stupid idea. Go do your shopping. Beat those lines." He's smiling, so I smile back and take the out.

"Okay." I give an awkward wave. "See ya."

But the blast of icy air as I enter the store shocks the stupid out of me. Josh isn't a creepy internet stranger. And I already know some things about him: Violinist. Florida. Technology-impaired. Has a sister. Likes dogs. The sum of all this information might not equal a whole person yet, but it also isn't nothing. It's more than he knows about me, anyway.

What's the worst that can happen? We get together, confirm we are polar opposites who have zilch to talk about, and go our separate ways. The end.

Or maybe we'll end up as friends. That wouldn't be terrible.

I'm CeCe Ross, I remind myself. *I am strong. I am an influencer. People like me.*

I duck back through the still-open automatic door. Josh has

already started a new song, but if I wait for him to finish, I'm going to lose my nerve.

"Hey, sorry," I say loudly enough for him to hear me over the vibrating strings.

His bow screeches to a halt and he opens his eyes. "What? I couldn't hear you."

I smile. "Do you like donuts?"

@Hi_Im_CeCeRoss: All the beauty bloggers seem to be talking about this season is long hair—'90s-esque French braids and '60s-reminiscent middle parts.

I love my short hair—it feels very "me." But I suppose it WOULD be nice not to have to get so many haircuts all the time. What do you all think??

Poll:

Should I grow my hair out?

Y/N

CHAPTER 9

"So you know that guy whose CD you're obsessed with?" I say to Mom as we unpack the groceries. "He was playing outside Trader Joe's again today."

Mom sets a bag of rice onto the counter and clasps her hands together in delight. "Oh, I'm so glad you got to hear him play! Isn't he talented?"

"He is," I admit. Too talented to not be findable online, that's for sure. "Actually, this is the second time I ran into him."

She tilts her head, surprised. "Really?"

"Yeah. I forgot to tell you. He was playing at the park a few weeks ago too."

"Well, that's quite the coincidence!" Mom says.

I bend down to offer Abe one of the dog treats I bought him. He carries it to his bed under the kitchen window and lies on top of it. Abe is a strange dog.

"Anyway, Josh is a junior too, and new to Ohio, so we figured, why not hang out?" I don't mention the part about me having turned him down at first.

"Hang out?" Mom lights up even more. "In person?"

"Yes, Mom, that's what 'hang out' means."

"Well, I didn't know if you meant in a chat room or something."

I burst out laughing. "A *chat room*? Do you still expect to hear 'you've got mail' every time you open your email too?"

Mom sticks her tongue out at me, but otherwise ignores my snark. "I think a new friend is exactly what you need right now, CeCe. And Joshua seems like a sweetheart. This is a great idea."

• • •

This is a great idea, I repeat to myself as I enter Holtman's Donut Shop on Monday. *This is a great idea*. My stomach takes a sickly little dip. The truth is, I've been nervous all morning.

Why is this great idea again?

I'm better in pictures and writing. I know my angles and how to find my light. I know how to market myself. It's easy to be witty when you can craft and delete and revise.

This, though. This is what I imagine going to a job interview would feel like. Josh and I have almost zero context. And apart from living in the same city and apparently frequenting the same places, I doubt we have much in common. What if we run out of things to talk about right away?

He's already here, sitting at the window counter, headphones on, sipping from a coffee cup. He doesn't see me. For a split second I consider bailing. Instead, I send off a quick text to Mackenzie: It seems I've forgotten how to function as a regular person. Or maybe I never did?? S e n d h e l p.

I sit on the stool he's saved for me. At least, I'm assuming it's for me. His foot is wrapped around one of the legs possessively. "Hi."

But he still doesn't notice me; he just gazes unseeingly out the window, wrapped up in whatever's piping through his headphones. Unreal.

I tap him on the shoulder. Hastily, he pulls the headphones from his head, his face becoming flushed as he realizes I'm sitting right here, and have been for who knows how long. "Hi! Sorry." He takes his foot back and carefully places it on his own footrest. "Hi."

"I really have to stop doing that to you," I say, laughing.

He shakes his head. "My fault. I'm not great at staying present." It's as if he's admitting some character flaw, but one he's grown to embrace.

"Your podcasts are that riveting, huh?"

He stares at me blankly. "No, I was just listening to music."

I smile. "No, I know. I mean, I figured. I was just . . . teasing. Sorry." Aghh, this is so awkward.

"Oh." After a beat, he smiles too, and visibly relaxes. I wonder if maybe he was nervous about today too.

"So . . . should we get a donut?" I ask. Holtman's is a Cincinnati institution; I can't believe Josh hasn't been here yet.

"Definitely." We hop off our stools. "What do you recommend?" he asks.

"Literally everything is good here. Want to get a few and share?" I haven't eaten today; I could devour three donuts myself, probably.

Josh agrees, and I step up to the counter—and immediately regret it. Of all the employees who could serve us, of *course* it's

Nikki who's come over. I'd forgotten about Nikki when I suggested Josh and I come here. She graduated from Armstrong High last year, and is very active on the app. She's also a massive #Cevie fan.

I'd hide, or grab Josh and duck us both out the door, but it's too late.

"CeCe! How *are* you? I heard about you and Silvie! What *happened*?"

I glance at Josh. His eyebrows are raised in quiet curiosity.

"Hi, Nikki," I say with an even smile. The same one I used on the busybodies at school right after the breakup. "How are you?"

"I'm fine, but oh my god, I've been thinking about you!" Her eyes actually begin to shimmer with tears. "I just can't *believe* it! You know Silvie and Jasmine came in here a couple weeks ago to see if we'd be able to cater the desserts for the prom."

"Oh?" I say as neutrally as I can. Having Holtman's donuts at the prom is a great idea—I'm annoyed I didn't think of it myself.

"So we got to talking about how, you know, prom last year was a disaster. And Silvie mentioned that you're not on the prom planning committee anymore?" Nikki frowns.

"No, I am. I'm just not vice—"

"I let her know that was very uncool," Nikki continues, "and that you two promised everyone you were still going to be friends, and she'd better not show her face in here again until she apologizes to you and lets you back on the committee."

"No, no, don't do that!" I say, horrified.

"Don't worry, I told everyone here what happened," she says

conspiratorially, her voice a little softer now. "We're all on your side."

"Nikki," I cut in, acutely aware of Josh watching me. I can't believe this. I could have chosen literally any other place to meet him today. Any. Other. Place. I just really wanted a freaking donut. "Everything's fine, don't worry."

She blinks. "So you two *haven't* broken up?"

Huh? "No, we have. I just mean . . . don't be mad at Silvie, okay? She didn't do anything wrong. We're both just trying to move on. As friends, like you said." I cross my fingers behind my back at that last part, to negate the fib. "Thank you for your concern, though," I add. "You're really sweet."

Nikki purses her lips and nods, somewhat mollified, if not totally convinced.

I clear my throat. "This is my friend Josh." I gesture to him and he gives a wave. "He just moved here so I'm introducing him to the best donuts in the world. Josh, Nikki is amazing. She knows everything there is to know about this place."

Pro tip: When you just want to drop the damn subject already, kill 'em with kindness. It works online too.

"We're going to share a half dozen donuts," I tell Nikki. "You pick! I trust your judgment."

Mercifully, a line has begun to form behind us, so Nikki has no choice but to get to business. She recommends a few of their staples, as well as a special s'mores donut and a blueberry and lavender cake donut, and cuts them all up into bite-sized pieces for us. I pay for everything (waving off Josh's protests), leave

Nikki a ten-dollar tip, and scurry us back to our seats.

After a suspended moment, Josh asks the obvious. "What was that about?"

"Try this." I hold out a crème brûlée custard–filled bite.

He obeys, and I watch in triumph as his eyes practically roll back in his head. "Okay. That's amazing. Wow."

It's almost enough to make me glad we came here, after all. Almost. But he's still waiting for an answer to his question. I guess I have to tell him now. He's going to find out the whole story eventually anyway. #sigh

"Nikki follows me online," I explain. "I haven't seen her since my girlfriend and I broke up, and I guess the whole thing came as a bit of a surprise to her. She shipped us big-time."

All of that is probably completely obvious from context, but I say it anyway, more for my benefit than Josh's. I need to make sure the situation is clear to him. We've spent about five collective minutes together and already we're at the first major test of our friendship or whatever this is. I'm a girl, Silvie's a girl. What will he have to say about it?

I watch him carefully for his reaction. He finishes his bite of donut, then says slowly, "What does 'shipped you' mean?"

I exhale in a short burst of laughter and relief. "It's internet slang for when you're a fan of someone's relationship, *or* for when you really want two people to be in a relationship. Like, I totally ship Eleanor and Chidi on *The Good Place*."

Josh takes another bite of his donut. "I haven't seen that. But they're fictional characters, aren't they? You and your girlfriend—ex-girlfriend, I mean, sorry—are real."

A rubber-band-snap twinges inside me at *ex-girlfriend*. "Right. You can ship anyone; it doesn't matter if they're real or not."

"Or if they're actually together or not?"

"Totally. It can be either—like, there are *lots* of Gigi and Kendall shippers out there, even though they're just friends."

Josh frowns. "Who are Gigi and Kendall?"

"Oh. Models, is the short answer."

Josh appears to be thinking really hard, trying to make this all make sense. For a second I think he's going to space out again, but then he bites into one of the cake donuts and it's like he's zapped into the present. He even makes a little gleeful noise.

"Good, huh?" I ask.

"Legitimately incredible."

I take a bite of the same donut. *Man.* What do they *put* in these things? A cup of sugar, two cups of flour, and a pinch of childhood whimsy?

"Anyway," I say through a mouthful, "when there's one relationship you worship above all others, that's your OTP. So, like . . . hmmm, what's a good example?" I'm thinking out loud now. "What kind of things are you a fan of? Have you ever watched *The X-Files*?" That's an old show, and Josh apparently likes old things, so . . .

"Wait." He raises a hand at me. It's that one tiny movement that does it—any lingering weirdness vanishes. He's teasing me now too. We're both here, both in this conversation, both amused in our own ways. "I have questions."

I laugh. "Lay 'em on me."

"What is an OTP?"

"Sorry. One True Pairing."

The next hour flies by, and the donuts disappear, as I explain OTPs, slash (same-sex) and plus (hetero) ships, shipper feuds, and stans.

Josh doesn't recognize a lot of the examples I use, so he tries to use his own, but they're all old and mostly music-related and I have no point of reference for them. Like, I've heard of the band Fleetwood Mac, but I don't know who the members are, let alone the intricacies of their marriages and affairs and divorces.

He has read Harry Potter, at least, so that helps.

"So I could 'ship' Hermione and Ron," he works out aloud, "but I could also ship Hermione and Harry, right? Even though one of those relationships actually happened in the books and the other one didn't?"

"Exactly," I say, irrationally proud. "Either one would be considered a ship. A lot of people ship Harry and Ron too. And Hermione and Draco."

"Draco?" he says, bewildered.

"Sure." I laugh. "Then there are portmanteaus—mashups of celebrities' or characters' names, to form a new word. A name for the ship." I'm about to say, "Like *Cevie*," but I stop. Josh obviously knows I'm on social media and that Nikki follows me, but he has no clue how internet famous Silvie and I really are.

Out of nowhere, it occurs to me that . . . maybe . . . I don't *want* him to know?

That can't be right. Can it?

Yes, Nikki spilled some beans I probably wouldn't have brought up so soon, and yes, Josh and I have spent a lot of time talking about internet stuff, but it's all been in such a *normal* kind of way.

Josh didn't come here with a single preconceived notion about me, facts about my life, or opinions about my opinions. He only knows what I've told him. We're just two people, getting to know each other organically. After the drama of the past several weeks, there's something very appealing about that.

Possibilities grip me, hard, and won't let up. It's not a friendship yet, this thing. But so far, it's easy, and uncomplicated, a teeny-tiny-baby seed of something that might grow into a friendship. I don't know what that growth will end up looking like, but I want to give it its best chance. Water it, give it sunlight, and let it flower however it wants to, free from outside pollution.

"How old are you? Seventeen?" I ask, mainly to change the subject, but also because I want to know. He *looks* young, but why are all his references so ancient?

"Yeah."

"Mm-hmm." I study his face. There's a little smudge of marshmallow from the s'mores donut below his bottom lip. "And you're not a vampire?"

I mean it as a joke, but it comes out so earnest that we stare at each other for half a second, then, at the same time, burst out laughing.

"What?!" Josh says when he's able to catch his breath.

"You *look* seventeen," I explain. "But Fleetwood Mac? Linda Ronstadt? Joni Mitchell?" I repeat some of his earlier references. "You're so . . . *old*."

His grin turns wry now. "You are not the first person to tell me that."

"And you're not on social," I continue, "and the whole CD thing . . ."

Josh shrugs, but unapologetically. "Music has always been my thing, you know? It's how I make sense of the world. And when you play violin, you're always surrounded by classical music."

I nod.

"I had a violin teacher back in Florida, from the time I was four years old. Renia. She had this massive record collection, and I was fascinated by them," Josh explains. "My dad worked full-time while also going to grad school full-time, and was a single parent to me and my sister, so more often than not he was late to pick me up from my lessons. After the official part of our lesson was over, Renia would let me choose a record, and we'd sit there and have a snack and listen to it while we waited for my dad to arrive."

There's a lot to unpack in there. I make a mental note to ask him about it all at some point. But for now, I just nod to show I'm listening and that he should continue.

"Renia had an affinity for women-led music. From almost all genres, but mostly folk, country, and rock. I can't really explain it, but that music, those records . . . it became part of me. Like a deep, under-my-skin, irreversible thing." He shrugs, as if to lessen the poetry of his words.

But I understand what he means. Not the music stuff, but finding a thing that infuses itself into your DNA. It's what political activism used to be for me.

"There was *some* modern stuff like Ingrid Michaelson and Kacey Musgraves," he continues, "but mostly classic stuff. Chrissie Hynde, Aretha Franklin, Tina Turner, Tracy Chapman, Ann and Nancy Wilson, Nina Simone . . ."

"Patsy Cline," I say, remembering.

"Exactly." He seems surprised.

"My mom said you were playing a Patsy Cline song when she met you," I explain.

"Ah. 'Walkin' After Midnight.' Right. It's on the CD too." He waits, as if he's asked a question. And after a second, I realize he kind of has.

"I haven't listened to it yet," I admit. I'm pretty sure Josh wouldn't think snippets overheard from Mom's car windows count as "listening."

He nods. "That's cool."

"I will, I promise." I can't help adding, "If it were on Spotify, I would have already."

He rolls his eyes. "I told you, I do listen to music online. And I *am* planning on putting my stuff up there—I just haven't gotten a chance yet."

"Okay, okay, fair."

"Also, I don't know if you've heard, but vinyl is back. Every hipster in Brooklyn and design snob in South Beach owns a turntable."

"Yeah, I guess I *have* seen some people talking about vinyl online," I concede.

After a pause, he asks, "Why is the internet so important to you?"

I wait for the rest. But apparently that's it. "Is that a trick question?"

"No."

"Um . . ." Even without going into the whole influencer thing, there are so many answers I could give. I mean, it's the internet. The most world-changing invention since . . . I don't know . . . electricity. Or modern medicine. Where could I possibly start? "It's convenient," I try. "No—not convenient. That's not the right word. What I mean is, it gives you *access*." Yes. Access. That's it. "We have access to all the information, all the people, all the music. Anytime. It's such a *privilege*. Albert Einstein didn't have that. Martin Luther King Jr. didn't have that. Why *shouldn't* we utilize it as much as we can?"

"I agree that it's a valuable resource," Josh says. "But, CeCe, you have to admit it's a lot of garbage too. Hacking of elections, cyberbullying, fake news."

Whoa. I dip back inside myself for another self-conscious second. Does this guy care about politics? Could that be something we could really talk about?

"It's like the more time people spend online, the less they know how to make decisions for themselves," he's saying. "Have of you heard of . . . wait, what are they called? 'Influencers.'" I can hear the air quotes. "They're these people online who tell their followers what to buy and wear and believe and do. And they make insane amounts of money for it."

The hope balloon inside me pops so hard it stings.

"Yeah, I've heard of that . . ." I say.

"Influencers." The disgust in his voice is not subtle. "More like brainwashers."

"They're not *brainwashers*." It comes out fast, and more indignant than I would like. "They don't tell people how to *think*. More like . . . they share things that align with their values or style. Things they think their followers—who are already following them because they found something interesting or enjoyable in their posts, for their own reasons—might connect with. And if they have the chance to make a living from it, and add some fun and positivity to the world, so what? I don't see what's so wrong about it."

Josh's eye-roll-adjacent expression makes it clear he doesn't agree. He shakes his head. "I don't get it. I also read about how actual dictionaries are adding words like *selfie*, *hashtag*, and *emoji* to the official English language. It just feels wrong."

"But *why* does it feel wrong?" I retort. "I know the internet isn't perfect. Obviously. But why focus on the bad stuff? Or rule out a natural evolution of a language and culture? Think of all the amazing things that couldn't have happened without the internet."

The person next to us at the window counter gives me a look, and I realize I've practically been shouting. My cheeks warm.

"Like what?" Josh asks.

I lean forward and lower my voice. "Oh, I don't know, like unprecedented access to education for girls and women in some developing nations? Or how it offers a human connection for incarcerated people serving long sentences for minor offenses? And, oh my god, it's been an absolute refuge for gay kids in the Bible Belt. I know finding an online community helped *me* when I was coming out, and I have a supportive parent."

Josh sighs. "I hear you. I guess it does do a lot of good too. Maybe it's just not for me."

"That's fair." And it is. I will *always* defend social media and everything that comes with it, even the bad, because it's valuable to me. But I also don't need to convince anyone that it must be valuable to them too.

If I suspected it before, I'm one-hundred-percent certain now: Josh won't look me up online. It probably wouldn't even occur to him to.

In a flash, I'm decided.

I'm not going to tell him about my online life. I'm going do my best to make sure the word *influencer* never comes up in our conversations again. He doesn't need to know that I make money from social media. That I get paid to post about beauty products and clothing companies, or that I've been asked to model even though I'm not a model, or that I have internet famous friends, or that my *dog* has his own fan base, or that a million people around the world know heaps more about me than Josh does.

He'll find out eventually, I'm sure. But for now, I'm just

Cecilia Ross, and he's just Joshua Haim, two people who like donuts.

It's exactly what I had no idea I needed.

I don't want to ruin it. I'm even willing to overlook the fact that he kind of, sort of offended me with all that *brainwasher* talk.

Josh's phone chimes with a reminder that it's time for him to leave to pick up his little sister from spring break camp. We wave to Nikki and the other employees, then hover outside the shop to say our goodbyes. "Thanks for asking me to meet up today," I say. "It was fun."

He hesitates. "Can I confess something?"

Oh no. What's he going to say? Did I have him all wrong? Is he really a rep for some pyramid scheme? A serial killer? A Republican?

"Sure," I say.

"I'd kind of thought, when you agreed to meet up today, this was going to be a date." He blushes and gives a little chuckle. "Stupid, huh?"

"Oh!" I wasn't expecting *that*. "Um . . ."

"Don't worry, I know now you're not into guys," he says hurriedly. "I'm cool with that."

"I . . . uh . . ." What do I even say? Do I come out to him as bi? I don't want him to misinterpret that as me saying this *was* a date, or that I like him that way. Or do I just let him assume I'm a lesbian, even though it's not exactly true, because that would keep us in our lanes here?

He shakes his head. "I'm sorry. I made it weird." He's toeing the ground again, like he did that day at the park. "I just really enjoyed our conversation today, so I felt like being honest might be the right thing. Never mind. Forget I said anything."

A car with its windows down cruises by, an upbeat '60s-sounding song I don't recognize pumping from its speakers. Josh starts to move, just a sway at first, but when the car stops at a red light, giving the music an opportunity to linger, his gangly wiggle grows into the kind of dance that is not at all cool but also pure joy.

I step back to give him room to do . . . whatever this is. Talk about a non sequitur.

"I love this song!" he says, moving his arms in a sort of ocean-wave motion.

I laugh. "I can tell!" A tiny part of me wants to start dancing too, but I can't bring myself to do it. What if people saw?

The car gets moving again, and the music fades into the distance.

"Okay, well," Josh says, the slightest bit out of breath. "I guess I'll see you around?"

I gape at him, trying to play mental catch-up. He's given me an out from the conversation, and I'm certain it was purposeful. The words *thank you* form on the back of my tongue, but I swallow them down. There's something else I need to say, now that the tension has been defused.

"Wait," I say quickly. Josh was honest; I can be too. "You're right. This was a just-friends thing."

"I know, you don't have to explain—"

"But," I continue, "I actually ID as bisexual."

I wouldn't have mentioned it today if the subject hadn't come up. But it did. And I still haven't managed to find a totally chill, #nbd way to come out to someone, so I might as well take the opportunity while it's in front of me.

"Oh!" Josh's eyes flicker with thought, as if he's going back and reframing his perception of me, just a little.

I find myself doing the same, studying him with an interest I usually reserve for when I zoom in on other people's app pictures, to try to read what their T-shirt says or figure out where they are by the street sign in the background.

Josh is the rare kind of person who wears his whole self right there on his expression. He's so . . . open. Genuine. Even when his views don't align with the rest of the world's, he still doesn't try to mask them.

I remember what it was like, to be like that. To be so certain of myself and my thoughts that I would tell anyone what I thought at any moment, without a single second of hesitation, and without caring what they'd think of me. Josh has that glimmer in him, even if he doesn't know it. And I want to hold on to it.

"Are you free tomorrow?" I ask. "I could show you some stuff around the city."

There it is—that earnest, unabashed smile. "Yeah. Cool."

We enter our numbers into each other's phones and exchange a quick hug. As we head off in separate directions, my footsteps are light with new-friend energy. I'm really glad I took a chance today.

@SilviaCasRam: I have NEWS! I wasn't sure if it was really going to happen, but I just got the green light to go ahead and share it with you all…I AM GOING TO BE A PUBLISHED AUTHOR!

I've been offered a book deal for my first book! I can't reveal too much about the project yet, but it's going to be all about #fashion and #identity and #thrifting! The book will be in bookstores next year! Someone pinch me! I can't believe it!!! And THANK YOU to each and every one of you for being on this journey with me—I literally would not be here without you all. 📖 📖 📖 📖 📖 ✳ ✳ ✳ ✳ ✳

CHAPTER 10

That afternoon, I go home, curl up on my bed with Abe, and click on Silvie's feed. Because clearly I have zero self-restraint.

When I see her latest post, I nearly drop the phone.

A book deal.

A *book* deal?!

Silvie's always wanted to be a writer. She used to share her short stories with me all the time, and I was happy to be given another window into the way her brain worked. Her stories were good. And she *is* the queen of thrift store shopping; publishing a book on thrifting isn't that much of a leap for her, in theory. But we broke up only a few weeks ago. It takes more time than that for a book deal to happen, surely. Even if she hasn't actually written the book yet, she would have had meetings, negotiations . . . I don't know the first thing about the publishing industry, but she *must* have been working on this when we were together. And she didn't share it with me. A whole new kind of rejection punches through my core.

We used to argue about her obsession with thrift stores all the time. I have no problem with buying used clothing; it's great for the environment, you can find great stuff, and it's important to have affordable options for people who can't buy new clothes all the time. The thing I *did* have a problem with was that Silvie didn't see any issue with shopping at certain religion-based charity shops, who donate a large portion of the money they make selling used goods to organizations that actively lobby against women's and LGBTQIA+ rights. It's well-documented information, and a two-minute Google search will tell you exactly which stores take money from people like us and then use it to hurt people like us. But Silvie didn't seem to think it was that big of a deal, and rolled her eyes at me when I'd get upset about it, as if to say, *Stop being so CeCe about everything. Lighten up.*

And now she's going to publish a book that will shine a favorable light on these places. I bet that's why she kept it from me—she knew I'd have objections, and she didn't want to hear them.

Um, congrats? I DM her, hoping it will induce an explanation.

No response. Even though she's replying to public comments and clearly online right now.

I pelt my phone across the room, and it lands on my beanbag chair.

Why is it so easy for her to ignore me? Am I really that inconsequential to her, after two years together?

It doesn't help that the messages of support from #Cevie fans have dwindled to practically zero. I get that life online is fleeting, and that people have short attention spans, but I hadn't thought everyone would forget us quite so quickly. Not our diehards, at least. It's been a few weeks post-breakup, and everyone has already moved on to whatever the next thing is. Everyone except me.

I pick up my phone again and select the MUTE option next to Silvie's handle. It's not an unfollow, but her posts won't turn up in my feed anymore. I'll have to seek them out if I want to see what she's been posting.

Then I text Mackenzie; it's four p.m. here, which means it's seven a.m. her time. She's probably up and out for a run by now.

Is there something wrong with me? I ask her.

Explain please, she writes back. That's one of the things I like best about Mackenzie—she's not one for offering baseless platitudes. She needs context.

Silvie's doing totally fine without me. She's having the best time ever in Mexico, and did you see she got a freaking book deal?? Like...how??

You didn't know about the book thing? Mackenzie asks.

Nope.

Ouchhh.

Yep. And she's ignoring me now. AND I searched #Cevie and no one's used the hashtag for two weeks. It's like that movie where that guy wakes up in a world where no one remembers the Beatles. I'm the only one who remembers Cevie.

Hold on, she writes. First of all, just because people have moved on that doesn't mean they don't remember. Second, yes, Silvie SEEMS to be doing great, but that doesn't necessarily mean she IS doing great. You know how social makes things look, babes. It's not real life.

That's true, I write back. Nothing is ever as it seems on social media. I know that better than anyone.

Thirdly, she says, you are not the Beatles. Get over yourself. 😊

• • •

Tuesday morning I'm getting ready to meet Josh, doing my makeup under the bright lights of the bathroom, when a DM pops up on my phone.

> Direct message
> From: @TawnAtDawn
> To: @Hi_Im_CeCeRoss
>
> Hey, CeCe!
> I'm Tawny Miller, VP of marketing at Treat Yo'Self. I noticed you follow us and have posted about a few of our products in the past—thank you for helping spread the word! Our whole team has been loving your posts lately. I'd like to talk with you about a more official partnership, if you're interested?

I stare at it for a full minute before allowing myself to believe it's real.

Treat Yo'Self is a hugely popular line of pop-culture-based novelty and self-care products. They sell things like bracelets with Leslie Knope's face on them, and massage oils with a #retro Spice Girls theme. The "Baby" Powder–scented one makes me gag a little, but I really like the "Scary" Cayenne. Lots of feminist, girl-power stuff, but things that are actually cute and trendy and funny.

They're *way* bigger than any of the other brands I've partnered with before. Like Tawny said, I have posted about some of their products here and there, just as a fangirl of their company. And they want to work with me! Not Silvie. *Me.*

Hi, Tawny! I reply right away, my fingers shaking a little. *Yes! Let's discuss!*

A few back-and-forths later, I send Tawny my cell number and she gives me a call. Turns out it was one post in particular that caught their attention—the one I posted from my solo lunch date, with the nod to Lizzo's song "Soulmate." Their CEO, Tawny's boss, is recently divorced, and approached Tawny and the rest of the marketing team with the idea of doing a social campaign around the universal experience of heartbreak.

"We'd love to have you come on board as a brand ambassador," Tawny says. Her tone is equal parts pep and business as she runs down the details. "You can be as personal as you want in your posts—in fact, that's what we're looking for. Talk about life post-breakup."

"But no one seems to care about Cevie anymore," I say, fully aware I might be talking Tawny out of her offer. No point in not being upfront about the situation, though. "What would I even talk about?"

Tawny volleys back to me. "*You* still care, don't you? You're still hurting?"

I'm silent for a beat. "Yes." I wonder how she knows that; I haven't posted about it at all since that first day.

"Exactly! Your breakup might be old news on social by now, but there are people of all walks of life struggling with heartbreak every single day, and who better to connect with them than someone who knows what it's like? Plus," she adds, "we absolutely *love* your style. We're confident this could be a great fit."

I couldn't agree more. The excitement bubbles back up.

Tawny runs down the basic points of the contract with me. It's a lot of the usual stuff, like the hashtags Treat Yo'Self wants me to use in each post (#treatyoself, #selfcare, #mystory) and the ones the Federal Trade Commission requires me to use (#ad, #sponsored). They'd like me to post at least three times per week for two weeks, with the option to extend. The posts can be in any format (photo, video, GIF) but each must include an image of me wearing or using at least one Treat Yo'Self product, with a direct link to the company's site. I'll also have to grant the Treat Yo'Self marketing department access to my app metrics for each day that I upload a post so they can view how many eyeballs landed on the posts. For each post I'll be paid $2,000 per 100,000 views. I have close to a million followers, so, even if only half of them view the posts . . . yeah. A lot of charities are about to get some big donations.

I accept on the spot, and Tawny promises to email me the contract by the end of the day and overnight me a bunch of products. Looks like I'll be doing a supersized #unboxing video tomorrow!

When we end our call, I place the phone gently down on the sink and look into the mirror. My expression is equal parts disbelief, joy, and disbelief that I'm feeling joy.

Everything's going to be okay. For the first time in ages, I'm certain of it.

I blot my smiling lips on a tissue, do one last check of my hair and outfit, and skip out the door.

Direct message
From: @Kathleen_A_Khan
To: @Hi_Im_CeCeRoss

Hi CeCe,

We're looking forward to seeing you at Pride in June. If you could send us a draft of your planned speech no later than one week before the event, we would appreciate it.

Please let us know if you have any questions!

All our best,
Kathleen, Indigo, and Xiomara

CHAPTER 11

As Josh and I stroll through downtown, I point out spots here and there, and Josh tells me about all the differences between here and Miami. I've never been to Florida, but from the way he describes it—the beach, the colors, the weather, the Cuban influence, the food, the music—Miami and Cincinnati might as well be on two different planets.

"Why did you move?" I ask.

"My dad got a new job."

"Oh." I nod. "What does he do?"

"He's a nurse anesthetist. Back home—I mean, back in Miami, he was working as an ER nurse and studying to become an anesthetist at the same time because the pay is so much better. So when he got offered this job at the medical center here, he couldn't turn it down."

I remember now what he said about his dad working and going to school full-time, and often being late to pick him up from violin lessons.

"Does he have more time off now?" I ask.

"Not really. The job is really demanding, so he still works six days a week."

I nod. "My mom's a vet tech. That's kind of like the

nurse version of veterinary medicine. She works a lot too."

"I bet the two of them would have a lot to talk about," Josh says.

"Totally."

On a whim, we hop on rental e-scooters and take them down to the water. It's a really nice day, and the wind on my face as we zoom through the streets feels good. I make sure to take a few quick selfies to post later.

"Can I ask you a question?" Josh asks after we park the scooters and stop to gaze over at Kentucky across the river.

"Sure."

"Have you ever dated anyone other than . . . what was her name? Silvie?" The words come out in a rush, as if he had to dare himself to say them.

I smirk at him sideways. "In other words, have I ever dated a guy?"

"That's not what I meant!" His cheeks have those specks of pink again.

"Uh-huh," I say, teasing. "Suuuure."

"No, really! I just knew you'd been together for a long time and, you know, you're only sixteen, and I've never even dated *anyone*, and, oh jeez, I don't even know what my point was anymore—" He scrubs his hands down his face.

"Josh, it's okay," I say, laughing. "I don't mind. I've had a grand total of two girlfriends, if you count the totally innocent thing with Rebecca H. at day camp the summer before eighth grade. I have had a grand total of zero boyfriends."

"Okay." He nods. "Got it."

"I'm definitely more drawn to girls than boys. Always have been."

"Have you ever kissed a guy?"

"Nope."

There's a brief pause, and I'm pretty sure I know what question is coming next.

"So how do you know you're bisexual and not gay?" he asks, and I smile to myself at his predictability.

This is something I've thought a lot about, and I have my answer at the ready.

"Because sexuality isn't experience-based. It's feelings-based. How do you know you're straight, even though you just said you've never dated anyone?"

More thoughtful silence as he takes that in.

"And I guess technically I'm *pan*sexual, because obviously there are more than two genders, and the person's gender or sex isn't the thing that makes me attracted to them anyway—" I stop, suddenly self-conscious. This is too much explanation. Josh literally only asked if I'd dated anyone other than Silvie.

But actually, he seems interested. He's nodding to show he's following, and waiting for me to continue. Huh.

"So, anyway, *bi* was the term I felt comfortable with when I came out when I was thirteen, so I've decided to stick with it."

The term *bisexual* also often requires less explanation and definition than *pansexual* to those not in the know, which I've found to be helpful in getting past semantics and straight to the point of the matter.

"Also, real talk, I've had a massive crush on this YouTube star Noah Lim forever, and I *totally* would, if he were offering."

Josh bursts out laughing. "Point taken."

I grin, partly because it's funny, but mostly because that's apparently the end of the conversation. Josh doesn't push back on anything I've said, or try to make his own point. He's accepted my answer as fact, and that's enough for him.

We continue our walk, meandering in the direction of the Krohn Conservatory. I pull a bag of gummy bears from my tote and we snack on them along the way. Josh prefers the orange and red ones, which is fine by me. #yellowandclearbearsforever

"Hey, is your last name really Haim?" I ask as we stand side by side on the lawn, gazing up at the majestic aluminum-and-glass greenhouse.

"Yeah." He squints. "Why?"

"It made me think of the band Haim. And I know you like women-fronted music, so I was wondering if that was, like, a stage name or something."

Josh laughs. "No, it's really my last name. No relation, though." He perks up. "Wait, do you like that band?"

"I do. They're great."

He sighs exaggeratedly. "Finally! A musical interest we share!"

"Guess you're not so out of touch after all, old man." I smirk, because he's totally still out of touch.

Grinning at each other, the sun warming us from top to bottom, we stand there. Just for a second, the trees and the greenhouse and the blue sky begin to fall away. Birds chirp from unseen places, all around us. Strange that I hadn't heard them before. Or noticed the slight dimple in Josh's left cheek.

Suddenly, out of nowhere, a big, shirtless, tattooed guy barrels toward us on his bike, picking up speed as he zooms downhill, yelling at us to "get the hell out of the middle of the path!" and Josh grabs my arm and yanks me onto the grass just in time for us to miss getting plowed over.

"Watch it!" he shouts after the guy, who doesn't turn around.

When my breath returns to me, I cough a little in shock. "Holy crap, that was close."

"Are you okay?" Josh asks, breathless too.

"Yeah, I'm fine. Thanks." I push my hair out of my eyes. "I don't think that guy was going to try to go around us."

He shakes his head. "Guess there are jerks everywhere."

I smile. "You mean you have jerks in Miami too?"

"You have no idea." His fingertips gently squeeze my arm, and in unison, we look down, as if we're realizing at the same time that he's still holding on to me. He quickly drops his hand down by his side and clears his throat. "His, uh . . . his tattoos were cool, though."

This boy is really good at knowing when I need a change of subject.

"I didn't get a good look at them," I say, and deliberately resume walking. "Would you ever get a tattoo?"

Josh takes a few quick steps to catch up with me. "I'm not sure. I've thought about it. I like other people's. I just don't know what I'd get."

"I've always wanted to get a little rainbow on the inside of my arm," I tell him.

"Like the rainbow flag?" he asks.

"More like an actual rainbow, done with five or six hand-drawn, semicircle lines. But yeah, the LGBTQ connection would obviously be a big part of the meaning. Silvie and I talked once about getting the same tattoo together, but it never happened."

"How come?"

"Lots of reasons. She didn't think her parents would approve, and I started to worry what people online would think."

Josh stops walking again. "Wait, what?"

I stop too, and look up at him. He's not smiling. No more dimple. "What?"

"Why would people online have anything to say about it?" He looks genuinely confused.

I can't help laughing a little at his naivete, though it is oddly charming. "People online have something to say about *everything*." But I decide to tell him the whole truth, the real reason behind my hesitation. "And sometimes people give bisexual people crap if they boast too much about their queerness."

"Huh?"

"You know, like 'You're not gay enough' or 'You could pass as straight if you wanted to, so why should you get to wave the flag as high as those who don't have that privilege?' That kind of thing."

He nods slowly, in thought. "So you didn't get the rainbow tattoo you wanted because you were worried those people would be mad at you for it?"

I shrug. "Kind of?"

This time, when Josh places his hand on my shoulder and pins me with his gaze, it's intentional. We're exactly his arm length apart. His eyes are so dark I can see my reflection in them. "CeCe."

"Yeah?"

"Why would you ever apologize for being you?"

I blink. That's the last thing I expected him to say. I don't have an answer.

"This is what I mean about the internet being . . . *unhelpful.*" I suspect he meant to use a stronger word, but censored himself.

"You don't get it," I say, shaking my head.

"Maybe not. But it seems simple to me. You are bisexual, right? That's a real thing about you?"

I nod.

"And you'd like to get this particular tattoo?"

I nod again.

"And the thing it would symbolize is not only something you're not ashamed of, it's something you're *proud* of?"

"Yeah."

"So then you should get it." He's so certain, so decided. "Who cares what anyone else thinks?"

It might just be because Josh is Josh, and the way he says things is always so earnest. But maybe it's also the nuance that comes with having a face-to-face, real-time conversation with someone. Hearing their voice and seeing their expression, not just their typed words—which, no matter how creative you get with them, ultimately end up looking exactly like any other person's typed words. But for a brief, precious moment I can't think of an argument. I even forget for a sliver of a second that caring what other people think about me is one of the central driving forces of my life.

Yes. I *should* get the tattoo.

But then I remember cancel culture, and the dad who peaced out because I was too strong-willed for our little family. There are so many risks, so many mistakes one could make. Josh's vision is nice, but reality is more complicated than that.

I gently take his hand from my shoulder and squeeze it once before letting it go. "Want to go to my house?" I ask.

Josh nods, and lets me lead the way.

For some reason, after all that, I can't stop thinking about how the gentle pressure of his fingers on my arm reminded me of how lovingly and confidently he handles his violin, as if it's the most precious thing in the world.

@Hi_Im_CeCeRoss: Poll results!

Should I grow my hair out?

Y: 18% (17,438 respondents)

N: 82% (79,440 respondents)

CHAPTER 12

The second we come through the front door, Abe waddles over as quickly as his old legs and click-clacky nails will allow, and flops upside down, all spotted belly and tongue lolling out the side of his mouth.

Just like the last time they met, Josh crouches down and showers Abe with pats and scratches and kisses.

"I'd love to meet Ears someday. And your dad and sister too," I add, pulling a pitcher of pomegranate juice out of the fridge.

"Anytime."

"Want seltzer in yours, or are you a purist?" I hold up the juice.

"Does anyone ever turn *down* a spritzer?" He seems appalled at the notion.

I set to work mixing the drinks and mutter, "My dad always did. Said seltzer was hippie nonsense."

Josh's eyebrows go high, but he doesn't press. A small part of me wishes he would ask, because then I'd be able to ask more about *his* family. I've been wondering ever since he mentioned his dad was a single parent, but he hasn't volunteered more information, and if there's anything I'm extra sensitive to, it's treading on uncomfortable family stuff.

"Want a tour of the house?" I ask instead, handing Josh his pink-filled glass.

"Definitely."

Our house is small, so the tour doesn't take long. Kitchen, with slate-gray floors and turquoise cabinets. Living room with the comforter-covered couch and the TV remote with the worn-away markings on the buttons. Hallway with the green shag carpeting that was here when we moved in and that Dad always wanted to pull up. Mom got that carpet shampooed after Dad left; pretty sure that little touch of TLC was her brand of peaceful protest against Dad. Bathroom that smells like lavender and vanilla and mint, with tampons on the shelf in full view because who cares. Mom's bedroom, which I gesture at from the doorway but don't enter. And my room.

"Whoa," Josh says as we step inside. He looks like he wants to start singing that song from *Willy Wonka*.

I haven't looked at my room through someone else's eyes in a long time. The only people who've ever really come in here before were Mom and Silvie, and they're as used to the decor as I am.

Quickly, and a bit belatedly, I do a scan to make sure there's nothing visible that would give away my secret-to-Josh life online. All clear.

"Yeah, so . . ." I say to Josh, sweeping a hand out before us. "This is me."

"Yes," he says. "It really is." I turn to find that glinty-eyed smile again.

I sit on the floor, and he does the same. There's a pen lying beside one of the feet of my desk chair, and Josh uncaps it and starts drawing on his canvas high-tops. I watch, mesmerized, as the bones in his right hand manipulate the pen as naturally as they work the violin bow, sprouting a plant bud on the white sole. The bud grows into a vine, and the vine spreads into a vineyard, all around the circumference of his shoe, with stems and leaves and the occasional grape.

"Is there anything you're not good at?" I ask. "Apart from online stuff, I mean." My voice is a whisper, but after the extended silence, it's jarring.

Josh looks up, his pupils adjusting. "Uh, yeah. Just about everything," he says with a self-deprecating grin.

I roll my eyes. "You play the violin like a professional. You dance without caring who's watching. You can turn a gym shoe into a freaking canvas. You connect with animals in a way that most people are incapable of or aren't interested in. I suspect you do the same with most people you meet too."

He scoffs. "I work really, really hard at the violin, and I'm nowhere close to professional level. Joshua Bell and Lindsey Stirling were way ahead of me at this age. I'm just trying to catch up." He begins ticking items off on his fingers. "I like to dance, yeah, but you definitely can't say that I'm good at it. This"—he lifts his drawn-on foot a little—"is just a doodle. I always have to be doing something with my hands, especially in uncomfortable or awkward moments." He looks away and his face goes red. "And yeah, I connect with animals, but that connection very much does *not* translate to how I interact with people. I actually think I like animals so much because I'm sort of bad at the whole people thing. Animals are simpler. More genuine. Easier to read."

"That's not true, though," I argue. "You connected with me. Like, right away."

Josh's gaze meets mine again, and stays there. "You're an exception, CeCe. Trust me."

I suck in a little breath.

This comfort between us, like we've somehow always known each other, is nice. Okay, it's amazing. But it's also horribly inconvenient, because it's so easy to just *say* things like that, all genuine and exposed. And then the lines go blurry, and then . . . what?

"Thanks," I say, for lack of anything better. "I still suspect you're one of those secret geniuses who's good at literally everything you try, but I appreciate that."

"I can't sing to save my life," he offers. "Which is unfortunate for a musician. I hear the notes perfectly in my head, but by the time they come out of my mouth, they're all wrong. My sister, on the other hand, is an amazing singer—she could be on one of those TV shows if she wanted."

"You should form a family band!" I laugh. "I bet your dad's good too, if the two of you are so musical."

He shakes his head. "No, my sister and I were both adopted. Dad can sing along with the radio just fine, but Gabby and I didn't inherit anything musical from him. Not in a DNA kind of way, anyway."

"Ohhh. Oh god, I'm so sorry." I hang my head in my hands.

"Why?"

"I *hate* when people assume things about me based on societal norms. And I just did the same thing to you."

"Oh. That's okay."

No, it's not. It's really not.

"Hey. CeCe." It's not until I'm looking at him again that he continues. "You're always so worried about hurting people . . ."

"Yeah, but that's the problem," I retort. "With, like, *the world. More* people should be worried about that."

"I know." He tilts his head like he's trying to figure out what he said that put me on the offensive. But it's not what *he* said, exactly—it's more that I'm tired of people acting like I care too much. "I mean, I agree. That's not what I was going to say."

I blink. "Oh."

"I was going to say that I wish you'd be nicer to *yourself* too."

I stare at him. "Oh," I say again. The only other person who's ever said anything like that to me before is my mom. "Ohh." It's all I know how to say, apparently.

Josh seems to sense my inner plea for a shift of focus. He keeps doing that. "So, what happened was," he begins, "my father was married a long time ago, and he and his wife decided to adopt a baby together. But by the time all the paperwork and vetting were done, and they were deep into the waiting process, their marriage kind of fell apart. For other reasons, not the adoption stuff." He shrugs. "So they decided to get divorced, but right around that same time, they got a call about a baby who'd just been born. That was me." He gives a toothy, overly posed smile. "So they talked everything through with the agency and their attorneys and my birth mother, and they decided that Dad would adopt me on his own. So he's my dad, but his ex-wife isn't my mom. Does that make sense?"

I nod.

"It was an open adoption, which means we've had some contact with my birth mother. Emails, photos, occasional visits. She lives in Florida still."

Wow. "What has that been like for you?" I don't know much about adoption, but on TV they make it seem like people who were adopted never get to know anything about their birth parents, let alone have a relationship with them.

"It's been great," Josh says. "She's a really interesting person. Very artistic and kindhearted." Artistic. Aha. "She wasn't equipped to raise her children herself, so she made the choice that was right for her. And my dad is one of the best people I know. I'm really glad she picked him to be my parent."

And here I am, still harboring resentment over my stupid father and his stupid stupidity. Josh is officially chiller than I am in every way.

"So your father decided to adopt again, later?" I ask. "Hence Gabby?"

Josh grins even bigger now. "Sort of. When I was ten, my birth mother found out she was pregnant again, and she reached out to Dad to see if he'd be willing to adopt her daughter. That's Gabby."

"So Gabby is your biological sister?"

"Half, but yeah. Cool, huh?"

"That's basically the coolest story I've ever heard," I say, amazed.

He beams. "Yeah. I agree."

There's a long silence, and I'm certain I know what Josh is thinking.

Sure enough, he puts voice to it. "What about yours? Your father, I mean. You mentioned that thing about the seltzer . . ." He says it so casually it's not casual at all.

I do want to tell him. But I don't want to blast all this happy energy to smithereens. "Would it be okay if we punt that story to another time?" I ask.

"Of course." Josh nods profusely, then goes back to doodling, on his other shoe this time. A series of semicircles emerge from his pen. They look a little like the rainbow tattoo I want, but the more intricate the pattern becomes and the more angles and turns the lines take, the more they take on an air of importance. Like a sharp metal crown, or icy mountain range, or big, toothy grins. When Josh looks up, a new glimmer has entered his eye. "Want to put on some music and dance?"

I only hesitate for a second. "Okay."

Josh gets to his feet and plugs his phone into the speaker cord on my desk. The music he selects is not anything I would have ever chosen. It's full-on country music, with prominent acoustic guitar and a kind of beat that makes you want to stomp your boots. Maybe if we were in a barn I'd know how to dance to this. But barefoot in my bedroom? It's so out of place.

"Really?" I say over the music.

"What?" he says, hopping from foot to foot.

"I'm not really into my-woman-left-me-and-stole-my-truck kind of music. Can we listen to something else?"

He rolls his eyes. "Just give it a chance."

The chorus of the song kicks in, and . . . *interesting*. The woman singing has a definite twang to her voice, but her tone is clear and pretty. And there's a line about kissing whoever you want—boy *or* girl—and another about loving whoever you love, 'cause you only live once. It's kind of great. And decidedly *not* what I think of when I think of country music. There's nothing about horses or trucks or America. It's just a love song.

"What is this song called?" I ask.

"'Follow Your Arrow.' Kacey Musgraves. She's rad," Josh says as his movements become more exaggerated. Okay, he's *not* a great dancer, but he's confident, and he's enjoying himself, and he's going where the music takes him; as far as I'm concerned, those are the three main requirements for dancing.

I take a deep breath and start some step touches.

"Finally!" Josh says. He grabs my hands and moves my arms in toward him and then out again. He doesn't pull me close, which I'm glad about. For some reason, I feel like that might be awkward. This way, it's easier to extend the leash on my inhibitions a little.

Josh sings along—terribly—and I join in on a word here and there, when I can remember them.

Another song, less country and more folksy-pop, comes on next, bleeding into the last without a gap. This one is more my speed, so I crank up the speaker. The next four minutes are a flurry of arm waving and jumping around and shout-singing and out-of-breath laughing.

"Hey," I say, dancing over to Josh's phone and scrolling through Spotify until I find "Elle me dit." "Have you heard this one? It's my favorite."

Josh shakes his head, but listens to the entire song attentively as I twirl around the room. I don't know how much of it he's actually picking up, since I'm pretty sure he doesn't understand the French lyrics, but he listens closely anyway. When the song ends, I switch to the English reimagining of the song—"Emily."

I notice Josh eye me thoughtfully at the "Don't leave your life to chance, or you'll end up like your father" line, but I don't meet his gaze. I've already let my walls down so much today; any further and I might crumble.

Another Mika song comes on next, then another. At one point, several songs in, Josh spins me around, then tucks me into a dip. Half upside down and giggling, I catch a glimpse of the bedroom doorway—and Mom's there, leaning against the door frame in her dark gray scrubs, an amused expression on her face. Josh must see her at the same time I do, because he pulls me upright and presses the PAUSE button on his phone. My heartbeat echoes in my ears.

"Hi!" I say to Mom, gasping for air and wiping the sweat from my forehead. "I didn't hear you come in."

"I can see that." Mom chuckles. She steps forward into the room and holds a hand out to Josh. "Nice to see you again!"

I'd forgotten they've already met. It seems weird now that Mom knew Josh before I did.

"You too!" He wipes his palm on his jeans before shaking her hand. "Sorry, I'm sweaty."

"Don't let me stop the party," she says, smiling. "I'm loving the playlist."

Josh beams. "Thanks!"

"I'll bring you up some ice water," Mom offers.

"It's okay," I say. "We can come down and get it." I look at Josh. His face is flushed, his hair slicked back a bit by the sweat at his roots. He looks . . . good. "I'm tired," I admit with a little laugh.

"Yeah, same. Ice water sounds amazing." Josh pushes up the sleeves of his T-shirt to his shoulders, and I allow myself the briefest glimpse of his surprisingly defined biceps. I should have guessed he'd have arms like that, with the way he plays the violin like his life depends on it.

I fix my eyes resolutely to his face.

As we follow Mom downstairs, my head is spinning, and not just from the dancing. It's rare that I think a guy is cute like that. I mean, yes, Noah Lim of YouTube fame, obviously. And there was a kid in eighth grade—my wood shop partner, Mark—who I found intriguing in a curiosity/new hormones kind of way. But this is different. I just legit checked Josh out, in the way I used to look at Silvie (and still do with her photos, in moments of weakness). *Josh.* A guy I know in real life, who I didn't even think was attractive at first.

My stomach is a gooey mess. No more arm ogling, I tell myself firmly. One and done.

We sit at the kitchen table.

"Josh, are you staying for dinner?" Mom asks. "I was going to make pasta. Nothing fancy."

"Oh, thank you so much, Maggie, but I actually need to leave soonish to pick up my sister—she's at camp this week while school is out."

"How old is your sister?" Mom asks, sliding two tall glasses of cold water across the table to us. We guzzle it down like we haven't seen water in days. Who knew dancing in your room could be such a good workout? I'll post something about that later, wearing the Jeremy Bearimy tank Treat Yo'Self sent me.

"She's seven."

"Wow, that's quite the age gap!" Mom says, sitting at the table too with a glass of white wine. She lifts Abe onto her lap and smooches the side of his snout. Two signs that Mom's had a hard day at work: She pours herself a glass of wine or she gives Abraham extra love and attention. When she does both, you know it was really bad. A dog hit by a car or some flagrant instance of animal abuse. I want to ask what went wrong today, but won't. I don't want her to relive whatever it was. "Second marriage?" she asks Josh.

I cough. *"Mom."*

She looks at me. "What? Divorce happens, CeCe."

"Yeah. *I know.* But . . ." I look at Josh apologetically. Two Ross women making the same mistake within an hour of each other.

He smiles at me, and I decide to take his earlier word for it that he doesn't mind. "That's what most people think—that Dad remarried and that's when Gabby came along. Either that or that she was a surprise for my parents." Josh laughs, and then gives her the same history he gave me.

This is Josh's *thing*, I realize. This and music. He lights up when he talks about his family, and adoption.

A loud sniffle sounds from across the table, and we both turn to discover Mom is weeping. "Sorry," she says, wiping her nose with a napkin. "It's just been a really long day, and that's such a wonderful story. I didn't realize how much I needed to hear something good." She looks at me through watery eyes. "CeCe, you should have Josh tell that story on your page. I bet all your followers would love such an inspirational—"

Oh no.

"Um, maybe!" I say hastily, plowing over whatever she was going to say next. The back of my neck grows hot. "But, you know, Josh doesn't really like social media stuff, so probably not. Anyway, Josh, what time did you say you had to pick up your sister?"

Josh and Mom stare at me.

It's not the words I've said. I think they're normal? It's the way too loud, abrupt way I've stopped the conversation mid-flow. It's not subtle.

What was it she said? *All your followers.* That could be a clue, if he were looking for one. But he probably wasn't. It's probably fine. Right?

"Six," he says after a beat, and glances at the clock. It's five thirty. The park where Gabby's camp is held is about fifteen minutes away, without traffic.

"Sorry, I'm not kicking you out or anything." I laugh awkwardly. "I just didn't want you to be late. Because, you know. Rush hour and whatnot." *Stop talking, CeCe.*

Josh's face clears. "You're right, I should be going." He stands up and says goodbye to Mom. As I walk him to the door, he says, "Thanks for today."

"It was fun. Yay spring break."

He laughs. "Let's do it again?"

I nod. "I'll text you."

"Cool." He hovers for a moment, as if unsure whether to reach out for a hug or not. Ultimately he just gives a quick "Okay, bye," and steps out onto the porch.

I don't breathe again until he's in his car and backing out of the driveway.

I know I can't keep my internet fame from Josh forever. And this would have been the perfect opportunity to tell him—Mom was there to be a buffer, we were in a sharing kind of mood.

But that day, back at Holtman's.

Influencers, he'd said, disgusted. *More like brainwashers.*

What if he finds this out about me and decides I'm not the kind of person he wants to spend his time with after all, and then I don't get to have any more days like this?

"I'll be upstairs!" I call to Mom, avoiding the kitchen and the many questions she probably has cued up for me.

I close my bedroom door and lean against it.

Josh seemed fine as he left. A smidge confused, maybe, but not mad. It's fine. Everything's fine.

Except . . . I don't know when it happened, but *fine* isn't good enough anymore. Not with Josh.

@Hi_Im_CeCeRoss: If you're anything like me, one of the hardest parts of having your heart broken is watching your ex be happy without you. And on top of that, the world keeps spinning. It's been a less than a month, but the world has moved on from #Cevie. Which makes me feel like…well, like there's something wrong with me for not doing the same. #truthbomb #realtalk

But the team at #TreatYoSelf reached out to me recently, to let me know they understand. They helped me realize that a lot of you understand too. Because loss is universal, and in a backward kind of way, it can bring us together.

Treat Yo'Self is all about #selfcare and finding what makes you happy. I've been obsessed with their stuff for a LONG time—shouldn't we all be wearing and using products that fit our own unique identities and make us feel good?

This denim romper has quotes from famous women stitched all across it. It's cute AND it's comfortable! It makes me happy. And you know what? I'm starting to realize that it's okay to be happy, even when you're sad.

#mystory #selfie #fashion #ad #sponsored

CHAPTER 13

I should have just told him, I think for the millionth time as I approach Procter & Gamble Plaza on Thursday. I've been feeling far too close to a right-wing lobbyist for comfort these last two days: like a selfish jerk who cares about nothing but their own interests, damn everyone else. I need to tell Josh the truth about my life online. And I will, when the time is right.

Josh is already at the plaza when I arrive, unpacking his violin. He'd initially wanted to meet later in the day because he needed to spend the morning practicing. Something about being determined to nail the third movement of Brahms's Violin Concerto in D Major, even though very few soloists ever achieve the skill level required to perform the piece professionally. He and his teacher back in Florida had been working on it together, and in her absence he's decided to "let the genius of Johannes Brahms himself remind him what he's been working so hard for."

I probably resembled the shrug emoji when he said that, but whatever!

Instead, I suggested he bring his violin with him, since I know he likes playing outside. His violin case has straps like a backpack, and he doesn't seem to mind lugging it around everywhere. He could practice at the plaza, which is surrounded by office buildings. Businesspeople tend to have deep pockets; maybe he'd sell some CDs.

"Are you sure you don't mind?" he asked. "Won't that be boring for you?"

This conversation took place over the phone, by the way—the actual *phone*. I'd texted him, and then my phone rang. I thought it had to be a butt dial. But then I remembered who I was dealing with.

"Of course I don't mind!" I insisted. "It'll be great."

"Hi!" I say now, claiming a spot on a nearby bench.

"Hey, CeCe," Josh says with a smile made of pure light and sunshine. His hands seem to act of their own accord, performing motions they've done countless times before: flipping open the case, tightening and rosining the bow, attaching a shoulder rest to the back of the violin, assembling the music stand. Josh's violin itself is a well-loved, beat-up old instrument, with nicks in the varnish and mismatched pegs. It's perfect for him.

"Don't mind me," I say, slipping my sunglasses over my eyes and pulling out my phone. "I'm just a regular bystander."

He laughs. "Okay."

Once he's satisfied with his tuning, he settles his left hand into position and lays into the first powerful chord with his bow. I'm surprised to realize I recognize the song. I don't know from where—it isn't on the CD that I finally borrowed from Mom and listened to in my car yesterday—and I couldn't distinguish Brahms from Bach from Beethoven if my own life was at stake, but it's familiar. Maybe it was in a movie or something.

For the next hour, Josh plays and plays and plays. I watch and listen from where I sit, and his music draws me in, making me feel like I'm a part of it, somehow. His eyes never leave the sheet music. His left-hand fingertips work in a kind of organized frenzy, pressing down on the strings in rapid, invisible patterns. Each note tugs him deeper into that musical place, the place he's always drifting off to, to the point where I legitimately wonder if he's forgotten that I'm here, or that he's in public at all.

I record long stretches of video on my phone, but don't post them, which, admittedly, is off brand for me. But this is one of the most peaceful mornings I can remember experiencing, and I don't want to share it with anyone else. I liked the meditation app, but *this* type of reflection and mindfulness is more my style.

People in the plaza stop to listen and murmur appreciatively. The violin case with the stack of CDs and little placard rests open on the ground a couple feet in front of Josh. A man in a dark suit tosses in a ten-dollar bill and selects a CD. Josh doesn't stop playing, but nods to the man appreciatively. When the man strolls away, Josh and I share an excited grin, and I give him a big thumbs-up.

But really, more people should be buying these. Or at least tossing some change into the case.

I study Josh's sign, the marketing part of my brain click-click-clicking. First off, he needs either better handwriting or a professional font. And some color—the black Sharpie gets lost on the brown cardboard. He should also really add a Venmo or Cash App handle.

I grab my phone and open the app to research what other Josh-like musicians are out there, and what they're doing to market themselves, but quickly get distracted. There's some hubbub happening across the feeds of many of the people I follow—lots of mentions of #culturalappropriation and #disrespect—and I click through them, trying to figure out what's happening.

Within a couple minutes, Josh's music scoring my scrolling, I get to the root of it all. A famous British pop star, a white woman, is using a giant, neon *om* symbol as a set piece in her new stadium tour. Some Hindu fans of hers saw it and posted the picture on social, and now the post has been shared thousands of times, with people calling for the singer to stop using the symbol immediately and some even urging her to cancel the tour.

Mackenzie has posted something too:

@AussieMackenzie: Om, or pranava, is a sacred symbol in many religions, including Hinduism, Buddhism, and Jainism. In yoga, we do often chant om at the start of a session, but this is done out of respect and with care and understanding of the word's purpose and meaning. The wearing or other use of the symbol should be reserved for those who practice the religions from which it is derived. Any other use is a sign of disrespect and blatant cultural appropriation.

Go, Mack!

Takedowns on the app are happening more and more, as online culture becomes more aware of the dangers of hate speech and the fact that even simple, hasty actions have the ability to cause lasting harm. An old photograph of a famous person doing something problematic emerges, or someone with a large following says something racist, and people on the app sound off, demanding not only apologies but consequences and retribution. And if the apology isn't heartfelt, or the person accused doesn't see what the problem is, matters only get worse for them. Online, one spark can ignite an explosion.

Most of the time, I agree with the callouts. I'm cheering on the masses from behind my phone screen, even if I don't do it publicly. I don't care who you are or how well-intentioned you are—if you do or say something without thinking it through or doing the appropriate research, and that thing harms someone else, or a whole group of people, you should not be given a pass. We *all* need to be held responsible for our actions.

Once, back before I made my app page a no-conflict zone, a television actress, after having a few drinks, posted something grossly prejudiced against a particular group of people. I joined the thousands of others and called her out online. And I was genuinely happy when she got fired from her TV show. It sounds extreme, but sometimes a second chance is one chance too many. The damage is done; calling it out and demanding action when it happens is the only way to move the needle of progress forward.

I'm grateful for, and a little in awe of, all the people out there who aren't scared like me, and who use social media to get loud and get *angry*.

Josh reaches the end of the piece, and the simple open note resonates through the breeze. I look up. His bow and fingers are lifted off the instrument entirely, and I think I can see sweat on his brow. I click off my phone; I'll log back on later to see if the singer has issued an apology.

It takes a few slow seconds, but Josh gradually comes back to himself. When his gaze unfastens from the music stand and finds me, he smiles. I shove my phone into my bag and spring to my feet, giving him a loud, resounding round of applause. A few passersby do the same, and Josh's cheeks go pink.

"That was *awesome*," I say as he begins to pack up. "I can't believe you thought I'd think it was boring!"

"It was okay," he says. "I'm more comfortable in third position than fifth, and that piece is like *all* fifth. I'll get there eventually."

"Well, it sounded professional to me. Even better than the CD."

"You listened to the CD?" Josh looks up, surprised.

One corner of my mouth lifts. "Well, it required tracking down a time machine first, but I made it work."

"Ha ha." He rolls his eyes.

"I do have one question," I tell him.

"Shoot."

"What does your shirt mean?" I've been trying to figure it out all morning. The text reads, WITHOUT MUSIC, LIFE WOULD B♭.

Josh slings the case over a shoulder, grinning. "Without music, life would be flat."

• • •

"Hey, thanks for telling me about your family yesterday."

We're in Josh's car, on our way to pick up Gabby from camp. I reach forward to lower the music a bit.

"Of course," he says.

"Want to hear my dramatic family story now?" I try to keep my tone light.

He glances at me out of the corner of his right eye. "If you want to tell me, yeah. I'd like to hear it."

I do want to tell him, and not only because I'm trying to make up for keeping him in the dark about the other thing. "So, my parents got divorced almost four years ago, when I was thirteen. My dad lives here in Cincinnati, but I haven't seen him in close to a year. That was my choice."

"Oh. How come?" Josh flips his blinker and makes a left-hand turn.

"It probably sounds bad," I acknowledge. "I know a lot of people would love to have a relationship with their parents, but . . ." I pause. I need this to come out right. "For me, it was the right choice."

Josh nods.

"When my mom and dad met, he was the opposite of who he

is now. He was pretty cool back then—he didn't eat meat, he had gay friends, friends from different backgrounds. He even went to protests against the Iraq War and filmed those events, with the goal of putting the footage together for a documentary. I've seen photos and clips, and heard stories from Mom. I didn't know him then, but I think maybe we would have gotten along. But after I was born, something changed in him."

"What do you think it was?"

I shrug. "I don't know. Maybe he was freaked out about being the father of a daughter? Or a father in general. Maybe his strict religious upbringing, which he'd pushed aside for a little while, worked its way into his consciousness again. Or maybe it was some fluke rearrangement of his brain chemistry. I don't know. Mom doesn't know. Whatever it was, though, it happened quickly."

"What did he do?" Josh asks. He pulls into the parking lot and keeps the engine running. In the distance, across an expanse of trodden grass, are dozens of kids in orange T-shirts, playing tug-of-war.

The clock on the dashboard reads 5:52. I can probably get the rest of the story out in eight minutes.

"He started watching conservative cable news all hours of the day. He repeated the things those people said at every opportunity—somewhere along the way, he developed such *hatred* for everyone and everything who wasn't exactly like him. Immigrants, queer people, people of color, people who needed government assistance, women fighting for equality in their workplaces, efforts to save the planet. Even people who were outspoken against the wars—though he used to be one of them!" I let out a breath. "It got worse after Obama left office and was replaced by that . . . other guy. Dad felt validated, so he got louder. Angrier."

"Wow." Josh has turned in his seat to face me fully. "I know Florida has its share of conservatives, but they weren't always so visible in Miami. We have—I mean, *they* have; I keep forgetting I don't live there anymore—flourishing immigrant and gay communities. Part of me always hoped people like your dad were caricature inventions of the media or something."

"Oh, they're real," I assure him. "And they are many. How else do you think the world became what it is?"

"I don't know—widespread propaganda? Hacking?"

The internet, he means. I sigh. "Yeah, but those things don't work without lots and lots of people willing to believe and defend those views."

A sad silence hovers in the car with us. "That must have been hard to live with," Josh says after a minute.

Understatement of the millennium. "It's so opposite of who I am. It wasn't just that I disagreed with it—everything in my soul actively *fought* it. I don't know how to agree to disagree, and I don't know how to respect someone just because he's my parent. You've seen my bedroom," I add.

Josh smirks. "Girls just want to have fundamental rights."

I laugh. "Exactly. And this girl"—I nudge a thumb at myself—"wants everyone *else* to too. Mom pushed back on

155

some stuff with Dad, but she was dealing with her own issues—I can't imagine what it was like for her, to suddenly be married to a stranger. She so badly wanted that picket-fence life."

"You know," Josh muses, "I don't think I've ever actually *seen* a picket fence. They must not have them in Florida. What do they look like?"

"They're overrated." I give him a side smile.

"So what happened?"

I shrug. "My dad and I fought. All. The. Time. Even when we tried to keep the conversation neutral, it ended up in a fight. He'd say something about a football game, and I'd get angry that he was still willing to support the NFL, after all the looking the other way about the brain injuries, or their players being accused of domestic violence. Or I'd say something about the weather, and he'd go off about how climate change isn't real. And that was before it became really personal. You know, with the LGBTQ stuff."

Josh nods.

"I remember arguing with him when I was five years old about his views on immigration and refugees and the freaking border wall." I shudder. The memory is crystal clear. "We were screaming at each other. Actually shouting in each other's faces. I was in *kindergarten*, Josh. I'm sure my argument was all feeling and no facts, but still. He should have listened to me. At the very least he shouldn't have fought back. He shouldn't have used the words he used. But he didn't have a filter, and neither did I." I fiddle with the seat belt some more, and finally just unlatch it. "About ninety-five percent of our conversations, my entire life over, have been filled with animosity. We don't like each other. We don't know how to coexist," I finish simply.

Josh's eyes are fixed on me. I can tell he's thinking hard. "Do you want to?" he asks. "Find a way to have a relationship with your dad, I mean."

I shrug. "In a perfect world? Yeah, sure. But the world *isn't* perfect. And demanding distance from him has become a self-preservation thing, I guess." Just like CeCe's Curated App World.

"I get that," Josh says, nodding again.

But there's more to say. "I didn't come out until after my parents' divorce," I continue, more quietly now. "Sometimes I think that if Dad found out I was bi while we were still living under the same roof, and for some reason my mom hadn't been around, he would have kicked me out."

Josh gasps.

"I mean, that's all conjecture," I say quickly. "It didn't happen that way. It wouldn't have happened that way, because Mom would have stood up for me. But the things he's said about gay and trans people . . . it's enough to make me wonder."

"Does he know now?" Josh asks.

I quirk an eyebrow Josh's way. "He found out on social media." Ah, the irony. "He's one of those people who do justice to your argument of the internet being a breeding ground for negativity."

Josh seems surprised I'd admit to that. But it's the truth.

"I'm not saying your argument *wins*," I say pointedly. "But, yes, people like my father love the internet because there's always something, someone, somewhere who is going to validate the hatred or superiority or whatever it is they're already feeling. Confirmation bias, I think they call it. He spends a *lot* of time online." Maybe even more than I do.

"What happened when he found out?" Josh asks.

I let out a one-note laugh. "What do you think? He emailed me a bunch of links to anti-gay websites, said some crap about how it's not natural, blah blah blah. I deleted the email without finishing it, then texted him to leave me alone."

"And you haven't seen him since then?"

I shrug. "He's reached out. I met with him a few times. It didn't go well." I leave out the part about *why* Dad wanted to meet those times. "Finally, last year, I told him to never contact me again, unless he's open to seeing things differently. So far, he's listened."

The mass of orange shirts is making its way toward the line of cars in the parking lot now. Josh opens his car door so Gabby will see him.

"I'm really sorry, CeCe," he says. "That's awful."

I shake my head. "It's okay," I say truthfully. "I'm glad for it, in a way. I've been able to set my own boundaries, and he's finally respected my wishes. It's better this way. Healthier. For me *and* for Mom."

"That makes sense." Josh waves to a little girl with a high

ponytail and grass stains on her leggings. She beams and sprints toward the car.

"So many times," I say, more quietly now, because Gabby's going to be in earshot soon, "I've wished I could just tune out. Mind my business, and not get so worked up when I hear someone say something closed-minded or cruel."

"Music is good for that," Josh offers.

"Yes." I laugh. "It is. Staying away from the news works too. And focusing your attention on lighter things. But then I feel guilty."

"Guilty?" Josh looks confused. "Why?"

I take a breath, and admit something to him that I haven't admitted to anyone. Not even Silvie. "Because I don't really *want* to tune out. I could have followed in my dad's footsteps. So many kids take on their parents' views as their own. For some reason, my brain magnets have been configured to repel my dad's, rather than cling to them. And I got the opportunity to figure out who I was really early in life. I was kind of forced into it, yeah, but I've come out the other side okay, I think." I'm whispering now. I'm not even sure Josh hears that last part.

Josh gets out of the car just as his sister reaches us. She gives him a big hug. "How was camp today?" he asks, beaming down at her. There's definitely a family resemblance—they're both fair-skinned, dark-haired, and lanky, with a smile that makes you eager to know what they're thinking.

"It was awesome! I got to row a canoe!"

"A canoe? All by yourself?"

Gabby laughs. "No, silly. That's really hard. You'll go in circles. Aly and Leanne and Benji helped."

"Ah." Josh nods.

"Did you get good practicing done today?" Gabby asks, heading over to the passenger side of the car.

"Some, yeah. Back seat today, kiddo. We have a guest."

Gabby startles when she looks through the window and sees me sitting here. "Hi!" she says, and seamlessly changes course to the back seat. "Who are you?"

Josh hops back into the driver seat. "This is my friend CeCe."

"Nice to meet you," I say, turning around to shake Gabby's hand.

"You too!" she says. "I didn't know Josh had a friend! Miracles do happen!"

"Hey, no editorializing from the back seat," he says, laughing.

I laugh too, and Josh catches me with the most heart-stopping smile. Then he whispers, just for me, "You've come out the other side more than okay, CeCe. You're amazing."

@Hi_Im_CeCeRoss: I've been thinking lately about how many things I've forgotten. Not big things like love and heartbreak and grief—I have a feeling I'll always remember those.

But the little things. Movies I've seen in the theater, socks I used to wear almost every day but that eventually got pushed to the back of the drawer, the crisp coolness of catching a snowflake on your tongue, the first time I got a cavity filled. Stuff like that.

That's why I'm LOVING this "5 Lines a Day" journal from #TreatYoSelf. It's so simple to keep up with, and helps you hold on to all the little things that make life LIFE.

Lots of designs available ([click here](#))! Mine has a collage of famous celebrity wedding dresses on the front! So #vintage and #timeless!

#selfcare #mystory #ad #sponsored

CHAPTER 14

"Read any good books lately, CeCe?" Josh's dad, Marty, asks me.

It's Sunday, the last day of spring break, and Josh and I are hanging out at his house. The weather is warm, almost summerlike, so we're sitting on his back patio.

Josh's dad lifts the grill lid and turns everything over—burgers, corn cobs, veggie dogs. I'm so hungry I want to eat the air.

Marty is shorter and chubbier than Josh, with a short, graying beard and surprisingly cool black-rimmed glasses. I have a feeling Gabby is going to out-height him by the time she's ten.

When I got to the house earlier, Marty opened the front door before I could even knock, boomed a "Welcome, CeCe!" and gave me a hug of the totally genuine, not-even-a-little-creepy variety. Which, I've found, is rare when it comes to older dudes. "It's so nice to finally meet you!" he said. "I'd begun to think you weren't real. But Gabby assured me you were."

I laughed. "Josh's assurances weren't enough?"

"That kid spends more time in his own head than in the real world. You never know what's real and what he's dreamed up."

"CeCe! Come see my room!" Gabby said, and I gave Josh a

fleeting wave hello before being whisked off to a stuffed-animal-filled bedroom. Posters of Ariana Grande, Janelle Monáe, and Billie Eilish were taped to the pink walls. "Oh! That's Ears." She pointed to the black-and-white cat curled up in the pet bed at the foot of her own bed. "He'll let you pet him, if you want!"

"Well, how can I pass that up?" I said.

We sat on the floor together, and I scratched under Ears's chin for a few minutes, listening to his purrs. That's when I noticed a small computer printout of Mika on the wall next to the larger posters.

"Do you like Mika's music?" I asked Gabby.

"I do now! Josh played me that song you played him," she said. "It's *so* good."

"'Elle me dit'?" My whole body went soft at the thought of music genius Josh sharing my song with his sister.

She nodded. "I've listened to it about a hundred times. Both versions."

"I've listened to it at least that much too," I confessed.

She beamed.

Josh appeared in the doorway then. "Gabby, Dad said you can have some screen time before lunch."

"Sweet! See ya, CeCe!" She hopped up and bounced down the hall.

"I figured you could use some rescuing," Josh whispered to me as we headed outside.

"No rescuing required," I whispered back. "Gabby's cool."

He smiled. "She is, right?"

Now on their patio, sharing the wicker love seat with Josh, I answer Marty's question about books. "I'm listening to *Between the World and Me* on audio now. I'm loving it so far."

"Ah, a nonfiction reader!" Marty replies, pleased. "We have that in common."

"What are you reading?" I ask. "I'm always looking for good recommendations."

"Right now I'm reading a book about gravity."

"*Gravity?* Wow. I don't really read much science stuff, actually . . ." I trail off when I see Josh's face. He's shaking his head at me while also rolling his eyes at his dad. "What?" I ask.

"Just wait," he mutters.

"The gravity book is so good," Marty says, turning the grill off and sliding the burgers and dogs onto the plate of waiting buns. "It's impossible to put down!"

There's an extended beat where Marty and Josh just look at me, waiting. Marty's grin is goofy/expectant, like the eyes-wide, big-smile emoji; Josh's is more embarrassed/apologetic, like the monkey covering his eyes.

And then I get it. Gravity. Impossible to put down.

I burst out laughing. A real, teary-eyed belly laugh.

"Oh no," Josh says. "I'm disappointed in you, CeCe." There's laughter in his voice.

Marty gives me a high five, still chuckling, pleased with himself.

"What's the matter with you?" I say to Josh, poking him in the ribs with my elbow. "That was hilarious."

He pokes me right back. "I'm glad you think so. Because there's more where that came from. Martin Haim *lives* for a good dad joke."

"Aw, don't be such a spoilsport," Marty says, ruffling Josh's already messy hair.

"Yeah, *Josh*," I say, mimicking Marty's tone. "Dad jokes are the best." I just decided this, right now. I'd never had the privilege of hearing a dad joke from a bona fide dad before. "And aren't you the person who was wearing an I'LL BE BACH shirt the first time I met you?"

Josh lifts his chin defiantly. "That's a *music nerd* joke, not a dad joke. Big difference."

"Uh-huh," I say. "Silvie loved to tell the kind of jokes that require a lot of setup. Like a whole freaking backstory that goes on for fifteen minutes before you get to the punch line." I always grew impatient at those. And even when they ended up being funny, I could never remember them when I tried to tell them to Mom later on. Give me a two-line joke any day.

"Who's Silvie?" Marty asks.

"My ex-girlfriend."

"Oh." He nods, but his forehead crinkles the slightest bit in confusion as he glances at me, then Josh, then me again. "Gabby!" he calls into the house. "Screen time is over! Come get some lunch!"

Barely a minute later, Gabby comes skipping outside, phone in hand. But she keeps it facedown on the table and doesn't check it once as we eat. I never thought I'd envy the restraint of a seven-year-old. I purposely left my phone in my bag in Josh's kitchen, ringer off, to make sure I wouldn't start auto-scrolling in front of his dad.

"I like your phone case, Gabby," I say. It's pink and glittery, and perfectly fits her personality.

She beams. "Thank you! What does yours look like?"

"It's silver and shiny—a little like yours, actually."

"Do you text with Josh?"

"Sometimes." I lower my voice to a fake whisper. "He's not very good at it, though."

"I *know*," she says, rolling her eyes dramatically. "He always says hi at the start of his texts."

"He does!" I laugh. "But everyone knows the best thing about texting is you don't have to say hi. You can just get right to whatever you were going to say, because the conversation never stops, it just pauses."

"That's what I tried to tell him!" Gabby says.

"Okay, I can hear you," Josh finally says, mouth full and eyes sparkling. "I promise I'll be better about texting, all right?"

Gabby and I share a look that says *Uh-huh, we'll believe it when we see it.*

The lunch conversation veers in a thousand different directions from there, but it's light and unfettered and the complete opposite of everything an afternoon with *my* dad would be. When the late-day sun crests our side of the house and begins to hammer us with its rays, we gather the empty plates and cups and head inside.

"Do you have dental floss?" I whisper to Josh after helping Marty load the dishwasher. "I feel like I have an entire corn cob wedged between my teeth."

"Sure." He nods in the direction of the hall. "Come on."

I follow Josh into a little bathroom off his bedroom, with white tile walls and a navy-blue shower curtain. It smells like Josh in here. His shampoo, his toothpaste, whatever else he uses. Not hair product. Pretty sure he doesn't know what hair product is.

He hands me the floss, and our fingers graze as I take it.

It shouldn't be anything, that touch. On its surface it's no more intimate than brushing hands with a stranger while sharing a handrail on a bus. And we've legitimately clasped hands before, like when we were dancing in my room.

So why do I inhale so sharply at this contact? Why does every inch of my skin erupt in prickles? Why am I so thirsty—no, parched? Why do I all of a sudden feel, deep down, miles inside me, so *tuned in* to this person standing beside me?

It's just our close proximity in this small bathroom, I tell myself. And the delicious shampoo smell. My guard is down, loosened from all the laughter. It's circumstance, that's all.

But then. Why has neither of us pulled away? Why are we still both gripping on to this tiny plastic square as if it's the last donut Holtman's will ever make? And why is my pinkie still on Josh's thumb? If it were a person on a bus, we would have readjusted, given each other our allotted space within a second or two.

It's been more than a second or two.

I watch Josh's hands with renewed interest as he finally, almost reluctantly, releases the box of floss and slips that same thumb through his belt loop, where it's safe. His hands are the best part of him. And there are lots of good parts of him. But his hands . . . the way those bones and muscles are capable of taking direction from his brain in such a precise way . . . of creating such *art* . . .

I need to snap out of it. I can't just stand here, clinging to a box of floss and ogling this poor guy's hands. They're just *hands*. Stop.

So I pull my gaze up to his face.

It doesn't help matters. His eyes are dark and intense and roaming over my face, searching, as if they expect to find the answers to the universe there. As I watch, his lips press together and he runs his teeth lightly over the bottom one. He's thinking again. But *what* is he thinking? What am *I* thinking, apart from wondering what he's thinking?

Oh, shut up, CeCe, I admonish myself. *You know what you're thinking.*

Yeah. What I'm thinking is, I like him. Like, *like*-like.

It's a revelation. It's also a disappointment.

I was just starting to get used to being alone; enjoying it, even. I haven't checked Silvie's feed for a couple days now, and I've cooked dinner for Mom three times this week—not because I was bored, but because I was legitimately inspired by some recipes I saw on the app. I texted Jasmine a new list of prom theme ideas, which she appreciated, since "Most of the ideas people had come up with so far were a snooze-fest." And the Treat Yo'Self partnership has been going so well that Tawny asked me to extend my contract.

Do I really want to be with someone again? And do I want to be with *Josh*? People say your significant other should also be your friend, but he's already my friend, and the rational part of me, at least, doesn't want to mess with that. Besides, does Josh even like me that way? I know that day we met up for donuts, he'd thought it was a date. But he hasn't said anything like that since then.

His eyes glint. What is he looking for when he searches my face? Are my thoughts printed on my skin, in my eyes, the shape of my mouth?

The fears, the feelings, the endless questions are filling up this tiny bathroom, echoing back at me off the ceramic tile walls. I can't think. I can barely breathe.

The moment is going on too long.

I look away first. Josh takes the cue. Looks down too. Toes the shaggy bath mat. Clears his throat. "I'll, uh, leave you to . . ."

"Yeah," I say, nodding too much. "Just need to . . ." I hold up the floss as a conclusion to the sentence.

"Okay . . . bye."

As he maneuvers his way around me, I hold my breath. My head is already filled to the brim with the scent of him. The brand-new idea of him.

He keeps his eyes down. Leaves the bathroom, closing the door quietly behind him.

I exhale.

. . .

"She's pretty," I hear Marty saying to Josh when I reenter the kitchen. "And fun."

I catch my breath and pause. Josh is busy transferring the leftover food into glass storage containers, and Marty is at the sink, washing the serving trays. Their backs are to me, and the sound of the running water makes them a little hard to hear, but they haven't realized I'm back, so their voices aren't as low as they could be.

Quickly, I tiptoe back around the corner, out of the kitchen. I'm out of sight now, but not out of earshot.

"Yeah, I guess," Josh replies noncommittally.

"You *guess*?" Marty presses. "Joshua, she's the first girl you've ever brought home. There's got to be a reason it's her and not someone else."

"Dad, please, stop." His voice is pained. "We're just friends."

"Uh-huh. If I had a 'friend' who looked at me like that, I'd marry her on the spot."

Looked at him like what? I only just realized I might have feelings for Josh. Like literally five minutes ago. What could Marty have possibly seen?

"Yeah, well, I'm not getting married any time soon. Thought I might give that another ten or twenty years."

Marty chuckles, undeterred. "You know what I mean, son."

"I know." A pause. "But she's not interested in me like that." The refrigerator door opens, then closes.

"Impossible." The tap turns off.

"Dad," Josh hisses, his voice lower now. "She just broke up with her girlfriend."

"Yeah, about that . . ." Marty says, lowering his volume too. "Is she a lesbian? Because the way you two were sitting by each other out there . . ." He trails off. I assume he's doing something with his body language, but I can't see. How *were* we sitting by each other? I had no idea.

"She's bisexual, but—"

"Aha!" Marty claps his hands, like *mystery solved.*

"But," Josh reinforces, "she's made it perfectly clear she's not looking to date anyone. End of story."

Does that mean he'd want to? If he thought I wanted to? Or is he just trying to get his dad off his back?

"What do *you* want, Josh?" Marty presses.

Yes, thank you, Marty. My thoughts exactly. I lean in a little, waiting for Josh's answer.

But he doesn't have a chance to give it.

"Hi, CeCe!" The voice from behind me is little. The volume is not.

I practically leap out of my skin. "Agh! Jeez, Gabby." I press a palm to my chest in an attempt to slow my racing heart. She's just standing there, cradling Ears in her arms, innocently beaming. "You scared me."

172

"Sorry." But her smile doesn't waver. Quite the opposite: When her eye line shifts beyond me into the kitchen, she grins even bigger and rocks up onto her toes, proud.

My face flaming, I turn to find Josh and Marty staring at me, putting the pieces together. Josh's face is bright red too. *Crap.* They know I was listening. And Gabby knew exactly what she was doing.

"All good with the flossing?" Marty asks, his eyes darting between me and Josh gleefully, as if he's trying to gauge who's more embarrassed.

"Yep," I say, aiming for normalcy. "Can't overestimate the value of good dental hygiene." That was so *not* a normal thing to say. I resist the urge to bury my face in my hands. Instead, I hastily step into the kitchen to retrieve my bag. Fumbling, I fish my phone out and thumbprint it on. No missed calls, no texts. Just the usual app notifications. "Actually," I say, palming the phone from one hand to the other, "I should be going. Abraham needs a walk."

Marty nods. "Thanks for coming over today, CeCe. I hope we'll be seeing more of you around here." He walks over and we exchange another hug. I hug Gabby too (even though she's totally my nemesis now), scratch Ears between the ears, and give Josh a little wave. It's kind of weird that I've now hugged every member of his family except him. But today is not that day.

"I'll walk you out," Josh says.

I swallow. Smile. "Okay."

"Hey, so," he says once the front door is closed behind us and we're halfway down the path to the driveway. "Did you hear what my dad said back there?"

I don't deny it. I don't say anything.

He takes it as confirmation.

"Just . . . don't overthink it, okay?" Josh says. "Dad's a total softie. Believes in soul mates, Cupid's arrow, all that stuff. He's always playing matchmaker." Josh rolls his eyes. "Tried to hook up the receptionist at work with the UPS guy last week. It isn't anything to do with you, don't worry."

"Oh," I say. "Okay."

But what I really want to say is *But what about the way you feel, Josh? Is that anything to do with me?*

"We cool?" he asks, his face unreadable.

I nod. "Of course."

He smiles in relief. "Great." Then, with an abrupt nod good-bye, he turns back toward the house.

I slide into the driver's seat and power the car on. Josh's CD begins blasting from the speakers. The windows are up, but I know he hears it, because he stops walking.

I hastily turn off the music, but I don't check my mirrors or put the car into drive. I can't bring myself to leave. I watch Josh, my breathing coming so heavy I can feel the rise and fall of my chest. Josh is stock still, facing the house, the bones and muscles of his back at full attention.

And then he does it.

He slowly turns back toward me. An endless moment passes,

as if he's deciding something. Then he moves closer to the car. One step, then two and three.

Something was set in motion when he heard his music playing from my speakers, and now neither of us is going to stop it. I know I don't want to.

I get out of the car.

@GabbySingsXoxo: My brother's new girlfriend is SO PRETTY. They're outside right now and I think they're going to kiss. 😆😆😆😆😆😆😆😆😆😆😆😆 😆😆😆

CHAPTER 15

I study Josh's dark eyes. Something is going on in there. Something deep and intense.

I take a breath to speak. For once in my life, I'm going to wing this.

"This is hashtag bonkers" is what comes out.

Josh laughs, just a little, and extends his hand, palm up. It's an invitation, a query. That beautiful hand. I grasp on to it, and he squeezes tight. It's amazing how good it feels, his perfect fingers wrapped around mine. "CeCe . . ." he begins, but I cut him off. I don't know why, but I need to be the one to say it first.

"I like you," I say, staring down at our hands. "*Like*-like." The words release the pressure that's been building since I met him. There. The hardest part is done. How simple it ultimately was.

"You do?" Josh breathes, half in disbelief, half in relief.

I glance up. His eyes are even darker now, if that's possible.

"Yeah," I say sheepishly. "I have a pretty terrible crush on you, if I'm being honest, which I think I'm only fully realizing right now, and—"

Josh cuts me off with a whispered "CeCe?"

"Yeah?"

"Can I kiss you?"

My body goes warm at the sweetness of the question.

This whole time, we've been slowly moving closer and closer together, but at my quiet, confident "Yes," time speeds up. In a flash, Josh closes the gap, pressing his lips to mine.

Oh my god.

Josh is kissing me. I'm kissing Josh.

Part of my brain registers that I'm kissing a boy for the first time ever, and that that's kind of momentous in its own right, but the thought falls away before I can properly acknowledge it, because, hello, this is not just any boy. This is Josh. He is so much more than just a boy. If Josh weren't Josh, I wouldn't have wanted to kiss him at all.

But he is, and I did. I am.

Our kiss is almost feverish, frenzied, like we're making up for lost time. Which is strange, because we haven't really known each other that long.

His hand untwines itself from mine and I feel a nanosecond of loss, but then he brings both his hands up to my face, my hair, and wow. Does he have any idea how much power those hands of his hold?

I wrap an arm around the back of his neck, tugging him closer. I want him as close to me as possible. He follows willingly.

Before long, we're both gasping for air, and we have no choice but to pull apart. Our eyes rove over each other's faces. I'm out of breath. Josh's cheeks are flushed, his hair hanging in his face. I reach out and brush it back. He captures my hand and presses his lips to my palm.

These tiny actions bring everything into complete and utter clarity. How many times have I wanted to touch his hair, his face? And by the way he just kissed my palm, so confident, so greedy, I know he's had that in mind before today too. And now we're suddenly allowed to. That thin thread of awkward tension that has been stitched through our friendship is gone, carried off in the breeze.

Josh's face breaks into an awed smile. "That . . ." His voice is scratchy. "That was . . ."

He doesn't need to finish his sentence. I know what he means. "Sorry not sorry," I tease.

He laughs. "Can we do it again?" he asks.

I launch myself at him. I'd forgotten how fun kissing can be. And Josh is *really* good at it.

Still kissing, we sit down on the pavement beside my car, on full view to the street but hidden from whoever might be watching from inside Josh's house.

"I thought you've never dated anyone before," I say at one point.

"I haven't," he breathes against my lips.

"Then where did you learn to kiss like this?"

"From you, I guess."

"Huh?"

"You're my first kiss, CeCe. This is all your inspiration."

"Oh." His first kiss. I shouldn't be so happy about that, but I am. I like that it was a first, of sorts, for both of us. I kiss him again, hard.

"I feel like I should tell you," he murmurs, "I've been enamored by you from the moment I opened my eyes to find you standing there, watching me play."

I pull back to get a better look at him. "Really?"

He rolls his eyes. "Oh, come on, it was obvious. I even asked you out on a date, as you may remember." He raises an eyebrow. "But you made it clear you only liked me as a friend, so . . ." He shrugs.

"Well . . ."

"Uh-huh." Josh brings a hand to my face again, caressing my cheek. I lean into it.

"I did only like you as a friend at first," I admit quietly. "But I wasn't over Silvie yet. The timing was wrong."

"I know," he says.

"But you had to be so damn cute and charming."

"Oh yeah, you know me," he teases. "Always being accused of being cute and charming."

"Josh, every person who's into guys at your school is probably already in love with you. I'm certain of it."

"I highly doubt that," he says. "But anyway, there's only one person I'm interested in."

I can't help the glow that spreads over me. "Same." I extend a hand for a shake, as if to seal the verbal agreement.

Josh takes my hand, but doesn't shake it. Instead, he pulls me in close and captures my mouth with his again. "You taste like gummy bears," he whispers against my lips.

Direct message
From: @QuietGuy1414
To: @Hi_Im_CeCeRoss

Dear CeCe—
I need advice. If this is too much to ask, I'm so sorry, and please ignore this message!

Anyway...

I'm gay. That's the first time I've said that out loud—if typing it can be considered saying it out loud. Ha ha. I'm terrified of anyone finding out. There's a kid in my class who everyone thinks is gay, because he's soft-spoken and wears a tie to school sometimes. He gets terrorized every single day.

Today he came to school with two black eyes and a bandage on his broken nose. The kids who attacked him at the bus stop yesterday afternoon walked away with a "talking-to" by the vice principal. That's it. It's so unfair. I wish I could talk to him, tell him that if he is gay he's not alone, see if maybe he wants to be my friend. But I'm scared. If anyone sees me associating with him, they'll turn on me too.

What should I do?

CHAPTER 16

"Is Mia going to be your prom date?" Jasmine asks at one of our before-school prom planning meetings.

We've had a ton of these meetings in the three weeks since spring break ended, and we've definitely made some good progress. Turns out DJ Rio was unavailable, but Silvie got a commitment from another DJ, so that's done. And our official prom theme is An Evening at the Symphony, which was one of my suggestions—and directly inspired by Josh, though no one knows that. But we've also been talking ourselves in circles on the subjects of paper tickets vs. digital, and plated dinners vs. buffet. One of the benefits of not being in charge anymore is that I get to tune out whenever I feel like it.

So I'm on my phone, reading QuietGuy's message for the second time, and at first I don't pay attention to Jasmine's question—she's probably talking to Deri or someone.

I get messages like QuietGuy's every now and then. Sometimes the writer asks my advice, but more often they just want to share their truth with someone who's willing to listen. I've shown Mom a few of them in the past (always covering up the writer's handle when I do so, to maintain their privacy), to remind her of the good parts of social media. I've been debating showing them to Josh too; I still haven't told him about any of this, and it could be a good gateway into the subject.

I begin to craft a response to QuietGuy—maybe there's a way for him to let the other boy know he's not alone, while also ensuring his own safety?—but after a moment my thumbs slow their typing.

The only response to Jasmine's question about the prom date has been a loaded, extended silence. That's weird.

I look up from my phone.

Jasmine isn't awaiting an answer from Deri. She's looking at *Silvie*, who is suddenly red-faced and half eyeing me. My phone clatters to the table.

Heartbeat spluttering, I ping-pong my gaze between Jasmine and Silvie and the rest of the GSA members, who are utterly silent and watching me for a response too.

"Who . . ." My voice is scratchy, and I clear my throat. "Who is Mia?"

Silvie fiddles with her pen. Her hair is shorter than it was when we were together, just brushing the tops of her shoulders, and there's a light blue streak at the front. It shouldn't work with her eye color, but it does. "I, um, posted about it. Her. A couple weeks ago. I was wondering if you'd seen it, because you hadn't said anything."

"You posted what? What did you post?" Hands trembling and moving in fast-forward motion, I grab my phone again and click on Silvie's handle. Sure enough, there are three pictures of Silvie and this Mia.

@SilviaCasRam: I want you all to meet someone very special. This is @MiaInIndy—my new girlfriend. 😊 We met in Mexico, but it turns out she lives in Indianapolis, which is less than two hours away from where I live in Cincinnati! Sound like #fate to you? Yeah, it did to us too. #TeAmo 💜 💜 💜 💜 💜

#girlfriends #girlswholikegirls

I swallow painfully.

Mia is really pretty. Dark skin, big hair, minimal makeup, amazing gold jewelry. The photos were taken from the same white-sand, blue-sky, blue-water setting of Silvie's other vacation posts. Their arms are around each other in all the shots, and there's no space between their bodies.

In the photos, Silvie is looking at Mia with an expression I know well. It's her heart-eyes expression.

And the hashtag at the end: *Te amo*. Does Mia speak Spanish too, like Silvie? And are they really already saying *I love you* to each other?

The air zaps out of the classroom, and I suddenly feel like I'm choking. I cough, hard, and someone—Ramsey, I think—smacks me lightly on the back. I shrug them off.

"Wow, tell me how you really feel," Silvie says sardonically.

I shake my head. "Sorry. Leftover cough from a cold I had last week."

"Right." She doesn't believe me for a second.

Ten attentive faces are still staring at me from around the table, waiting for me to say something. They've probably been waiting for me to say something since Silvie's first Mia post went up. But I didn't know. *How* could I not have known?

And I realize—I didn't know Silvie was dating anyone because I muted her on the app, and I haven't clicked on her page in ages. Because I've moved on too.

Over the past few weeks, the bubble around me and Josh has sealed shut—a more lasting version of that split second outside the conservatory when his fingertips were on my shoulder and the world started to disappear.

He and I have been spending most days together after school, usually at his house because Gabby isn't old enough to stay home alone. But sometimes he comes over for dinner with me and Mom. I think, because Josh and I don't interact online, we've been accommodating for it in other ways. In real time, with no publicly posted history to scroll through, we're learning each other's stories and quirks, likes and dislikes, reactions and expressions. There's always something to ask, or something to tell.

Small things, like when he showed me the trick of feeding ice cubes to my orchid plants rather than regular water. Or when we argued over whether fennel tastes good or not (I am firmly in camp "shoot it into outer space and never think of it again"). Or when he found out my mom had once gone to an Alanis Morissette concert, and they geeked out together over the photos she'd taken from the nosebleed seats.

And bigger things, like when I told him about my grandma who used to quote lines from old black-and-white movies, before the Alzheimer's got really bad. Or when Gabby got a new email from their birth mother, but he didn't get one.

It's special, this place of isolation with him. Comfortable. Warm. I wonder if this is what it's like for him when he's playing his music.

I study Silvie's photos on the app again. Mia looks nothing like me. But then, Josh looks nothing like Silvie. I can't believe it, but I'm actually . . . okay with it? Even if that okayness *does* have the slightest tinge of sore-loser-ness to it.

"You should bring her," I say, putting as much certainty into my voice as I can. "To the prom. You should bring her."

Silvie looks stunned. But after a moment, she smiles. It's a small, close-lipped smile, but it's there. "Okay."

"Great!" Jasmine claps her hands. "Now, let's talk party favors."

• • •

After the meeting, I catch Silvie on her way out the door.

"Hey," I say.

"Hey."

"Can I walk you to your class?"

She hesitates, like she's worried I'm about to unleash my *real* reaction about her new girlfriend. "Sure."

We slowly make our way through the halls, which are filling up with more and more people as the school buses unload. It's weird how much about walking with Silvie is the same as it was before. The crane of my neck as I look over and up at her. The way she hugs her books to her chest, because she's never been one to carry a backpack. Our matching strides, despite the fact that her legs are a lot longer than mine. So much has changed since we last did this that it feels like *everything* should be different.

"So, a book deal, huh?" I say. It's not the main thing I wanted to talk about, but it *is* a lingering elephant in the room. We've only spoken about GSA stuff these past few weeks, and barely even that.

"Yeah. Sorry I didn't tell you about it. A lot of things were still up in the air with it back when we were together, and I didn't want to jinx anything . . ." She trails off. She knows her excuses are flimsy. I don't need to tear them apart for her.

I nod. "I hope it goes well. I'm sure it will."

"Thanks."

We round a corner and dodge a few oncomers.

I take a deep breath. The corridor smells like bleached floors and the musty insides of lockers. "Anyway, I wanted to let you know—not in front of everyone—that I'm actually dating someone too."

I peek over at Silvie in time to watch her eyebrows go skyward. "Really?"

"Yeah."

"For how long?"

"Since spring break, I guess."

Silvie nods. "Same."

"Yep."

"Where does she live?" Silvie asks.

My stomach dips nervously at her assumption. Why do I feel like I'm coming out all over again? But this is *Silvie*. No matter what we've been through, I can be honest with her. Right? I clear my throat. "Um, actually, it's a he. Josh."

"Oh." A beat goes by. "Wow. That's new."

I nod, staring down at the tile floor. "I wasn't looking for it," I say quickly. "You know I like girls more than boys."

"I know."

I can't shake the feeling that I've betrayed her somehow, by dating a boy. It doesn't make any sense, especially for me— gender is truly not the thing that makes me attracted to someone. Silvie knows that. But this girl vs. boy thing is complicated. The image thing is complicated. And okay, maybe I still feel the need to justify it to myself too.

I always assumed I'd just date women. Like, forever. It's what I know, and I know I like it, and I'm so entrenched in the queer community already . . . I've always been totally okay with boys being nothing more than a possibility.

And then Silvie left, and Josh showed up.

"He lives here," I continue, answering her earlier question. "In Cincinnati. But he goes to Delilah Beasley. He's a musician."

We've reached Silvie's classroom. I'll have to book it to the other side of the school for my first class, but I can't leave her yet.

"So . . ." I look up at her cautiously. "What do you think?"

She chews on the inside of her bottom lip for a minute. Then she meets my eyes and smiles. "Is he an ally?" It's like she's an old-school parent asking if he comes from good breeding.

I laugh in inexorable relief. "He is. You'd like him, I think."

"I hope I get to meet him someday. Maybe we can double-date."

Yeah, that's never going to happen. "Totally," I say noncommittally.

"Cool," Silvie says, tightening her grip around her books, and I know she has no intention of this double date ever happening either. "Well, thanks for telling me. I'd better get to class." She nods toward the open classroom door.

"Me too." I pause. "Hey, Silvie?"

"Yeah?"

"Is Mia part of the 'finding out who you are without Cevie' thing?" I ask, hitching my backpack strap higher on my shoulder and forcing myself to meet her gaze.

She nods.

"Are you happy?" I ask.

The corner of her mouth curves up, and she nods again.

"Good." I'm not totally sure if I mean it or not, but it feels like the right thing to say.

Silvie disappears inside the classroom, and I slide my phone from my bag as I walk to my own class. I need to send out another Treat Yo'Self post today, and until a few minutes ago, I had no idea what I was going to write about. Things have been good—better than good. I've even been considering asking Tawny if it would be all right if I veered away from all the #heartbreak talk.

Now, though, the words come easily.

@Hi_Im_CeCeRoss: I just found out my ex-girlfriend has a new girlfriend. And I'm feeling FEELINGS.

The most confusing part of all of this is that I really thought I'd started to move on. I was focused on self-care, and beginning to look forward instead of back. I was even starting to be…dare I say it…HAPPY.

But this threw me for a loop. And I'm not even sure I have the RIGHT to be jealous or sad about it. Shouldn't I be happy she's happy?

I honestly don't know. But for tonight, I'm going to take a bath, curl up in my #treatyoself <u>Mars Investigations pj's</u>, and hope for good dreams.

#selfcare #mystory #ad #sponsored

CHAPTER 17

The following day, after school, I sit cross-legged on my bed with my laptop. The cursor on the blank page blinks, waiting.

I have to get my speech to Kathleen by May 29, which is less than three weeks away. And I haven't started writing it. I've barely even let myself *think* about it, since that day Silvie bailed and it became clear that I'd be doing it all alone.

When Cincinnati Pride invited Silvie and me to speak, I accepted the invitation with an *OMG! YES! This is the biggest honor of my life, I will be there with bells on, thank you SO MUCH*, and Silvie and I immediately began brainstorming speech ideas.

I wanted to talk about coming out in middle school, and having a long-term, same-sex partner in high school. Even now, with marriage equality, and antidiscrimination laws, and more diverse representation on TV and in movies, my experience is far from the norm. Especially in the Midwest. I was going to use my share of our time onstage to gush about Silvie, and talk about all the ways in which I'm lucky, and how I want every queer kid to have the same experience, if they want it.

I was going to allow myself to be political in public for the first time in a long time.

Now what?

The cursor blinks. And blinks. And blinks. I'm not going to get any speech writing done today.

I close the laptop and text Josh.

My birthday is two weeks from today. Want to know what I want?

About a half second after I push the SEND button, I recognize how flirty the words sound. That's actually not what I meant. But I don't clarify.

The phone lights up with a response: Hi. Wouldn't have pegged you for a Taurus.

I burst out laughing, and thumb back a reply.

I wouldn't have pegged you for someone who knows anything about astrology.

Gabby's influence, he writes back. And then: 👻

Josh! Look at you with the emojis! 👻 👻 👻 👻 👻

Ha ha, he says. So what do you want for your birthday?

I want to help you get your music online and redo your photos and press materials.

I count the seconds, my whole body made up of heartbeat, waiting for his answer. Unlike speech writing, *this* is something I'm good at. Marketing. Curating. I know how to help Josh; I just hope he'll let me.

Sixteen endless seconds later:

OK.

I throw my arms up, touchdown-like, and hop around my room in victory.

Photo shoot, I text before he can change his mind. Sunday morning.

· · ·

"Josh. Lower. Your. Arms," I say for the fiftieth time.

We met up in the trendy Over-the-Rhine neighborhood, Josh armed with his violin, me with my phone's camera already set to portrait mode. We took off on foot, walking around the neighborhood, stopping for pics whenever I spotted a cool brick wall or mural for Josh to pose in front of. Well, "pose." Turns out he's *terrible* at it.

This photo shoot is the complete opposite of the ones Silvie and I used to do together. We knew what we were doing.

Josh does not.

I've never met anyone less comfortable in front of a camera. Every time I point the phone in his direction, his shoulders hunch, his chin goes rigid, and he suddenly seems to know only two facial expressions: mug shot or squinty-eyed, toothy-mouthed cheeseball. I'm starting to understand why he used that grainy picture for the CD cover. It was probably the best one he had.

Right now, he's leaning, as instructed, against a stack of banana crates we found. One leg is propped up, his dark gray T-shirt is rumpled in just the right way, hinting at the suggestion of abs. He wouldn't let me put product in his hair, but luckily the humidity is low today and he didn't really need it. He looks totally hot. Like, so hot that I can't believe I didn't find him attractive from day one.

195

These photos are so close to what we need. Except he keeps insisting on holding the violin and bow up like he's playing.

"But why?" he asks, also for the fiftieth time. "I'm a violinist. I should be playing the violin."

"You can play the violin all you want," I say, trying hard to keep the exasperation from my voice. "Later. Right now we need to see your freaking face."

I swipe from the camera setting to the web browser on my phone and do a quick image search. *Famous violinists.* About a zillion images of old white men come up. Nope.

I try again. *Famous violinists. Sexy.*

There we go.

I click on a picture but don't show Josh yet. "You like Joshua Bell, right?" I ask.

"He's one of my heroes."

I hold the phone up for him to see. Taking up the full screen is a photo of Joshua Bell in a T-shirt and jeans, holding his violin and bow in front of his midsection, one hand in his pocket. His face is completely unobstructed.

Josh's expression changes as he takes in the image. "Ohhh."

I do another search, then another, showing him the results each time. David Garrett, Lindsey Stirling, Ray Chen, Charlie Siem, Vanessa-Mae. All violinists. All unreasonably gorgeous. All totally happy to pose for the camera in a way that actually shows what they look like.

Josh nods. "I get it now."

I grin triumphantly. "Good."

Josh goes back to the banana crates with, praise Oprah, a much more casual hold on the violin and bow. CeCe: 1, Josh: 0.

I snap a few more shots and study them on the phone screen. Much better, but he's still a little too tense.

A mischievous smile creeps onto my lips as another idea strikes me. I do a new Google search. Commit a few of the search results to memory. Swipe back to the camera.

"Hey, Josh?" I say, my finger hovering over the image capture button.

"Hmm?"

"What do you call someone with no body and no nose?"

His eyes narrow. "What the hell are you talking about?"

"Nobody knows!"

I wait for it. And . . .

Yes!

I snap picture after picture as Josh first registers, then reacts to the joke. The transformation is incredible. His body relaxes into laughter, his eyes warm, his smile radiant. I check the snapshots on my phone.

Finally.

"Hey, Josh, why can't you hear it when a pterodactyl goes to the bathroom? Because the pee is silent!"

When his laughter calms enough that he's able to breathe again, he says, mock-appalled, "Did you really just dad joke me?"

"Desperate times." I wink.

Suddenly it's as if the joking and the photography and the back-and-forth of the afternoon were all threads in a thick rope, binding us together tighter and then tighter without us realizing it, and now we're tied up in something from which there's no quick release.

Our eyes are locked. The street sounds and clinking of glasses from a nearby gastropub fade into the background. The last traces of humor leave Josh's face, replaced by something more intimate, something . . . delicious. Enticing.

Without breaking our connection, without looking at the phone screen, I snap another few photos. I'll look at them later. If they capture even half of his intensity in this moment, if people online feel half as warm looking at them as I do right now, he'll sell a million albums.

Slowly, I lower the phone.

My mouth is dry. My lips part, ever so slightly, of their own accord.

Josh notices. His eyes drift down to my mouth, then back up. He takes a step forward. Just one.

And I launch myself at him.

Laughing, he pulls me close. The moment our lips touch, my thirst is instantly quenched. I melt into him.

Eventually someone walking past whistles at us, and we pull apart, embarrassed. I'd forgotten for a minute we were in public. I'd forgotten there were other people in the world at all. I don't let go of his hands, though, and he doesn't let go of my gaze.

"I think we're probably done with the photo shoot portion of the day," I whisper, swinging our linked hands between us.

"Thank god." He rolls his eyes good-naturedly, and I let go of one of his hands just so I can mock-punch him. "So if we're done with photos, what's next?" he asks. Before I can reply, he tacks on, "Birthday gift–wise, I mean."

"Right. Birthday gift–wise." I nod. "Next I start work on your new website."

Josh wrinkles his nose. "Are you *sure* you want to do this? It seems like a lot of work."

"I'm looking forward to it. I'm good at this kind of thing," I assure him.

Briefly, I hope he'll ask me more about that. *Why* am I good at it? In what way? And then I'd have no choice but to tell him, because lying by omission is one thing, but lying by *lying* is another.

A few times I've considered just pulling up my profile page and holding it out for him to see. It shocks me, sometimes, how badly I want him to know my whole story. The experiences I've had, the people I've met, the additional three thousand followers I've gained since starting the Treat Yo'Self posts. I want to tell him about the day, back in middle school, that changed my life—the day my mom got me a phone and I opened my app account.

I still remember my first post:

Hi, I'm CeCe. 👏

I didn't realize at the time that I was introducing myself to literally nobody, since I didn't have any followers yet. #fail #Iwasonlytwelve

I want him to understand how, much later, when people finally started to reply, they became my world. They were handles, not names, and avatars, not faces, but they were real. Still are.

I want Josh to meet them. All almost-million of them.

If I were sure he'd like them, I'd introduce them in a heartbeat.

But I'm not sure. And I like what we have. I don't want to ruin it.

And I don't have to. Not right now.

"Well, if you're looking forward to it," he says, "how can I say no? Happy early birthday, CeCe." He grins that beautiful, dimpled grin, and kisses me again.

@SilviaCasRam: The most beautiful girl in the world, @MiaInIndy, came down to Cincinnati today!! And she ate a literal PILE of my dad's chilaquiles, so basically he's now her number one fan. 😄

#selfie #girlswholikegirls #love

CHAPTER 18

Hello, Cincinnati! I type, sitting at my kitchen table the following Saturday. The weeks have been saturated with school and prom stuff and spending time with Josh and Gabby and keeping my app feed current, and I've had zero time to work on my speech. But Josh is on Gabby duty on Saturdays while Marty's at work, and I did all my homework last night, so I finally have some time to dedicate to the speech. *Happy Pride! And thank you for having me! I can't believe it was only two years ago that I attended my first Pride parade, with my girlfriend, Silv—*

Nope. *Delete.*

Why does literally *everything* I attempt to commit to paper almost immediately loop back to Silvie? She's not my girlfriend anymore. Mia's the one having Silvie's dad's chilaquiles for breakfast now, apparently. And, okay, that stings a little, because Silvie's family was like an extension of my own, and I miss them. But Josh is . . . well, Josh is the best surprise ever. Things are good between us—really good. We don't even bicker.

I should be motivated. *Excited.* Like I was when Silvie and I first accepted the invitation. But that was when I knew what I wanted to talk about. Now, no matter how hard I try, or how long I sit in this chair, the page remains blank, the brightness of the illuminated white screen stinging my eyes.

I wish I could text Josh, see if he has any ideas. But he still knows nothing about the parade or speech or any of it.

So I text Mackenzie instead. SOS. Need ideas for Pride speech. Help?

Mackenzie's cis and straight, and this isn't exactly her wheelhouse, so I'm not expecting any major revelations, but she's also smart and level-headed, and I value her input.

I'm surprised when, a minute later, I get a reply.

Think of the speech like a post, only bigger, she's written. Stick with what you know.

That's . . . actually helpful. Thank you, I text back. Why are you awake? It's before five a.m. her time.

Early flight to Tokyo, she says. 🍪

I don't bother asking what she's going there for—I'm sure it's work. She's always being flown places for promotional gigs. Fly safe. Xoxoxo

I place the phone down and bring my fingers back to the computer keyboard. *Think of it like a post*, I repeat to myself. If I were allowing myself to be political, just this once, on the app, and I wanted to tie it to LGBTQIA+ issues, what would I choose to talk about?

Elections is the first thing that comes to mind. Then: *voting*.

Okay. That doesn't feel too far off base. Maybe there's something there. Instead of attempting any narrative structure, I keep listing words and phrases. *Congress. Local. Canvassing. Supreme Court. Public schools.*

When the clock on my laptop screen flips to noon, I *finally* allow myself to scroll over to my website-designing software. I did the thing; I've made some progress on the speech. Now I get to work on something fun.

When I open the email Josh sent me with his bio for the website, I start laughing. Hard.

I'm from Florida. That's it. That's all he's written. It's adorable.

Words come easily to me now as I craft and mold Josh's bio into something a bit more . . . more. *As a young child toddling along the Miami shore, Joshua Haim dreamed of his music one day spanning oceans—reaching, and perhaps even creating, a new generation of classical music lovers worldwide.* He'll roll his eyes at my changes, but I know what I'm doing. When you're a public persona, it's crucial that the picture you paint of yourself online gives people something to grasp on to, to connect with. Too generic and they'll click away, forgetting you before they even had a chance to learn your name.

This morning, I could have sworn time had crawled to a stop. Now the hours pass in a blur.

I text Josh some small questions, like whether he wants his email address on the site or not. But mostly I follow my own creative instincts. That, and I spend an inordinate amount of time gazing at the photos I took of him.

They turned out even better than I could have hoped. The ones from later in the day, when he's relaxed and laughing, are so good I have trouble picking just one for his Spotify and

Pandora artist pages. He emanates such joy and confidence in these pictures that I'm certain every single person, guy or girl or enby, will look at him and immediately want to be his friend— or more. Like when you watch the thank-yous at the end of an episode of *Saturday Night Live* and think how much fun they all seem to be having, and wish you could be a part of it.

The three pictures I took after the laughter had faded, though . . . those are the ones I can't stop looking at. Part of me wants to post one on my feed with about a thousand fire and alarm emojis and hashtag it #smoldering #hotguyalert, but I don't.

I can't help wondering, though—what *would* people online think, if I ever did share Josh's existence with my followers? I haven't gotten the rainbow tattoo because of the prominent online opinion that bi isn't as worthy of the rainbow as gay. If I start openly dating a cisgender guy, what would people say then?

I take a break from working to whisk up a coconut and jojoba oil deep conditioner for my hair. But though my laptop is closed, my brain won't stop whirring. What about the other parts of me that I've kept hidden online? I consider as I apply the mixture to my head and cover it with a hot towel and shower cap. The partnership with Treat Yo'Self has been going so well that a couple times I've thought about maybe leaning into the personal side of things with my other posts too. What would happen if I spoke from the heart on *all* the things that matter to me? If I posted photos not just from my neighborhood and city, but in front of the protest wall in my room? Or if I reposted news stories that I thought deserved more attention? My followers stuck with me through the end of #Cevie. Maybe, now that we've had time to get to know and like each other, they'd stick with me through this stuff too?

It's a lot to get my head around, and I haven't made any decisions either way—if I'm being totally honest with myself, I'll probably *never* work up the nerve. I wish I could do the thing that Josh makes seem so simple, and just not care. But I do care. I want to be liked. I want to be included.

By Sunday evening, the laughing photos have been edited and posted to Josh's new website, along with a bio and contact form, links to buy and download his album, and widgets so visitors can stream some of his tracks from the site for free. It all looks pretty awesome, if I do say so myself.

The only thing left to do is set up his social media.

Mom's working late, so I order a pizza and share a few bites with Abraham as I create Josh's app profile. That part is easy enough. The part that has me tripped up is the question of whether to follow him from my own account or not. What if he clicks on my handle and sees everything I've been keeping from him? If—when—he finds out, I want to be the one to tell him, in person.

"What do you think, Abe?" I say.

He just gazes back at me with an expression that can only mean *More pizza?*

Ultimately I decide that the odds of Josh even logging in to his account are pretty much nonexistent, so I click FOLLOW and become his first official fan. I even feel a little tremor of excitement over the notion of being able to say "I knew you when" when Josh inevitably gets rich and famous and has people creating fan accounts for him online.

I text him that night. After many hours inventing new curse words to shout at my website-designing software, I'm pleased to announce you are now the proud owner of your very own official website, Spotify and Pandora artist pages, and social media account. I add a balloon filter over the screen. Want to meet up this week so I can walk you through everything?

Yes! he responds immediately. I have a late orchestra rehearsal tomorrow, but how about we meet on your birthday? Donuts??

• • •

"Happy birthday!" Josh practically shouts as he comes through the door of Holtman's on Tuesday after school.

"Hey." I grin, hopping off my stool. "Thanks."

He comes right over and, without a moment's hesitation, cradles my face in his hands and kisses me tenderly. "I missed you."

"I missed you too."

"How has your birthday been so far?"

I shrug. "Silvie met me at my first-period class to say happy birthday and ask if I wanted to eat lunch with her and our GSA friends in the cafeteria, like we used to."

Josh's eyes widen, just a touch. "Did you?"

"Yeah. It was okay. Kind of weird. But I was getting sick of library lunches. And she and I are trying to be friends."

"Should I be jealous?" He says it kind of jokily, but I can tell there's some measure of concern in there.

I shake my head. "Definitely not."

He smiles. Holding out his hand, which I grasp, he leads the way up to the counter. "Donuts are on me." I open my mouth to protest, but he stops me with a hand up. "No arguments."

"Okay, okay."

Nikki isn't working today, so an employee named Anthony helps us. Josh has been back to Holtman's a couple times with Gabby, so he knows the ordering drill by now. It's cute how he's all take-charge about it, proudly making his donut selections and ordering us two lattes.

We sit at a table and I open my laptop, walking him through the features of his website. "Your email address isn't posted anywhere on here, but people can contact you through this little form, and the message will go right to your email inbox," I explain. "And then you can reply to them from there. Does that make sense?"

Josh nods. "Thank you again, CeCe," he says. "I can't believe you did all of this in two days. Do you know how long it would have taken me? And it wouldn't have been nearly as good."

I laugh. "I know."

"You were right about the photos too. The new ones are *so* much better."

"Well, the bar was low." I roll my eyes. "But I have to admit the new ones are really good. You look like a model."

Josh's cheeks go pink—he knows how hot he looks. Good.

Everyone should have confidence-boosting photos of themselves.

When I show him how the music-playing widgets work, his eyes widen like he's witnessing real-life magic. "Cool, huh?" I say, pleased.

"Very," he says.

"I only included three tracks, sort of as a sampler, because you want people to buy the album, or at least listen to it on the streaming sites."

"How did you pick which tracks to use?" he asks.

"Oh. I used 'Walkin' After Midnight' because it's my mom's favorite. And the other two are my favorites. But if you want to use other ones instead, it will only take me a couple of minutes to change—"

He shakes his head, cutting me off. "The Mendelssohn and Bartók are my favorites too."

"Really?"

He studies my face like he's seeing something new there, and kisses me. He tastes sweet, like sugar and dough and too-good-to-be-true-ness. "For someone who claims to not know much about music," he says, "you have a good ear."

I shrug. "I don't think I've even heard of Bartók before. I just know how listening to it makes me feel."

Josh picks up a piece of donut but doesn't eat it yet. "How does it make you feel?"

I take a sip of my latte, thinking. "Peaceful? Grounded. Like maybe the state of the world isn't that bad after all. It gives me a chance to breathe and stop worrying, just for a minute or two."

Josh is smiling at me again, and it's like in the photos but better, because he's right here. I could fall in love with this person.

"Anyway," I say, clearing my throat and turning back to the computer screen, "you also have this little area for 'news.' So if you record another album, or book any gigs or anything, you can post updates here. But it's not a blog, so you don't have to constantly keep uploading new content."

"Okay, that sounds good. I don't think I'd be able to keep up with a blog."

I smirk. "You definitely wouldn't."

"Ha ha," Josh fake laughs.

"Actually, speaking of . . ." I click over to his profile on the app. "This is you. @JoshuaHaimViolin. And look, you already have one follower." I point to my handle, which is the only one in his followers list.

I hover over the link, suddenly feeling bold. It's the effect of Josh's presence. His whole being, just like his music, makes me feel like maybe . . . I can do this. I can tell—show—him the truth about me. About my life on the app. And it will be okay.

Appropriate that it's a Tuesday. I like Tuesdays. Elections are held on Tuesdays. Tuesdays can change the world.

I hold my breath. I'm about to click on my handle and bring up my page.

But then Josh's confusion clears and he realizes he's looking at the app. Suddenly his face changes. Gone is the awe at my tech skills, and the glint in his eyes from our teasing banter. His whole expression flattens.

"CeCe, you know how I feel about social media." He puts his donut down and takes a sip of latte as if to wash away the bad taste I've suddenly put in his mouth.

I'd forgotten for a minute there that sometimes Tuesdays are for disappointment. That in elections there are just as many losers as there are winners. But either way, you get your answer.

"I know," I say quickly, trying to regroup. "But you need to be on here if you expect anyone to find you." There's an edge in my voice that wasn't there a moment ago.

"I don't even know how to—"

"Which is why," I interject, "I'll post your updates for you. I'll be your one-woman social media team." I click on the draft of the post I started yesterday but haven't uploaded yet. It's the video I took that day at the plaza. I've captioned it: *New city, same #goals.* And I've tagged a Brahms fan group I found that has a ton of followers. "What do you think?"

He looks unsure.

"I don't have to post it," I say.

"No, that's not what . . ." He trails off, then appears to collect his thoughts. "I just . . . you don't mind?"

"Do I *mind* posting about how awesome you are on your feed?" I'm baffled. "Josh, this is where I thrive."

"Are you *sure*? I feel like I've asked too much of you already."

"Hello, that makes no sense. You haven't asked me to do *anything*. I asked you if I could, remember? For *my* birthday gift?"

He rakes his hands through his hair, making it messier. "You're one of a kind, CeCe."

My legs turn to jelly at that. Good thing I'm sitting down. "Look who's talking."

Josh goofily pops the donut chunk into his mouth.

"Anyway, your password is GabbyMarty305, in case you ever need to log in. Three-oh-five is the Miami area code, right?"

His mouth quirks up at one corner and he nods.

I click POST and the video goes up. If the Brahms fan group watches and reposts, Josh'll start collecting followers within minutes.

I close my laptop. "Do you have anything to do for the rest of the day?" I ask Josh.

"Nope. Dad got out of work early today to pick up Gabby so I could spend the afternoon with you."

"Oh." My cheeks heat in realization. "Oh, Josh, I'm so sorry! I didn't think about Gabby when I asked you to hang out. Your dad really left work early? For me?"

He places his hand on my knee. "CeCe, it's your birthday. He was happy to do it. My family loves you."

What I don't say is: *I love them too.* Even though it's the truth. "That's really nice," I say instead.

"So what do you feel like doing? I'm at your disposal." He does a cute little bow, like he's a valet on *Downton Abbey*.

When I was a kid I used to *love* my birthday. More than

Christmas or the trip to Disney (before it went bad) or summer vacations. Mom would make a cake or cupcakes or pie in the morning, and she and Dad would sing the happy birthday song for me at breakfast. Then, after school, Mom and I would go to the mall, and I'd get to pick out something impractical— platform sneakers or too-heavy earrings or fingerless gloves. The things I always wanted but my parents couldn't afford to buy very often.

Last year, for my sweet sixteen, Silvie threw a lunchtime surprise party for me at school—I walked into the cafeteria and was greeted by cheers and confetti and a candle stuck in the middle of my veggie burger. Even the hairnetted lunchroom staff joined in. We livestreamed the whole thing; it was pretty epic.

Today, though, I just want to be low-key. Famous Birthdays featured me on their homepage this morning, so I spent most of the day fielding happy birthday messages from followers, which was really fun, but a little overwhelming.

Josh is still waiting for an answer. "Honestly?" I say, leaning over to rest my head on his shoulder.

"Always."

"I kind of want to go to Trader Joe's and buy a bunch of junk food and then go to your house and listen to you play for a while. Ooh, and then maybe we can watch the news and shout at the anchors and throw popcorn at the screen?" I peek up at him. "But if you'd rather do something more exciting, that's good too."

Josh is staring at me, his expression unreadable.

"What?"

He blinks a few times, then wraps his arms around me in an embrace so powerful it literally lifts me off the ground. "I can't believe I went seventeen years without knowing you," he whispers in my ear.

. . .

I've never had more fun grocery shopping in my life. We try the free samples, and Josh shows me how to tell if a mango is ripe (which is apparently something all Floridians just *know*). I introduce him to cinnamon bun spread, which is my favorite thing about Trader Joe's, and we stock up on peanut-butter-filled pretzels and microwavable mac-and-cheese balls and cocoa batons and Thai-lime-and-chili almonds and of course gummy bears.

We can't seem to physically stay away from each other for very long. Our hands are linked as we cross the parking lot, and before we even get to the car, Josh stops walking and pulls me close for a kiss. Which leads to a full-on make-out session up against a random car, the grocery bags abandoned to the pavement. This boy is addictive. And I love it.

When we do finally get to his house, Marty greets us at the door, an apron around his waist. "Happy birthday, CeCe!" he booms so loudly the whole neighborhood probably hears.

"Thanks," I say, blushing.

"Hungry?" he asks. "I'm making lasagna."

"CeCe requested junk food for her birthday dinner." Josh

215

holds up the Trader Joe's bags and kicks his shoes off. "We're going to hang out in my room for a while."

Marty nods. "Have fun. Keep the door open!"

Josh rolls his eyes, but when we get to his room, he does make sure to keep the door open a crack. If Marty only knew how many afternoons we've spent in here together with the door closed.

Josh sets up our junk food picnic on his bedroom floor as I grab the fuzzy green blanket from his bed and wrap it around myself like a cocoon. It's become something of a routine for me—the first few times I did it, Josh asked if I was cold. But by now he knows that I just like to be cozy.

He's smiling to himself, big, as he lifts his violin from its open case and begins flipping through the sheet music on his music stand.

"What?" I ask.

"Hmm?" He looks up, all nonchalant.

I scoot forward. "What is that smile?"

"Nothing," he insists. But it doesn't take long for him to give in: "All right. I love that you love that blanket. It smells like you now."

"A good smell, I hope," I tease.

"A *very* good smell. I don't know what all those products you use are, but they're amazing."

I laugh at the image of Josh alone in his room smelling the blanket and trying to figure out what each of the scents are. "People pay a lot of money for that stuff, you know. The lotions and makeup and spray shampoo. I wouldn't use half of it if I didn't get it for free."

I don't realize what I've said until he halts the rosining of his bow and his expression wrinkles in confusion. "Why do you get it for free?"

Oops.

I grip the blanket in my fists, frozen, as my brain wars with itself.

TELL HIM. Now's your chance. Do it.

But if you tell him now, and he doesn't react well, your birthday will be ruined. And it was starting to shape up as one of the best birthdays ever.

You're going to have to tell him eventually, CeCe. This can't go on much longer.

One more day. That's it.

Okay, fine. But don't lie.

"Umm," I say hypercautiously, as if I'm tossing a live grenade from hand to hand. "It's a long story."

"I like long stories."

Of course he does.

Marty sticks his head in the room then, saving me from having to reply. "Wow, that *is* a lot of junk food." I spot him eyeing the cocoa batons, so I offer him one. He takes it and devours the whole thing in three seconds.

"Dinner of champions," I say, holding up a baton of my own and crunching into it.

"Have you ever been to a Reds game, CeCe?" Marty asks.

"Reds?" I repeat. "Like the baseball team?"

Josh quirks his head, apparently also trying to get a hold on the non sequitur.

"That's the one," Marty says. "The great American pastime."

"No," I admit. I walk Abe past the ballpark all the time but have never actually considered going inside.

Marty reaches into his back pocket and produces two tickets. "One of the doctors gave me these today. They're for Friday night. I thought you two could go, if you wanted. Consider it a birthday gift."

I look at Josh. "Are you a secret baseball fan?" I ask him.

He laughs. "Definitely not."

"Do you know anything about baseball at all?"

"Nope. You?"

"Nope."

We read each other's expressions in silence for a moment, and I know we're thinking the same thing: It could be fun, going somewhere together neither of us have been before. An #adventure. Kind of like our relationship. I turn back to Marty. "We'll take them."

Once Marty's left, Josh looks back at me.

"Sorry about that," he says. "What were you saying before? About the free products?"

Sometimes I think Josh is the only guy in the world who truly wants to listen to what women have to say. Usually I love that about him. Usually.

"Can I tell you more about it on Friday?" I ask. I'll explain

everything at the ballpark. No one can be mad while surrounded by nachos and stadium lights, right?

Josh looks confused, and intrigued, but I give him a big,
innocent smile and bat my eyelashes at him exaggeratedly, and
he relents. "Of course." And he lifts his violin and starts playing
the happy birthday song.

@monica1864: Happy birthday, CeCe!!!!!

@DudeWheresMyBar: You're only 17?? How did I not know this.

@Grad_School_Gal_6: You're my #style inspiration, CeCe! Hope you have an amazing day!

@LOL12345: Follow me back pleeeez!

@BirdyFan444: That selfie is 💯 👌

@December_Capricorn: You are so beautiful, CeCe! How are you still single?!

@PeanutJellyButter: Happy birthday to you, happy birthday to you, happy birthday dear @Hi_Im_CeCe_Ross, happy #birthday to you.

@Deaf_And_Fabulous: OMG! It's my birthday today too! Twins!

CHAPTER 19

Mom meets me at the door, candle in cupcake, cupcake in hand. It's funfetti. Her hair is in a messy bun on the top of her head, and she's changed out of her scrubs into jeans and a flannel shirt.

"Sorry I had to work late," she says, lighting the candle.

"It's okay, Mom," I assure her. "I had a good day."

"What did you do?" She holds the lit flame out to me.

I close my eyes, and on the hope that the "influencer CeCe" conversation with Josh on Friday goes well, I blow out the candle.

Friday. In three days, Josh will know everything.

"CeCe? You in there?" Mom waves a hand in front of my face.

I blink myself back into the room. "Yep. Sorry. Just spacing out."

She leans in closer, inspecting my face. "Did you get bitten?" she asks. "Am I going to have a full-fledged zombie daughter on my hands in a couple of days?"

I laugh. Her question reminds me of that time I asked Josh if he was a vampire. Feels like lifetimes ago now.

"I don't smell any rotting flesh," I say, looking down at my bare arms. "I think we're good."

"Excellent." Mom nods. "So? Tell me. How did you spend

your birthday?" We sit on the couch together and pass the cupcake back and forth until it's gone. My stomach whines over the newest injection of sugar.

"Josh and I went to Holtman's and Trader Joe's, and then hung out at his house. He played me music and we watched MSNBC."

My phone chimes from my bag with a new text, but I ignore it.

Mom smiles. "Trader Joe's, huh? If you guys get married, you might have to have the wedding there. It's kind of your place."

"*Married?*" I balk. "Jeez, Mom. Settle down." She sounds like Marty.

She laughs. "I'm kidding, CeCe. You should wait until you're at least thirty to get married."

"*If* I decide I want to get married at all," I remind her.

"Of course." She nods. But for all her progressiveness, Mom's still old-fashioned in some ways, and I know she hopes to someday get married again. She'd have to start dating first, though.

All this long-term-relationship talk makes me think again about Friday's impending moment of truth. If Josh doesn't react the way I want him to, it's very possible I'll be single again sooner than any of us think. My stomach takes another little swoop.

"What?" Mom asks. She must have noticed my expression change.

I sigh. "There's one thing I haven't told you."

Her eyebrows raise.

"Remember that time when Josh was here talking about his family, and I kind of . . . rushed him out the door?"

"Yeah. That was weird."

I nod. "Well, it was because you said something about posting his story online for all my followers."

"And?"

"And . . . he doesn't know about my followers." I bury my face in a pillow to hide from Mom.

I can't see her expression, but after a moment she asks slowly, "What do you mean?"

"I mean, he knows I'm on the app, obviously. And that I . . . like the internet."

"You 'like the internet'?" Mom repeats, as if double-checking she got that right.

"You know, like, I made his website for him and stuff."

"Uh-huh . . ."

I lift my head and blink against the spots as my eyes readjust to the light of the room. "He doesn't know I'm internet famous, or that Silvie is internet famous, or about the Pride speech, or that I get paid to promote products, or . . . anything."

It sounds really bad when I say it out loud like that.

Mom stands up. "*Cecilia.*" She's aghast. "How could you not tell him that? *Why* wouldn't you tell him that?"

My phone chimes again. And again. I need to check my texts.

"You don't understand!" I say to Mom, in full defense mode now. "He thinks all that stuff is stupid and problematic and offensive. He told me so pretty much the first day we met. I didn't want him to dismiss me so quickly, so I kept quiet. And then it turned out we had so many other things to talk about, and it was . . . nice, getting to know each other without the app in the way."

Mom considers this, and her body language goes a little less rigid. Just a little. "Okay, I get why you didn't mention it at first. But you can't build a relationship on lies, CeCe. Keeping things about yourself secret from the other person is a one-way ticket to a breakup." I know she's thinking about Dad, and all the ways he changed over time.

"I know that, okay?" I'm shaking my head. "I'm going to tell him this week. But . . . what if he decides he doesn't like me anymore? That I'm not the person he thought I was or something?" My heart squeezes at the thought.

Mom sighs. Sits back down and holds on to my socked foot. "First of all, I'm not into any of that app stuff either, but you and I manage to get along just fine. Who's to say the same thing won't happen with Josh? But you have to give him the chance."

"Yeah," I say. "I know."

"That said," Mom says, "if he does overturn a table and run down the street screaming bloody murder, or whatever it is you think he's going to do, then . . . did you really want to be with him anyway?"

I roll my eyes. "Well, when you put it like *that* . . ."

"Exactly." Mom crosses her arms, smug.

But not *exactly* exactly. Because, yeah, if Josh reacted that badly, then obviously he's not the right person for me. But it would still be a rejection, based solely on *who I am*. And I'm not sure I can withstand another blow like that.

This is not one of Mom's two-choice situations, though. I *have* to tell him. I should have told him from the start, and I didn't, and now it's way more complicated, and I have no one to blame but myself. And maybe Silvie, a little. Just because it feels good to blame her for something.

"Luckily, there will be no tables to overturn. We're going to a Reds game."

Mom's entire being jolts. "A *what*?" She reaches over and touches the back of her hand to my forehead.

"What are you doing?" I duck away.

"Checking your temperature. Surely 'a sudden interest in sports' has to be a symptom of some rare illness I've never heard of."

"Ha ha, very funny. The tickets were free, and you know I can't turn down free stuff."

My phone chimes again.

"Who *is* that?" I grumble, getting up off the couch and grabbing my bag.

My phone is lit up like a warning flare. A loooong string of app notifications is lined up one by one, and at the top there are seven texts from Mackenzie.

Girl. OMG.

Are you dating a BOY?

WHO IS THIS BOY???

Why didn't you tell me????

Where are you???

You're not on your phone, I guess. Where ARE YOU? Why no phoney-phone???

CeCe, check the app. You're blowing up.

I freeze. What the . . . ?

@CutiePumpkinPie1998: Breaking: @Hi_Im_CeCeRoss has been LYING to us. Just look at these pics. She's not heartbroken. She's not even GAY.

#unfollowCeCeRoss #spotted #Cevie #spreadtheword

CHAPTER 20

I'm going to throw up.

Someone with the handle @CutiePumpkinPie1998 saw me and Josh making out in the Trader Joe's parking lot. They recognized me and they took about a zillion pictures. And they posted them all to the app.

The photos are good quality. You can tell it's me. You can't see Josh's full face, but it's clear he's a guy. You can also totally tell we're super into each other. The person must have been only a few yards from us, but Josh and I were too preoccupied to notice.

I should have been more careful. But the parking lot felt private, and I wasn't exactly thinking clearly.

But who would *do* this? I kind of recall seeing @CutiePumpkinPie1998's handle in my comments before, but not in any way that made me take real notice.

I click on the name. Blocked. All I can see is their profile pic: a cartoon dog.

Whoever this person is, they live in Cincinnati. Or at least they're in Cincinnati today, and happened to need groceries. They know who I am, they have a really stupid handle, and they're probably feeling pretty damn powerful right now.

Within minutes the photos were shared hundreds of times.

Now, little more than an hour after they were posted, they're *everywhere*, shared thousands of times. They've even made their way to the influencer gossip sites.

My hands are trembling, causing the screen to shake, but my eyes refuse to go anywhere else.

#UnfollowCeCeRoss is trending. I'm losing followers by the second. 50,000 gone, in a finger snap.

I have more @s and direct messages than I ever have before. They're accumulating like snowflakes in a blizzard; I can't possibly process them all. And they're all . . . so . . . *mean*.

Some are brutally long and detailed:

> @happyfaceJen: I really thought I'd found a kindred spirit in CeCe Ross. I thought HERE'S someone my age who understands what the queer experience is like. I thought she shared her life with us, not for attention or money but because she cared about us. Because she was one of us. I was GRATEFUL for it. I didn't even care that she did all those sponsored posts, because CeCe said she donated a lot of the money to charity. Was her relationship with Silvie even real? Was ANYTHING she told us real? I bet she's never given a dime to charity in her life.

Others are remarkably short and to the point:

> @Jellybeanqueen1: Screw you, CeCe.
>
> #unfollowCeCeRoss

"Oh my god," I whisper to my phone. "Oh my god. Oh my *god*."

If you're not visible, you're forgotten.

Online, one spark can ignite an explosion.

Those were my words to live by. But this . . . this is all wrong. This isn't how I'm supposed to be seen. Everywhere I look, people are turning against me. I feel each punch as if they're physical.

"What is *wrong*?" Mom's practically shouting in my face, and I realize she's been trying to get me to talk to her for a while.

But I can't look at her, can't form words other than *oh my god*. I sit on the edge of the couch, my spine rigid. My trembling thumb keeps scrolling, my eyes and brain struggling to keep up. Out of the corner of my eye, I see Mom thumbprint her own phone on.

The fire is spreading. Posters are feeding on each other's anger. Each post, each message, each comment seems to be worse than the last.

I don't understand. How is this happening? And how is it happening so *fast*?

I really am going to throw up.

Thrusting my phone at Mom, I bolt down the hall and slam the bathroom door. But instead of leaning over the toilet, I turn on the shower. I don't know why. My whole body is shaking, and nothing makes sense. Without waiting for the water to heat up properly, I strip down and step in, then sink down to the tub floor and sit there as the water pounds down on top of me.

I can't hear anything except water, can't feel anything except water. But I don't see the water at all. The scrolling messages are imprinted on my corneas, taunting me whether I open or close my eyes.

Not really gay.

Lying to us.

I never said I was gay! I wouldn't have! I've always been bi; that was never a secret. Why is everyone acting like I duped them? Why is no one stepping up to say "Um, hey, CeCe's bi, remember?" or even "Let's give her a chance to explain, okay?" I haven't seen a single message like that.

Mom pounds on the bathroom door. "CeCe?"

I don't answer. My mind is still folding in half and turning itself over like a ball of dough.

"Are you all right in there?"

"No," I whisper. But there's no way Mom can hear it.

"I'm coming in!" she shouts, and a burst of cold air hits me as the door opens. She sees me sitting there, arms around my knees, shivering, water dripping from my nose, and runs over.

"Cevie," I say through shivering lips.

"What?" Mom turns off the water and wraps a big, fluffy towel around me. With her help, I stand. Step out of the tub.

"I thought no one would like me anymore. After Cevie."

"Okay?" Mom says, treading carefully.

"I was worried. I didn't want to disappoint them. But . . . they were nice. They understood." I look up at her, blinking

230

away the moisture clinging to my lashes. "People can be nice online sometimes too, you know."

"I know, honey." Mom's walking me across the hall into my room.

"And with the om thing. People called her out, but there was a reason for it. They weren't *bullying* her. They weren't being mean. They were trying to help."

"What's the om thing?" Mom asks.

I'm not in the mood to explain. "But this . . . this is *mean*. Why are they being so mean?"

It's not a rhetorical question. I really want to know. But Mom either doesn't realize that, or doesn't have the answer. She digs through my closet and comes up with an old bathrobe I got as a Christmas present from my grandparents, like, three years ago. I've never worn it, but I shrug into it now and pull the belt tight around my middle. Mom sits in my desk chair and faces me.

"Did you see it?" I ask after a minute.

She nods, but hesitates before saying anything. I can practically see the words she's thinking, floating around in space around her head. *I told you so.*

"This was what I was worried about, CeCe," Mom says with a sigh. "There's so much room for error online."

The word pierces my skin.

"Error?" I shriek. "You think this is *my* fault? You think I did something wrong?"

She's waving her hands in front of her face, shaking her head. "No, that's not what I meant! I meant there's so much room for things to go wrong. For misunderstandings to happen, or lies to be spread, or people to turn against each other. It's not real life, CeCe! It's words and pictures on a screen."

"Yeah, but they're words and pictures I've been able to control," I say, teeth chattering.

This is the exact thing I was scared of. It's why I didn't get the tattoo I wanted. It's why guilt burrowed deep inside me when I started to date Josh. I *knew* admitting to the world that I liked a cisgender guy could get my queer card revoked. It's why I haven't owned up to my new relationship to my friends in the GSA, and it's one of the main reasons I've tried so hard to keep my app life and my Josh life separate. I wasn't only scared of what he'd think; I was scared of what *they'd* think. And now I know.

But I have to defend the app. I have to. It's part of me. "This is some jerk who took and posted pictures without permission. It should be illegal."

"It should," Mom agrees. "But it isn't. And that's part of why the app is dangerous."

I circle the terry-cloth belt around my wrist, then unravel it and do it again. It's soft. Soft is good. I wonder if they make pants and shirts and underwear out of terry cloth. I'd buy it. "It's not dangerous," I mumble, despite the mounting evidence to the contrary.

My relationship with Silvie was one of the realest, most important, most defining things in my life. Do they *really* think I was faking it all?

"Where's my phone?" I ask Mom.

She doesn't reply right away. She just looks at me shiftily, pursing her lips.

I blink at her. "What?"

"What have we always said? If things on the app ever take a turn, and your self-confidence begins to suffer, you're out."

"No way." I shake my head wildly and hold out my hand, palm up. "Give me the phone."

"CeCe . . ."

"I won't go on the app, okay?" Not right this second, at least. "I need to text Mackenzie back."

Two, three, four seconds tick by. Then Mom sighs. Reaches into her back jeans pocket and reluctantly produces the phone. I grab it from her.

Just saw, I text Mackenzie. Freaking out. What do I do??????

She texts back immediately. Who is that guy???

He's just a guy. That guy I got donuts with that time, remember? His name is Josh.

You're dating him? Why didn't you tell me??

It hasn't been that long. He was just a friend at first.

He seems cute. Hard to tell because his face was all over your face. 😊 😊

I ignore that. I know the internet loves a pile-on. But I tried REALLY hard to not ever be at the bottom of one of those piles, Mack.

You've done great, babes. Look at how far you've come from Little Newbie CeCe. 💋

So then why do people keep saying I LIED to them?? I never kept the fact that I was bi secret.

Mackenzie's typing bubble goes and goes and goes. Finally: People see what they want to see. They think they've read the news when they've really only read a headline. They see a photoshopped picture of a celebrity, and believe that person has gained fifty pounds. You know?

Yeah...but how does that apply to me?

Your relationship with Silvie was OTP epicness. It spoke louder than words.

I think about that. It sort of makes sense. People may have heard me say *B*, but they *saw* me and Silvie, and *saw* the Pride announcement, and they decided that meant *L* or *G*.

But what was I supposed to do instead? I type.

Mackenzie sends three shrug emojis all in a row. I don't know, she says. Reminded people more often that you swing both ways?

I hate that term. Especially when used by straight people.

Sorry. ♥ You know what I mean, though. The app is visual. They needed visual reminders.

Like what?

Hmmm...like maybe pics of you with hot dudes?

That's stupid. While I was with Silvie??? I text. No way. And anyway, I've never even LIKED a guy before Josh.

Not true, Mackenzie counters. Noah Lim.

He's not a real person!

He totally is a real person.

You know what I mean—not a real person in my life. Not an actual possibility.

Still though. Maybe if you'd posted more about your not-a-real-person crush on him, this wouldn't be happening now?

That's insane, Mack.

This is an insane life we lead, CeCe. ♥

I read back through the text thread. I love Mackenzie, but her world is hot yoga and clean eating and Icelandic mud baths. She doesn't get it.

So you're saying it's my fault. For not being more "visibly bi," whatever that means.

NO! I'm saying your followers just need a chance to get used to it. This is new for them.

It's new for me too, I remind her.

It WILL blow over, I promise. Drink some water and get some rest. Tomorrow is a new day! ☀

I send her back a heart, and click the phone off.

Mom is still here, sitting at my desk, watching me, concern shaping her features. I hold out my arms. Immediately, she crosses the room to me, and I allow myself to sink into her hug and close my eyes. We stay like that for a long time.

@RoaminRamen: #unfollowCeCeRoss

@MarryMeTylerPerry: #unfollowCeCeRoss

@HollywoodBowlofCherries: #unfollowCeCeRoss

@Meena1717: #unfollowCeCeRoss

@Maaatt: #unfollowCeCeRoss

@PodcastsAndPlaylists: #unfollowCeCeRoss

@GIJaney: #unfollowCeCeRoss

@SmithEllie: #unfollowCeCeRoss

@Texarkana720: #unfollowCeCeRoss

@HTVMT1: #unfollowCeCeRoss

CHAPTER 21

I'm so tired. All I want to do is crawl into bed. But I can't go to sleep yet. I need to post a response.

After Mom leaves my room, I sit on my bedroom floor with my phone in my hands. Maybe this is a "don't engage with the haters" situation. I don't know. I also don't care. If I stay quiet, won't it be interpreted as a guilty plea? *Yup, I've been faking my queerness all along! Ya got me!* ✌️

Problem is, I can't exactly give clarifying details about my relationship with Josh either. People are already trying to find out who he is; any additional information from me would only amp up their motivation. And thanks to me and my idiotic birthday request, he now has an online presence.

Josh didn't choose this. He's entitled to his privacy.

I open the app.

Down another 60,000 followers. *Don't think about it*, I tell myself.

I start a new post. Text only.

Y'all, I'm bisexual, remember? That little "B" between the "G" and the "T"? Search through my page. I've never pretended otherwise.

I'm not in the mood for sugarcoating. And I don't think I've ever used the word *y'all* in my life, but it's better than *guys*, which I'd written at first but then deleted because it might be taken as gender exclusive, and that's the last thing I want right now. I hit POST.

I'm about to shove my phone under my pillow, hopefully for the rest of the night, when a new text message comes through.

Can't wait to see you Friday! It's from Josh.

After everything, it's this that makes me burst into sobs.

Oh, and guess what! he continues. I've gotten 12 new song downloads already! People are really paying for my music, CeCe!! This is all your doing. I can't thank you enough.

He has no idea. He thinks everything is as happy and perfect as it was this afternoon. How am I supposed to tell him the truth now? The prospect of coming clean to him about this part of my life was scary enough. But now I'm caught up in this firestorm, and as much as I tried to keep my app life and my Josh life separate, somehow he's in it too. Am I really supposed to go, "Hey, Josh, surprise! Not only am I internet famous, but there's an angry mob after me! And guess what? You're the reason! Wheee! Play ball!"

Yeah, I don't think so.

This is everything he hates. I can't loop him into it. It's too much.

Before I can talk myself out of it, I write back, Hey, I'm so sorry, but I think I need to cancel Friday. The prom decorations are getting delivered that day, and I need to help unpack everything. 😔

Guilt grips me in its claws. But going to a very public baseball game, where followers of mine might be in the stands, or watching on TV, is definitely *not* what we need to be doing right now. I need time. I need to figure out how to get this all under control before I see Josh again. And it's not a *total* lie— the decorations *are* being delivered that day. We're just planning on unpacking them during the day, rather than after school.

Oh. Ok. I understand, he writes back immediately. Can I help?

Nah. Thanks though. 😒 Please apologize to your dad for me too.

A pause, then: Will do. Get some sleep. Talk tomorrow.

I start to reply *xoxoxo* but delete it. Yup! I send instead.

I check Josh's app profile. The Brahms fan group must have stepped up, because he's already got over seven hundred followers. And apparently twelve of them have bought his songs. And his photos have gotten a *ton* of likes.

It's a stroke of luck that his face isn't visible in the pictures of us kissing. Just to be safe, though, I log in to his account and set his profile to private. It's better if he's not findable right now. No one would expect me to be dating someone with no social media presence.

Once that's done, I go back to my endless stream of notifications, just for a little while. It's my birthday and I'll cry if I want to.

· · ·

I must manage to get some sleep because before I know it, the sun is up.

It's a school day, but I can't bring myself to get out of bed. Maybe if I stay just like this, under the covers, socked feet, no makeup, curtains closed, white noise machine whirring, everything else will stay the same too. If I don't look at my phone, the notifications will stop coming. If I don't talk to Josh, he won't think about me. Like when you're a baby and think the whole world disappears when you close your eyes.

A knock sounds at the door, and as I'm debating whether saying "go away" or saying nothing would be more effective, Mom peeks her head in.

"Good morning," she says quietly.

"The good-est," I mumble.

She comes into the room and sits on the edge of the bed on top of all the blankets and a little bit on top of my leg. "I thought the response you posted was great."

"You read it?"

"Of course."

"I haven't checked my phone yet today. What's the response been like?"

Silence.

With some effort, I push myself up on a little more of an incline and look at Mom. "Tell me."

"It's not *all* bad."

"Meaning what?" My fingers inch toward the phone.

"Some people are defending you now. More than before, for sure."

Okay, that's good. "But . . . ?"

Mom sighs. "I don't know."

Sitting up fully, I thumbprint the phone to life and quickly scan the comments. Mom's right—there are more messages in my defense today than there were yesterday. I guess my rebuttal had some effect, at least. But I'm still shedding followers.

And there are a lot of comments to the effect of:

@Allegra4Ever1: Even if @Hi_Im_CeCeRoss IS bi, by dating a cis guy she's left any semblance of her queer life behind.

and

@XmasElf1225: I don't care how she IDs. She's defected into breederdom. I'm done. Bye. 👋 #unfollowCeCeRoss

The comments that hit the hardest, though, are the ones that go something like this:

@BlueChipppChick: What do you have to say about all of this, @SilviaCasRam?? Did you know she wasn't really in love with you?? Is that why you dumped her?

Silvie hasn't responded to any of them. I wish she would. I turned off the "Silvie has viewed your post" notifications weeks ago, but there's no way she hasn't seen what's going on.

Everything I've built is on the verge of being destroyed, no matter what I do. Silvie's word means more than mine right now—if she defended me, it would help, I'm sure of it.

A probably-terrible idea occurs to me. A nothing-to-lose kind of idea. I push it back for now.

Meeting Mom's gaze again, I nod, resigned. "I'm starting to see what you mean about the app."

Her mouth drops open in shock.

But before she can get too excited, I amend that statement. "I'm *not* going off it, though," I say resolutely. I'll never leave it. Maybe I'm lacking a crucial survival gene, I don't know.

Mom smiles. "I didn't think you would." She stands up. "Breakfast?"

"Just tea, please." My insides are still all tied up, and if I'm going to follow the probably-terrible idea to its probably-terrible conclusion, I'd rather do it on an empty stomach.

• • •

With a deep breath and a second, third, fourth straightening of the bottom of my jean jacket, I ring the doorbell.

On the other side of the door, Silvie's dogs start barking. I always thought it was funny, the way those two little monsters flipped out at the slightest change in their environment. But that was back when I was allowed to just walk in without ringing the bell. Now the barks feel ominous, even though I know they're coming from two teeny Yorkies.

The door opens.

"Oh. Hi," Silvie says, blinking as if to clear her vision and make sure it's really me. She's in her version of pj's: oversized basketball shorts and an off-the-shoulder T-shirt. It's early— seven a.m. But I wanted to catch her before school.

"Hey," I say. The dogs stopped barking when they realized it was only me who'd rung the bell. They scratch at my shins now, tails batting back and forth. I crouch down to pet them, and whisper, "I've missed you guys too." Then I look up at Silvie. "Can we talk?"

"Sure. At school, though? I need to go shower."

I'm not going to school today. Mom okayed it. Everyone will have seen the callouts online, and I just can't deal with their opinions yet. But all I say is: "It's kind of urgent."

Silvie hesitates, but only briefly. "Of course." I expect her to open the door wider to let me in, but instead she closes it, and joins me on the porch. We sit on the steps, making sure to keep almost a foot between us.

"So, how are you holding up?" Silvie asks. She doesn't need to qualify the statement; there's only one thing she could be referring to. I'm thankful for the conversation starter.

"I don't know." I shrug weakly. "Not great."

"Yeah."

I turn my phone over and over in my hands. "How many takedowns have we seen before?" I murmur.

"A lot," Silvie says.

"Right?" I shake my head. "I can't believe I thought they were justified. Not the bullying part, but, like, usually the person had done or said something really messed up, so I thought people had a right to be upset."

"Yeah," she says again.

"But *this*? The pictures with Josh. *This* is what people are mad about?" I look at her. "Do you think it's justified?"

Silvie's gaze meets mine for only a second, then darts away again. My heart pounds so loudly as I wait for her answer that I'm a little worried I won't hear it when it comes. "No," she says finally. "I don't. I think your privacy was violated and people are being jerks." Her response is so simple, like it's a fact. After she says it, she peeks at me out of the corner of her eye and smiles.

That friendly, understanding smile is everything. *Everything*.

I exhale, and tears spot my vision. "Really?"

"It's messed up, CeCe. You didn't do anything wrong."

I sniffle, and I don't fully know if I'm crying out of hurt or relief. "So why are they doing it?"

"Probably because it's fun to point fingers and feel like you're better than someone else for a little while? The internet is a giant clique of mean girls."

"You sound like my mom," I say wryly.

Silvie laughs at that, and it takes a moment for the sound to fade.

"You know," I say softly, "you were one of the only people I told about Josh. I didn't even tell Mackenzie."

She looks surprised. "Why?"

I take a breath. "Because he's a boy."

Silvie tilts her head a little, and I shift my position on the porch step, turning to face her more. She won't judge me if the words that come out haven't been entirely thought through yet. She won't go posting about some stupid thing I said that I wished I could take back immediately.

"It's not that I care about gender," I say quickly. "Like, at all."

She laughs a little. "I know you don't. I've always been jealous of that."

"Really? Why?"

"Because it feels so closed-minded of me to *only* consider women. So not enlightened."

I laugh. "Silvie, you are the least closed-minded person I know. Shut up."

She smiles and shrugs sheepishly.

"Anyway," I continue. "I don't care about a person's sex or gender. But I knew that *they* would care about it. The people online."

Silvie nods. "You've always cared so much what they think, CeCe. I mean, yeah, everyone on the app equates likes and followers with value at least a little. But for you . . . it's at another level. It's your entire support system and your identity and your *family*, in a way. You can't stand to disappoint them."

She's right. Of course she is. I'm glad we're talking without hesitation now; I needed this.

"Do you remember when we almost got tattoos?" I ask her.

"Of course."

"We never really talked about why we didn't. It just kind of faded away."

Silvie runs a hand through her hair. The blue has faded, but the bleached streak still looks cool. "Yeah."

"The reason I decided against it was . . . this." I gesture around us, as if to indicate the entirety of my current situation. "I was scared of pushback. That people would think I wasn't 'gay enough' and didn't deserve to wear the rainbow."

By the expression on Silvie's face, she didn't know that. That doesn't surprise me—Silvie has never worried about the same things I do. "Wow. Really?"

"Yeah. Were your parents really the reason you decided not to?"

She looks off to the sky. "They were part of it."

"What else?" I press.

"I don't know." She sighs. "It kind of felt like we'd be doing it to prove something. Like the two of us getting matching tattoos would be another way to show the whole world how *perfect* our relationship was. Even though . . ." She glances at me quickly, then looks away again.

"Even though we weren't even close to perfect," I whisper, finishing the sentence when I realize she isn't going to.

Silvie nods. "A lot of the time I felt like I was the only one in the relationship who knew it, though. It was a lot of pressure, to match what you were putting out there on the app."

Ouch.

But after a few moments, I understand what she's saying.

"I'm sorry," I say, and it's the truth.

"It's okay." She smiles.

"Can I ask you something?"

Silvie rests her elbows on her knees, and looks at me. Waits.

I shake my hair out of my face and say cautiously, "If I keep feeding the trolls, it will mean one thing, but if I go silent, it will mean another."

She nods.

"But people seem to want *your* input on all of this. And I thought, maybe you could . . . weigh in? To try to put it all to rest? Everyone is more likely to listen to you than me right now." I look at her pleadingly.

Silvie chews on her lip, studying me for a moment. My heart races. I feel like such a jerk for asking, but I'm out of options. Finally she nods once and says, "Okay."

I inhale sharply. "Okay? Really?"

"I'll do anything for you, Ceece. You know that." She grins, and her eyes go all sparkly, and for a split second, it's like nothing ever changed, and we're still up in her room, lounging on that teal rug and taking selfies. "Consider it a belated birthday present."

Swallowing my heart back down into my chest, I cross the invisible line and hug her tightly. "Thank you."

CHAPTER 22

@SilviaCasRam: Hey, guys. As you know, I usually try to avoid controversy, especially controversies that are already in full flame, but there are a few people in this world that I'm willing to brave the fires for. @Hi_Im_CeCeRoss is one of those people. And what's been going on lately isn't cool.

CeCe is bisexual. It's one fact in a long list of facts about her. She and I loved each other very much, and yes, we are no longer together, but no, it's not because she was secretly straight all along. She is free to date whomever she likes, and I hope you'll support her like you've supported me. Xxx. 🖤

@TinaTina1999: No way. She LIED to us, Silvie. 👎

@GayMike_NYC: So bisexual people get to just be in hetero relationships and still claim to be queer??? Doesn't seem right.

#unfollowCeCeRoss

@blueberrystudio: Bi people should really step back and let the rest of us do the talking.

@That_enby_life_37: Bisexuals have it so much easier than trans, gay, and lesbian people. It's not fair.

@MizEllenPatiro: I wish I could take a break from being queer sometimes too, but I CAN'T. Why should she get to??

@SilvieIsMyHero1: Watch, @Hi_Im_CeCeRoss is going to be another housewife married to a dude, insisting she gets to march in the parade. #girlbye

@Books-Are-My-Life: Don't defend her, Silvie! Have some self-respect. 🌈

@CaliforniaGirl1969: Silvie and Mia 4-ever!!! 🖤🖤🖤🖤🖤🖤

• • •

Direct message
From: @TawnAtDawn
To: @Hi_Im_CeCeRoss

Hi, CeCe!
Thank you again so much for your AWESOME work representing Treat Yo'Self! We are so grateful for everything you've done to bring attention to our brand so far.

250

That said, our marketing team has determined that our partnership with you is no longer as effective as it once was, optics- and sales-wise. For that reason, we'll be suspending your sponsorship. If and when things change, we'll reach out to reconnect!

xoxoxo,
Tawny

Direct message
From: @Hi_Im_CeCeRoss
To: @Kathleen_A_Khan

Hi Kathleen,
I'm really looking forward to Pride next weekend! As requested, I've attached my speech for the pre-parade rally. Please let me know your thoughts—I'm open to making changes.

Thanks again for this incredible honor. See you next week!

CeCe Ross
—1 attachment—

Direct message
From: @Kathleen_A_Khan
To: @Hi_Im_CeCeRoss

Dear Cecilia,
Thank you for your message.

As you know, Pride is meant to be a joyous celebration of the LGBTQIA+ community. We've been closely following the developments on your social media account, and unfortunately the current conversation taking place there is the antithesis of the positivity we aim to embrace at our event. Therefore, it is with a heavy heart that we must rescind your invitation to speak and be the grand marshal at this year's event.

Apologies for the late notice.
Sincerely,
Kathleen Khan
Cincinnati Pride

• • •

Josh: Hi. I missed you this weekend. How are you feeling? Still sick?

CeCe: Yeah. 🫠

Josh: Gabby's really into making soup lately, and she put the ingredients for lentil soup into the slow cooker this morning. We'll bring you some after school today! We can all hang out and watch TV. What's it called when you watch a bunch of episodes in a row again? Deep-diving?

CeCe: Bingeing.

Josh: Right. Bingeing. We can do that, if you want.

CeCe: Actually, I think I need to be alone. I mean, I don't want to risk getting you and Gabby sick too.

Josh: Are you sure?

CeCe: Yeah.

Josh: Ok. Maybe this weekend then?

CeCe: Maybe. Not sure. I'll call you when I'm better.

• • •

Direct message
From: @Joseph_E_Ross
To: @Hi_Im_CeCeRoss

Hi, honey. Dinner tonight? My treat. Anywhere you want to go.

Dad

After Silvie's post backfired, I should have seen the rest coming. But man, I really didn't.

Being dropped by Treat Yo'Self stung, but whatever. They'll find someone else to rep them, I won't get any more free swag, the world will keep on spinning.

The unceremonious disinvitation from Cincinnati Pride, though—that one cuts deep. Isn't Pride about celebrating and protecting one's right to identify any way they choose? About cutting down the bias? I guess the organizers just didn't want to involve themselves in my mess.

But the Pride event was the biggest, most meaningful thing I'd ever been asked to participate in, and—though I was nervous, and not totally in love with the speech I'd written—I'd begun to get really excited for it. I was going to talk about the influx of anti-LGBTQIA+ judges who have been appointed to state and federal benches in recent years, and remind people that, apart from running for office, the most impactful action they can take to protect queer interests is *vote*. If not for themselves, then for all of us who aren't old enough or eligible to vote ourselves. It wasn't a groundbreaking speech, but it was *something*. And I was proud that I'd somehow managed to finish it despite everything else going on.

Pride was supposed to be the perfect start to the summer— and maybe even a start to a new public persona for me. An important stepping stone toward being fully *CeCe*, as much online as off. And then those stupid pictures came out, and my one chance was squashed before it was even really real.

I haven't seen Josh since my birthday, which was over a week ago. I told him I had the flu. I just can't be around him. Not right now. It doesn't mean I don't miss him like crazy, though.

At least things at school haven't been terrible. I'm back to eating lunch with the GSA kids every day, and Silvie's been extra nice lately. She's been helping me with my posts—finding new ways to be positive and stay relevant, despite the hate and unfollows I continue to get in response. She even connected me with someone online who runs a dog rescue organization, and I've done a few posts for them. It feels good to be able to call Silvie my friend, and mean it.

As for the DM from Dad . . . It arrived in a fresh message bubble at the top of a fresh page—I haven't heard from him in so long that the app isn't even registering any previous conversation threads.

I have no idea what to make of it.

He knows I'm making money and have achieved some level of fame; that's public information. In the past, each time he reached out, I stupidly hoped maybe he wanted to talk about things, maybe he missed me.

But the thing is, my father only ever reaches out when he wants something from me.

The first two times, he needed a "loan." Just a little money to get him over a hump. He's never been great at holding down a job—he claims it's because he's a "creative type" and can't be boxed in. (His dream is to be a documentary filmmaker.) That's just an excuse, though. It's mainly that he doesn't like taking orders from other people. I mean, anyone who's going to engage in a full-on shouting match over politics with a *child* isn't going to keep his mouth shut when the boss man (or god forbid, boss lady) asks him to do something he doesn't think he should have to do.

The first time, I gave him the money (again, *stupid*), but never saw a penny of repayment. The second time, I held my ground and said no. That's when he changed tactics—the third time he asked me to meet, he promised he wasn't asking for anything. So I went. And he didn't ask for money. But that didn't mean he wasn't after something else. Apparently he'd been working on a new documentary, and thought my connections could get him an audience with a producer. I didn't bother asking what the documentary was about. I didn't want to know.

In that same meeting, he said some pretty horrible stuff about Silvie and her family. Well, about Mexican people in general, but he *knew* what my girlfriend's background was, and he didn't let that stop him. I started to tell him that he should keep that crap to himself, but the branch that had begun to bend and break all those years ago finally snapped clean off the tree. I was done.

I made it as clear as I could, through all the hurt and disbelief and rage, that he was actively and consciously choosing these "ideals" over his actual family, real people in the real world who had already given him too many chances. I'd made a choice to live my life openly and proudly, and family or no, I could not be around his rhetoric anymore.

So I told him he shouldn't reach out to me again—*ever*

again—unless his priorities changed. I'd be willing to have a civil conversation, to try to forge some sort of relationship with him, but only if *he* was willing to put his hate behind him and listen to other points of view.

So far, he's respected that request.

Wednesday after school, I stare at the DM so long, the words start to look strange.

Hi, honey. Dinner tonight? My treat. Anywhere you want to go.

Yes, he only reaches out when he wants something. But he also never uses terms of endearment. And he never, ever offers to pay.

After spending so much time at Josh's house, being around a dad who is fun and caring and accepting and cooks dinner and tells jokes and gives gifts and who *listens*, I can't help it—I want that too. I've always wanted it.

I stare at my phone, debating.

I should say no. Now is not the time for me to invite more drama into my life.

But could Dad be contacting me now because he really has reconsidered his perspective? Could this request to meet be a drop of glue meant to attach the branch back onto the tree? Has he seen the firestorm on the app? Could he want to offer his support?

Despite everything, I can't help hoping.

Okay, I write back, and name the time and place.

@CincinnatiPrideOfficial: Breaking: RuPaul's Drag Race fan favorite contestant to step in as grand marshal of Cincinnati Pride parade, replacing CeCe Ross. Additional details to follow.

CHAPTER 23

That evening, I'm on my way out of the house to go meet Dad, when a car turns into the driveway.

My heart drops. *What is Josh doing here?*

His car door slams. As I catch a glimpse of his expression, my feet grind to a halt, taking my ability to breathe with them.

Oh no.

He's holding up his phone as he walks toward me. "What is this?" he calls. Because he's Josh, it comes out less like an angry demand and more like a plea for clarity. Which is way worse.

"It's . . . a phone?" Playing dumb will only delay the inevitable, I know, but every extra second is a chance to get my explanation in line.

He glances at the screen, which has gone dark, and lets out a grumble of exasperation. He thumbprints the phone back on and holds it up again, stopping right in front of me. "No. *This.* What is this?"

I know what it is, of course. I knew the moment I saw his car. My pulse is racing. He knows. But how much?

"It's my page on the app." @Hi_Im_CeCeRoss, right there, in brilliant HD.

"Yeah, I can see that," Josh says. The phone is still in his hand, his arm jutted out straight toward me, as if he's hoping I'll point out something on the screen that will make it all make sense. "But . . . why do you have a million followers?"

"Eight hundred thousand," I whisper in correction.

He doesn't appear to hear me, which is probably for the best. "Why are so many people talking about you that my *seven-year-old sister* heard about it before I did? Why are there pictures of *us* on here?" His eyes go a little wilder with each question he asks, as if the scope of it all is only just sinking in now.

"Gabby saw it?" I whisper. I didn't count on that.

"Apparently everyone on the planet has seen it, CeCe. I'm the only idiot who had no idea." Josh's face is drawn, and I realize it's not anger I'm seeing—well, it *is* anger, but it's something else too. It's embarrassment.

No. This isn't what was supposed to happen. I was protecting him. I was protecting our relationship.

Shame washes over me, all the way down to the ends of my hair. It's obvious now: I didn't only lie to Josh. I made a fool of him. It wasn't my fault that those pictures were posted, but it did only happen because of who I am. And I didn't even trust him enough to clue him in.

"Oh, Josh," I whisper. My throat burns. "I'm so sorry."

He finally drops his arm to his side. His fingers release, and the phone plunks into the grass. My first instinct is to grab it and check to make sure the screen didn't crack. Nothing worse than a dropped phone. But I stop myself. That wouldn't be helpful.

"Come inside," I say, digging my key out of my belt bag and opening the door again. After a brief hesitation, Josh follows me into the house. But instead of heading to my room, he veers toward the kitchen. Which I guess is as good a place as any.

With shaking hands, I make us two pomegranate spritzers and quickly text Dad. Going to be late. Sorry.

He texts back right away. No problem.

Josh is being cold, Dad is being accommodating. Hello, Bizarro World.

I leave my phone on the counter and join Josh at the table with our drinks. Tension is heavy in the air.

"Why didn't you tell me?" Josh finally asks, his voice flat. His phone sits on the table beside him.

I trace shapes in the condensation on the side of my glass, trying to figure out where to begin. "About which part?" I regret it the moment I ask it. *Stop stalling.* Josh already knows; no reason to dance around the subject.

He rolls his eyes. "Come on, CeCe."

"Yeah. Sorry." I shake my head. Inhale. "So, you know those 'influencers' you hate?" I look up at him. His cheeks are flushed. "I'm one of them."

"I never said I hate—"

"It's fine," I say, cutting him off. "I get it. The internet *is* scary and fake and huge and small, and everything at once. But before I met you, it was my whole life. I'm . . . *part* of something on the app. Or, I was. I don't know how much of my page you read . . . ?"

"A lot," he says. He swallows visibly.

I remind myself to breathe. "Okay, so then you can probably see why I didn't tell you the whole truth at first. I didn't want to scare you away."

Josh frowns. "Why would you think I would be *scared*? That makes no sense."

"Okay, maybe not scared. More like . . ." I search for the right word. "Uninterested? In me. You made it clear you didn't see the value in the app. So I thought if you knew how big a part of my life it was, you wouldn't give me a chance."

Josh sighs. "That's not fair, CeCe. You didn't have any interest in music, but I still shared it with you."

"Yeah." I swallow. "That's true. Josh, here's the thing—I care a lot about what people think. Of me." It's embarrassing admitting this to Josh, of all people. Like confessing to a scientist that you believe in magic. "And . . . it's caused a lot of problems." I clear my throat to get rid of the crack that's turned up in my voice.

Josh nods. He's probably remembering what I told him about my father. "But what about later?" he asks. "After we'd gotten to know each other better? You could have told me then."

"I know," I whisper. "I should have."

Josh spins his phone around and around on the tabletop, staring at the dark screen. "You've posted *so much* since we've known each other. You must have been posting constantly, and I had no idea. There were so many times you could have just told me the truth, but you didn't." He shakes his head. "It must have taken some real effort."

"Yeah." It's all I can say. He's not wrong.

"Gabby said you're *famous*. Is that true?" He's looking at me as if through new eyes. It's horrible.

"Internet famous," I clarify. "It's different from, like, movie- or pop-star famous."

He rolls his eyes. "Whatever. You have a million followers. You make money just from having an opinion."

"Eight hundred thousand," I say again, this time so he can hear. "Followers. It *was* at almost million, until last week."

He studies me long and hard, and for the first time ever with Josh, I feel uncomfortable. I don't know what he's thinking, I don't know what he's feeling, I don't know if my explanation is helping or hurting.

I take a tiny sip of my drink. His remains untouched, moisture pooling around the glass onto the table. "I was going to tell you," I say, scrambling for a positive slant. "Last Friday, at the game. I'd decided it was time."

"It was 'time' to tell me the first day we met," he bites back.

My insides twist. "I'm so sorry, Josh. I didn't know the pictures were being taken, I swear. I'm suffering the consequences too, believe me—"

"Yeah, I saw. *So* sorry that's happening to you." His tone is derisive now, and he levels me with his gaze.

I swallow. "I didn't mean it's equal to what you're experiencing or anything. I just mean I understand what—"

"No, CeCe. You *don't*." He sits back in his chair, his jaw tense. "You're not the one who got pulled into this garbage against your will. At least you *knew* what was happening. If Gabby's friends at school hadn't been talking about you, she never would have seen the pictures of us, and I never would have seen them, and I would have had no clue that this *thing* was happening. Or that my freaking *girlfriend* was responsible for it and didn't see the need to mention anything to me."

"You can't see your face in the pictures," I say, desperate to make it better.

It doesn't work. "*Really*, CeCe?" Josh asks, his posture turning rigid. "That's what you're going with? That it's all totally fine because it will take people an extra five minutes to figure out who I am?" Then, after a pause in which I can tell he's thinking hard: "Who knows who I am? I mean, that it's *me* you're dating? My name?"

It's not the question I expect. But at least it's one I can answer easily.

"Silvie does."

"Anyone else?"

I swallow. "My mom. And Nikki from Holtman's—but she only knows your first name. Mackenzie. She lives in Australia, though. And Silvie might have told Mia, I don't know. And Gabby's friends, maybe? If she told them she knows me? I don't know." It's not a long list, and I know he realizes that too. I *should* have told more people about him—he's my boyfriend. But I'm also relieved I didn't.

"But it's *not* just them," he emphasizes. "*Anyone* who's seen us together, or will see us together, will be able to connect the dots.

They know you, and they'll have seen the pictures. So even if only a few people know now, *everyone* will know eventually." There is no question mark at the end of his sentence; he knows it's a foregone conclusion.

I lean forward. "Josh, I'm going to do as much damage control as I can, when it comes to you and your privacy."

He doesn't look hopeful. "Like what?"

"Like . . ." I hate that I'm going to say this. But I have no choice. "Like eliminating any further opportunities for the public to spot us together."

Something clicks behind Josh's eyes, and I know he understands. It's a stab to the heart, clean through. "That's why you've been blowing me off."

"Nothing makes sense right now. We needed . . . we need some time."

"Time away from each other."

I nod. The effort it takes is obliterating. My palms are clammy. "I guess so. Yeah."

Josh shakes his head. "Did you ever stop to think what *I* needed? I didn't *need* to be your boyfriend, CeCe. I wanted it, but that was when I thought I knew you. There were things I needed, though. I needed a friend, I needed to be able to focus on my music and on my family and on getting through high school without being dragged into . . . *this*. Whatever this is."

"I know. I'm sorry, Josh," I whisper, my lower lip beginning to tremble. "I screwed up."

He holds my gaze, but there's so much hurt in his that I have to blink. Tears I didn't realize were there spill down my cheeks. And then . . . that's it.

Josh scrubs his hands through his hair and stands up. "I'll see you around, CeCe." He picks up his phone and leaves the kitchen, stopping briefly to crouch down and rub Abraham's face. The screen door bounces behind him.

I watch through my tears as he drives away. I should feel lighter—Josh knows. It's all out there now, no more lies or secrets. But I'm heavier than ever. My body wants to crumple to the floor, pulling Abe's warm body against mine.

A new text pops up on my phone. It's from Dad. Got a table in the back.

Another weight stacks itself on top of me. I'd almost forgotten.

On my way, I text back, and grab my keys.

@Joseph_E_Ross: Meeting my daughter @Hi_Im_CeCeRoss for dinner tonight. Proud dad right here! Like to think she got her talent and work ethic from me.

By the way, trailer coming soon for my new documentary short on #immigrationcrisis.

#BuildTheWall #USA

CHAPTER 24

I weave through tables to the back of the café, where Dad's scrolling on his phone.

Anyone would be able to pinpoint us as father and daughter—same nose, same smile, same straight hair. I've always resented how much I look like him; there's literally zero chance it's all been a huge mistake and my true biological father is somewhere out there, ignorant of my existence.

With a nervous breath, I slide into the seat opposite him. He looks just as I remembered, but with a little more gray in his hair. A deeply familiar stranger.

He looks up. Smiles. Clicks his phone off. "Hi, CeCe."

He starts to stand up to hug me, but I remain firmly seated and stop him with a guarded wave hello. "Hi," I say. I was going to say, "Hi, Dad," but I refuse to give him a single thing he hasn't earned.

"What can I get you?" He nods at the big menu above the counter.

"Just a mint tea, please." It's dinnertime, but I'm not hungry.

He gets up to order, and in the two minutes before he returns to the table, I start to second-guess this whole thing. I should have canceled, after what happened with Josh. At the very least

I should have asked Mom to come with me. But didn't even tell her I was coming here. I used to think I could handle anything on my own. Maybe it was true, once.

Dad places a mug in front of me and sits back down with his own mug of coffee. I square my shoulders and keep my gaze trained on the steady flow of steam, using the tea bag's string to dip it in and out of the water. I wish I had a tether like that attached to *me*, with someone holding on tightly, making sure I don't sink or float away or keep bobbing long after the water has gone cold.

"How have you been?" Dad asks, wrapping his hands around his mug. His cuticles are jagged and scabby, like he's been picking at them.

It's the dumbest question I've ever heard. Isn't it obvious? I've been very much not okay.

"Fine," I say, set on single-syllable words only.

"How's Maggie?" he asks.

"Mom's fine."

"And Abraham?"

"Fine."

He nods. "Good."

We lapse into awkward silence. He's probably waiting for me to ask how he's doing. But I don't want to.

The air between us grows thick and sticky, more uncomfortable with each passing second. I can't help but notice the glaring lack of a "happy birthday." In a flash, I'm certain he's forgotten that I'm seventeen years and one week old, that him reaching out today was pure coincidence. I don't really care, ultimately—it just adds an extra layer to it all. Like a blurry filter over a terrible snapshot.

We don't know each other, my father and I. And the parts we do know, we don't like. I take a sip of tea just to have something to do. It's too hot, and my tongue goes a little numb from the shock. Even more perfect. I almost want to laugh.

"School is out soon?" Dad asks, and you can practically hear the effort it took for him to dig the question out of his stock of old, dusty standbys.

I nod. Take another scorching sip. "Three more weeks." There. A whole phrase. Hope he appreciates it.

"You're a junior now, right?"

Part of me thinks he shouldn't have to double-check; the other part of me is impressed he got it right. "Yup. One more year."

He sits back in his chair, pulling his mug closer to him with one hand. "Does your boyfriend go to school with you? Or does he go somewhere else?" He says it so casually, his face so placid, that it takes a second for me to remember this is not a normal question. Not from Joe Ross.

My eyes narrow. "What?"

"Your boyfriend. Where does he go to school?"

There are those warning bells again. "I don't have a boyfriend." *Not anymore.*

Dad nods congenially. "It's not official yet, then?"

A lighter flickers to life, deep in my gut.

271

I'm pretty sure my father stalks my app page regularly. He may even have a Google Alert set up for my name—back before I cut off contact with him, he was always bringing up things to me that he couldn't have possibly known about otherwise.

I hate that he has this access to my day-to-day life; I've always hated it. A million strangers seeing me in my pj's or knowing what I think about scrunchies being back in fashion? Great! My father getting access to that same information without having to work for it? Infuriating.

"Are you referring to the photographs that were taken of me and my friend without our permission?" It nearly kills me, but I manage to keep my tone level the whole way through that sentence.

Dad ignores the question, and asks one of his own. "Are you saying they weren't real?"

"No, I'm not saying they weren't real. I'm asking if that's what you're choosing to bring up right now." The lighter touches its flame to the walls of my belly, and the fire spreads.

Dad holds his palms up. "No need to get defensive, CeCe. We're just having a conversation."

I push my tea away. "Did you bring me here to talk about those pictures?"

I'm fully expecting him to say, "No, of course I didn't. I brought you here to talk about XYZ." I don't know what XYZ is, but surely it's something other than those damn photographs.

But apparently the man still has the ability to surprise me. "Actually, yeah," he says, shrugging. *Yeah? YEAH?* "When you broke up with that girl, I'd hoped it was a sign that you'd seen the light. But I wasn't sure until I saw the pictures."

SEEN THE LIGHT?

The words are gasoline on the flames. I'm actually surprised it took a whole ten minutes to get here—roaring blaze of fury is the level my father and I exist at.

"WHAT?" I shout, gasping for air, not caring who can hear us, not caring who around us might recognize me, not even caring that people could film this on their phones and put *that* online too. "You're not seriously doing this right now." I shake my head in disbelief.

Dad's looking back at me all innocently, like there's nothing horribly, terribly wrong. "I'm trying to tell you I'm *proud* of you. Can you just let me say it?"

"Proud of *what*?" I shout. "What are you *talking* about?"

He blinks, actually confused. "You'd asked me to stay away unless I found a way to embrace who you are, did you not?"

I gape at him, struggling to play catch-up.

"Did you not?" he asks again.

I nod once.

"And did I not respect your wishes?"

I nod again.

He puffs his chest out a little, like he's proud of his ability to follow a simple directive. "Then you and that girl split up—"

"Her name is Silvie," I say through clenched teeth.

"And you started seeing this boy. I knew you'd come around, CeCe."

He is worse than the thousands of anonymous, faceless trolls online. I want to scream, cry, throw a chair, throttle him, do whatever else I can in a desperate reach for him to *see me*. Seventeen years and one week of fighting, of pushing, of protecting myself, of using the scalding pain to do something *good*, to give back to the world in a way that feels positive.

After the divorce, I closed off a part of myself. I stopped shouting. I'd thought it was self-care. I'd thought it was productive, me being kind to myself, allowing myself an injection of happiness.

But the truth is, it wasn't proactive—it was *reactive*. It was because I was broken. Beaten down, so tired, so utterly sick of losing. The energy left me; it flew off and found a new home.

When I stand up and open my mouth, all that comes out is a weak croak. "This was a bad idea."

I could scream at my father until I'm purple in the face, and nothing will ever change.

"CeCe, please," he says. "Sit down. Let's talk."

There are people watching; I can feel their eyes on me. I should save face, sit back down, act pleasant. They have no context for any of this; my father is acting calm, and *I* seem like the irrational one.

But that's the thing, isn't it? No one ever knows the whole story. They think they do, because of a few overheard words or some stolen photographs, but they don't. And when you keep forcing a curated, fake life into their feeds, day after day, hour after hour, they never will.

Suddenly the bubble I've been floating around in pops. It's been stretched too far. I blink away the residue.

Maybe these people, online and in this too-public café, don't *need* to know the true story. Maybe that's not what's important. They're going to see what they want to see anyway.

Maybe what's important is the few people who *do* know you, faults and mistakes and all, and love you anyway.

Tears fill my eyes again and begin overflowing. I let them do what they will. It doesn't matter. None of this matters.

"Sorry," I say lightly, looking around at the people working and dining at the café. "Father-daughter disagreement. You know how it is."

I'm exposed. I'm a mess. But I don't sit down. Bracing my hands on the back of the chair, I lean in so that my father is the only one who can hear me.

"Bye, Dad," I say, and with the words comes a sense of peace I haven't felt in ages.

I can't just keep going as I have been, hoping things will magically get better. I hoped Silvie's post would make things return to a place of shiny, happy placidness; it didn't. I hoped my father wanted to see me because he missed me—that we could find a way to have the tiniest fraction of what Josh and his dad have; we can't. I hoped Josh would understand why I kept so much from him; he didn't. Of course he didn't.

I need to stop hoping. I need to *do* something.

CHAPTER 25

Direct message
From: @Hi_Im_CeCeRoss
To: @Kathleen_A_Khan

Hi again Kathleen,
I'm writing to follow up on the status of my appearance at this weekend's Pride celebration. While I understand your team's decision to go in a different direction, I recently had a burst of inspiration, and I rewrote my speech from scratch. The updated version is attached.

I believe the community may be interested in what I have to say. If you agree, I'd be happy to present the speech at the rally.

Thank you for your time and consideration.

Cecilia Ross
—1 attachment—

• • •

It's Saturday. Pride day.

Three days ago, mere hours after I turned the tables on my father and walked out on *him*, I sent Kathleen my revised speech. I couldn't get the words out of my head and onto the page fast enough. Once it was all down on paper, I knew this was the speech I should have written all along. I had a feeling Kathleen and the other organizers might agree, so I took a chance. I'm so glad I did. It would have sucked to miss this.

The city has been transformed. News vans are everywhere you look. Helicopters hover high above the streets, getting overhead shots. Security scrambles to redirect traffic as eager participants overflow onto streets that haven't been officially closed off. Shouts and cheers and chants and bursts of music rise up from the massive crowd at Fountain Square, where the pre-march rally is taking place. Thousands of homemade signs bob above people's heads, declaring IF BEING GAY IS WRONG, WHY ARE WE ALL SO FABULOUS?? and BINARIES ARE FOR ELECTRONICS. Rainbow flags wave in the breeze, as far as the eye can see.

"Are you ready?" Silvie asks, straightening my necklace. Her voice cracks on every syllable.

"Are you crying?" I ask, aghast. "Don't worry! It's going to be great."

She nods, sniffling. "No, I know. I'm just really glad we ended up here."

I know she means "here" both literally and figuratively—and I'm glad too. Here and here are both very good places to be.

Mia's standing a few feet away, listening to the current speaker and giving Silvie and me space to talk. Mia and I met for the first time this morning; she's really nice.

"Thank *you* for being here," I tell Silvie now. "I'm not sure I could do it without you."

Her smile is a freshly charged battery to my operating system. "Of course you could. You've never needed anyone, Ceece."

I shrug. Maybe, maybe not.

My phone, gripped tightly in my palm along with my printed-out speech, chimes with a new text.

Rooting for you today, babes! Mackenzie has written. *Watching your and Silvie's feeds for the livestream—will repost as soon as it goes up. I'm so excited I even skipped bedtime!* 💪 😵

I shoot her back a long string of heart emojis.

Kathleen Khan comes over, headset on. "We're about two minutes out," she tells me. "Once the current speaker is done, she's going to introduce you. Any last-minute questions?"

I've never been more ready to give this speech, but I do have one question. "You'd said you were going to send me the livestream link?"

Her expression jolts as she remembers. "Right. Sorry about that. Organizing this thing has been a logistical nightmare; it slipped my mind."

"No worries. Just wanted to share with my followers." And one non-follower.

She takes out her phone and types something. "Of course. Thanks for the free press." She looks back at her phone as the text goes through. "There you go."

"Cool, thanks." The link comes through to my phone, and I quickly share it on the app and air drop it to Silvie. She shares it on her page too.

Then I open a new text window. *Hey, Josh. I know you want nothing to do with me, and I promise I'm going to respect that. But here's a tiny piece of my apology. Hope you'll watch. Xx*

I attach the livestream link, and send it off.

"Thank you so much," the speaker on the stage, an attorney who represents trans and nonbinary kids involved in court battles with their school districts, is saying. "And now it is my great honor to introduce today's next speaker, social media sensation Cecilia Ross."

Sensation, huh? I'm not sure whether to take that as a compliment or not. I wonder how long it took them to land on such a perfectly nonspecific word.

Silvie beams at me, and I drop my phone into her palm for safekeeping. I don't need it right now. "Break a leg," she whispers.

With a final check to make sure my outfit—a pink jumpsuit with blue heels, green bangle bracelets, red-and-purple beaded necklace, orange headband, and my little yellow house earrings—is in place, I step onto the stage to the sound of applause. It's very possible that I look more like a clown than an esteemed speaker at a major political event, but I don't care. I wanted to wear every color of the rainbow, so that's what I'm doing. I actually think it looks pretty good. Maybe I'll set a trend.

I stand behind the podium and look out at the crowd. There are *so* many people here. And not just any people—my people.

The livestream cameras are trained on me from every angle.

"Hi, I'm CeCe," I begin. "That was my first ever post to the app: *Hi, I'm CeCe.* It's my handle too. It was the start of everything. So it feels fitting to begin that way now." My hands are shaking; the stapled speech pages wobble in my hands. I place them carefully on the podium, and take a steadying breath. "I'm CeCe, I'm seventeen, I'm from Cincinnati, Ohio"—cheers sound at the mention of our city, and I smile—"and I live my life online. Openly in lots of ways, but not entirely. I've edited myself a lot over the years, with the goal of getting people"—I wave my hand across the sea of faces—"to like me. To think I was special."

I squint out at the crowd. Mom and Silvie are beaming up at me from the very front row. Their presence means everything.

"But despite my obsession with making my life look perfect, things still went haywire. I still made people upset, and I still lost a ton of followers. If you missed the backlash somehow, go ahead and search 'unfollow CeCe Ross.' And make sure you have popcorn at the ready. I like to put chili powder on mine."

That gets laughs. A whole roar of them. The sound relaxes me a little bit more.

"So. I'm going to try something new," I go on. "I'm going to stop curating my posts so much. From now on, when I go online, I want to be the real me. And I'll warn you—sometimes that means I'm going to be loud, and political, and angry. I *will* piss people off, I guarantee you. But, hey, why should my online relationships be any different than my real-life ones?"

More laughs. I wonder if my dad is watching this. If he is, I hope he can tell how much love and support and joy is emanating from this little section of our city today.

"For now, though, I want to focus on one aspect of my identity. One small but important sliver of who I am." I pause. Take a breath. "I'm bisexual. Always have been, always will be. I am that *B* that people rarely talk about, even online, even today. Bisexual people in opposite-sex relationships are often seen as straight, and bisexual people in same-sex relationships are usually presumed to be lesbian or gay. But bisexuality is a thing, and it's time we do better at recognizing and celebrating that."

Some applause ripples through the sea of spectators, and even more than the laughs, this boosts my confidence.

I hold my chin a little higher. "Years ago, when I was first working through all this stuff, it was the online community who helped me realize that bisexuality doesn't look the way most people think; it's very rarely a fifty-fifty split of feelings for boys and feelings for girls. It can be different for everyone—some bi people are ninety-nine percent attracted to the same sex, some are ninety-nine percent attracted to the opposite sex. And guess what? It still counts!" I look up to see a few people nodding. "The definition gets even more delightfully muddled when you acknowledge that there are far more than just two genders out there, and that, yes, bi people may be attracted, or not, to individuals who identify as any or none of them."

I turn the page. "This idea was simultaneously a revelation and a redemption for me. Personally, I tend to be primarily attracted to female-presenting individuals, and that was something I was aware of even as a preteen. But I kept getting hung up when it came to landing on a label. I thought, well, it really does seem like most of my crushes and daydreams are directed at girls, so that must mean I'm gay? But oh, hey, there's that one boy who I wouldn't mind having as my boyfriend. So . . . straight, then? Bi didn't feel like a real option. Not until social media told me it was." I glance at the crowd again; they're still with me, still listening. *Whew.* "Isn't it funny how our brains work sometimes?" I ask them. "How susceptible we are, even at a young age, to such internal and societal biases? Funny, and also depressing."

"Preach!" a man in the crowd yells.

I grin and look back at my speech. "A little later, through those same online conversations, I realized that those 'percentages'—the 'I am seventy-eight percent attracted to A, nineteen percent attracted to B, three percent other,' or whatever—aren't set in stone. How could they be? The human heart and brain are complex organs. Figuratively speaking, they can change and grow just as much as any other aspect of a person. And when you consider the other big factor—that attractions vary based on the people the attractions are directed toward—all bets are off. When you're bi and single and looking, you never know who your next partner may be, or how they'll ID. You can guess, based on your feelings and your history, but you can't be sure. You're just a person looking for love. I think that's pretty cool."

For the first time, I notice the bottle of water sitting on the podium. I take a sip and continue. I'm not shaking as much now, thankfully, but it's really hot up here, under the sun and camera lights. I hope my makeup holds up.

"When I came out to my mom at thirteen," I continue, "*bisexual* was the word I used. When Silvie and I were getting to know each other, it's one of the first things I told her about myself. If I was misleading in my interactions on the app, I apologize. My friend Mackenzie says you can't just say something a couple of times online and hope it sticks—you need to keep the visual going. Maybe that's true. But either way, despite all the self-censoring I've done, I would *never* lie to you. And if I'm being honest, which is the point of this whole speech, it hurts that you'd so easily believe I would."

I pause again. Clear my throat. "When Silvie and I broke up, I couldn't see myself falling for someone else—ever. I loved her so much." I dare a glance at Silvie in the audience, and she shoots me a smile. "I thought we'd be together forever, even though, intellectually, I'm aware that the odds of marrying your high school sweetheart are incredibly low. So imagine my surprise when, after Silvie and I broke up, I did start to have feelings for someone new. Someone who happens to be a guy. I wasn't seeking it, but there it was." I try to push the image of Josh out of my mind. If I dwell too much on whether he's watching right now or not, I'll lose my nerve and never get the rest of the words out. I take another sip of water. "We kissed, as you saw. I'm not going to apologize for that. And you should never have to apologize for kissing the person *you* like either, no matter what gender they are. Provided that it's a consensual kiss, of course!" I add.

Another page turn. "The thing about social media is it's never the full picture. Feeling like you know someone's life isn't the same as actually knowing it." The corner of my mouth lifts, and I shrug. "If you follow me, you know my dog Abraham's scruffy face and screwy teeth, you know my favorite food is gummy bears. You know how embarrassed I was to come clean with my Spanish-speaking girlfriend about that D-minus I got on my

Spanish test last year. You know my mom is camera shy. But did you know I have a father too? One who doesn't support a single thing I stand for? Who is so ashamed of me that he would rather I were someone else completely? No. I know you didn't. Because I don't share that stuff."

I quickly swipe my fingertips under my eyes just to make sure there's no moisture there. Yes, the irony of wanting to look okay while talking about wanting to look okay is obvious. But I'm leaning in.

"I didn't need you all to tell me that if I dated a guy it wouldn't fit in with what the world saw and knew and loved me as. That fear has been deep inside me for a long time."

My ankles start to wobble, and I realize my knees have been locked this whole time. I try to focus on my breathing and let my muscles relax, like the voice in that meditation app says to do.

"I've had a lot of time to think recently," I say, "and I keep coming back to the same questions: Why do I suddenly have to define what it means to be bi? Why do people's identities and relationships need definitions anyway? If you like me, and follow me online, why not choose to be happy that I found a moment of happiness?"

The atmosphere in the crowd grows quieter than it was a few minutes ago. Thousands of people are giving me their undivided attention. It's unreal. But I need to focus.

"I've noticed that many of the people who were mad about me dating a guy are the same people who claim to be open-minded and progressive about sexuality and gender," I continue.

"Yes, I understand that cisgender bisexual and pansexual people have the luxury—the privilege—of being able to date someone of the opposite sex and fly under the radar in everyday society, whereas gay and lesbian people, and many trans people, don't. I agree it isn't fair. But does that mean bi and pan folks don't get to wave the flag quite as high or shout quite as loud? Do they not get to stand up and be counted too? What happened to supporting and welcoming someone no matter how they ID or who they love, regardless of if it fits a certain narrative?

"And what if the guy I kissed, the guy whose life has been turned upside down because of all of this, weren't cisgender? What if he were trans, or male-presenting nonbinary? What if he were cis but *I* were trans or nonbinary? Would that be 'better'? Why or why not?"

I pause to let that sink in, and find Mom in the crowd again. "My mom and I do this two-choice thing. Like: Paninis or wraps? Bike ride or a walk? Beyoncé or Halsey?" The crowd laughs appreciatively, and I go on. "A two-choice system can help things feel easier. But there are more than two choices in life. There are *infinite choices*. And even when something isn't a choice, like sexuality, you have a choice in how to talk about it." Mom is wiping her eyes, a wadded-up tissue clenched in her fist, and my heart squeezes.

"Yes," I say, turning another page, "the labels, the letters in the initialism—LGBTQIAP—are important. Owning your identity is powerful, and something to be proud of. But sometimes the letters also box people in, put margins and rules on what does and doesn't qualify, and who is and isn't welcome, and what someone who IDs a certain way is and isn't allowed to do."

I realize I know the rest of the speech by heart, so I don't need to look down at the paper anymore. I glance out into the crowd, meeting the eyes of person after person. "Remember when I said I'd felt like I needed permission to ID as bi? Well, I'm giving you permission to be you, if that's something you need. No matter who you are, or how you identify, or who you do or don't love, or how confident or confused you may be, you are doing great. And your story belongs to you alone, whether you decide to share it with a million people"—I smirk—"or no one."

A pocket of applause bursts from the audience, and I bask in it. They're not only listening, they're agreeing.

"If you do decide to share your story, or it gets shared against your will, there are people who aren't going to understand. *And that's okay.* It's not your job to change them, or change *for* them. I'm not saying to not care what other people think—of *course* we care what other people think. But maybe we should put *more* weight on what the people *who love us* think."

My chest starts to feel tight; I've been breathing way too shallowly. I make myself take a long, deep breath before looking straight into the camera. "I didn't follow that advice. And I hurt someone important. Someone who, until he met me, thought a 'ship' was just a big boat. Someone who doesn't know how to take a selfie, and who has a remarkable ability to leave the planet for the length of a single song."

I look down, suddenly feeling too exposed, too vulnerable. But I can't stop now; I'm almost there.

"My time on the app has given me more than I could have ever dreamed of. But it's taken some stuff from me too. Through it all, here's what I've learned: Be proud of who you are, online *and* off. Kiss and flirt however your heart tells you. And when you find someone who loves you for you, whether that's a romantic partner or a friend or a caregiver or a child or the teacher who runs your school's GSA, put your phone down, let them see you with hashtag no filter, and give them a hug."

The last word reverberates through the mic, and . . . that's it. Speech over.

I can't quite believe it.

The crowd erupts into deafening cheers, and I stand there, my grin stretching my face, my heart beating a million miles a minute. Silvie and Mom and even Mia are jumping up and down, clapping and screaming. By the time the next speaker comes onstage, the adrenaline has worn off. I'm shaking again and there are spots in my vision as I make my way down the metal backstage steps.

But then Mom is there, and Silvie is there, and their arms are tight, tight around me, and it's all okay.

When we part, Silvie hands me my phone. "You have a text from Mackenzie," she tells me. Bypassing the mile-long list of app notifications, I open the text message.

It's just one word: Rockstar.

@Michelle1717: Thank you, CeCe!

@FashionDistrictMaven: OMG what a QUEEN.

@LondonCalling888: That's what we call a #truthbomb

@TinaDancer: CeCe Ross is my hero.

@IronWaffle: Talk about a hater smackdown! Go, CeCe!

@CurlyHairDontCare901: That person who posted those pictures is a miserable human being. What a jerk.

@JackInTheMountains: I hope all my friends on here are following @Hi_Im_CeCeRoss because she's an absolute goddess.

@DanielMontez71: Cecilia Ross for president!!!!!!

CHAPTER 26

The speech repeats in my dreams all night, and when I wake the next morning, it takes me a minute to remember that it wasn't all a figment of my unconscious imagination. I really did that. I really stood up there and bared my soul. That was *me*.

Mom and I watched the video three times last night (she kept pausing it and rewinding her favorite parts), but I have a feeling it's going to take several hundred more viewings to feel real.

I slide my phone out from under my pillow. Maybe Josh has seen the video by now.

No texts. No missed calls.

My heart drops. I didn't think the speech would be a guaranteed ticket to reconciliation or anything, but I'd hoped it would at least bring us a step closer.

I just wish I knew if he's watched it. I should have never taught him how to turn off the read receipts on his texts.

The scent of fresh-brewed coffee, mixed with something sweet, wafts into my room, and I glance at the clock. It's eight thirty a.m. Mom should be at work by now. I pull a loose sweatshirt over my head, grab my phone, and head down to the kitchen.

Mom's there, singing along with the radio, pouring blueberry batter into muffin tins.

"What are you doing home?" I ask, shuffling over to the coffeepot and pouring a healthy serving into the Rose Apothecary mug I got from Treat Yo'Self.

Mom grins. "I took the day off."

"You took yesterday off." Not that I'm unhappy she's here; far from it.

"I told them I needed a whole weekend with my daughter. I figured we could both use a mellow day at home after yesterday."

I smile. "Sounds perfect."

After the rally, Mom and I marched in the parade for a little while, but I was feeling drained from the speech and needed some time to decompress, so we peaced out early. Anyway, there were tens of thousands of people there—I knew no one would miss me.

Mom slides the muffins into the oven, then joins me at the table. "So," she says, nodding at my facedown phone. "Have you checked the app yet?"

I shake my head. I stayed off the app for the rest of yesterday, which at once felt freeing and very wrong. But as part of new-and-improved CeCe, I'm thinking I might try to keep taking mini-vacays from the app every now and then. Not for too long, of course, but it would be nice to get to a point where a half a day without checking my notifications doesn't feel like the end of the world. We'll see.

"I think you should." It's literally the first time my mother has ever told me to log on to the app.

Curious, I thumbprint my phone on and tap the app icon. I'm back up to 925,000 followers. That's an increase of over 100,000 since yesterday! And I have so many messages it takes me over a minute just to speed-scroll to the bottom of the list. Almost all of them are overwhelmingly supportive. What a difference a day makes.

I look up at Mom. "Wow."

She's nodding, teary-eyed and proud. Just like yesterday. "Your story really resonated with people, kiddo."

When the muffins are done baking, Mom piles them onto a plate, I crank the AC, and we snuggle under the couch comforter with Abraham. In between episodes of *Killing Eve*, I work my way through my app messages.

One of the first ones that came through, time-stamped yesterday before my speech even ended, was from Tawny, inviting me back to Treat Yo'Self. I thank her profusely—and politely turn the offer down. I really did mean what I said yesterday—it's pointless trying to please people who don't actually care about you, who drop you at the first sign of a challenge—and I'm trying to follow my own advice. To Tawny's credit, she says she understands, and will continue to root for me in my endeavors.

I'm not going to stop doing sponsorships—at least not while I still have the opportunity to do them—but I think from now on I'm only going to rep products and companies that have a direct political or environmental impact. There's an app that gives voters easy-to-understand info on their candidates—maybe I'll reach out to them. What's the worst they can say? No? I've heard worse.

It takes most of the afternoon, but I get through all my notifications and messages. Yeah, there are a handful that say "Shut up, CeCe" and "Stop trying to be relevant," but for the most part, it does seem like the bulk of the haters have lost interest. #win

I take a selfie on the couch with Abraham. I'm wearing zero makeup, and my skin looks pale and bumpy. I can't help myself—I soften and smooth it out with filters before posting. But, hey, at least I own up to it in the hashtags. Baby steps.

> @Hi_Im_CeCeRoss: Back home with Honest Abe. Thanks for having me, Cincinnati Pride. 🖤
>
> #filter #brightness #structure #warmth

It feels surprisingly good to be so transparent—to be honest just for the sake of being honest, and to not let my fear of how it will be perceived stop me. And I didn't reread the post twelve times before posting.

Quickly, before the momentum fades, I add a few new frames to my stories, inspired by the signs and chants and other speeches at Pride:

We may have achieved marriage equality in the US, but we cannot and will not rest until every citizen of every country around the world has the right to marry the person they love, openly and without fear of retaliation from their family, community, or government!

and

Protect trans youth! No more bogus "bathroom bills"!

and

Fight back against the rampant voter suppression efforts in this country! Know your rights! Register to vote, volunteer, and offer a ride to a neighbor on election day!

When the likes start pouring in, a mangled sob of joy escapes me. Abe's head pops up at the noise, and he gives me a look that says, *Shhh! I'm trying to sleep!*

When Mom takes Abe out for his walk, I pull my fuzzy socks up to my knees, put on the British *Office* to stream on the TV, and allow myself a few moments to be an observer. To let the #lastdayofschool kid pics, pretty lattes with steamed milk art, and early summer vacation photos wash over me. Snapshots of lives lived. Today, I'm very liberal with that little heart button.

As I scroll, a single hashtag keeps popping up in my feed, and I slow down to pay more attention. *#definebi*. Define bi.

Hmm. I do some quick recon.

I didn't realize it at first, because many of the posts didn't tag me, but it seems the video of my speech has had a chance to circulate. People who didn't see it live are catching up today, and sharing it to their feeds. But they're not just sharing the link and moving on—they're telling their stories too. About being bi. About what it means to them.

My heart hammers as I try to absorb it all. People from all corners of the internet, of all genders and ages, of different nationalities and careers, are sharing their experiences with being bisexual.

@AnnieLennoxFan73: I'm a cisgender woman married to a cisgender man. Everyone assumes I'm straight. My husband and close friends have known for a long time that I'm bi, but this is the first time I'm saying it publicly. HELLO, WORLD, I'M BI!!! #definebi

@This_Is_Nathan1981: When people see me with my boyfriend, they think we're just another gay couple. When they find out I've had girlfriends, they think it was a long time ago, before I was out. Wrong on both counts. #definebi

@DenverLennon: I'm genderqueer and bisexual. My parents are confused by my labels, but they're trying. #definebi

@KnittingChampion12: I'm cis. My girlfriend is trans. We are both bi. #definebi

@DebbieInCali: I'm straight but my teenage son is bisexual. We have a Pride flag sticker on our car, right next to our stick-figure family. #definebi

@LibrarianJulie: I've only ever dated men, but I kissed a woman once and it was amazing. I'd like to do that again, maybe. Does that mean I'm bi? Help! #definebi

> @JEC1234: I'm single, bi, and looking. I'd like to date someone else who IDs as bi. Maybe it's you??? #definebi

> @NYGiantsGuy27: I'm a dude in a monogamous, happy, hetero marriage, but…sometimes I think dudes are hot too. My wife and I bond over it. #definebi

This is *the best thing ever.*

I follow the hashtag closely; there are more posts every minute. Some of them tag me, but most of them don't. The movement is taking on a life of its own, and I suspect many of the people participating haven't heard of the speech or know who I am. Somehow, that makes it even cooler.

"Yes!" I leap to my feet on the couch cushions and shout, "*This* is why I love the freaking internet!"

Mom hurries in from the foyer, Abe's leash still in hand. "Now what?"

"Look at this!" I show her my phone.

"'Define bi'?" She scrolls through a few of the posts, and looks up at me, wide-eyed. "You did this."

I shake my head. "I didn't!"

"No, you did, CeCe," Mom insists. "It's because of your speech!"

"Nope." I jump off the couch, scoop Abe into my arms, and dance with him around the living room. "My speech helped start it, maybe, but this is its own thing."

I can't stop smiling. When I was first figuring out my identity all those years ago, the internet helped me. Ever since, I've wanted to give back. But I always questioned how far one person can really push the needle, even if they do have a million people watching and listening and . . . judging.

No, it's *this* kind of movement, this wave of honesty from *lots* of people—hundreds, maybe even thousands—coming together to share their experiences, and what being bi looks like to *them*, that is huger than anything I ever could have hoped to achieve. The posts are all incredible. Each unique, special, and powerful. And they're going to live online forever. This can help kids and teens and adults coming to terms with their own identities. It can help shift the cultural perspective as a whole.

The freaking app, man. Gotta love it.

#socialmediaforever

• • •

That night, I'm helping Mom with dinner, listening to her hum and trying to pinpoint what song it is, when another notification pops up on my phone. I take the opportunity to put the knife down and wash my hands. I need a break anyway—my eyes are so watery from chopping onions it's like I'm seeing the kitchen through two fishbowls.

"Still trending?" Mom asks as I wipe my eyes on my sleeve.

#Definebi *was* still trending at last check, but that was an hour ago. "Let's see . . . yup!"

Mom pumps her fist in the air.

I swipe over to my notifications.

And I stop breathing. There's one new mention, from a

handle I know well, but who has never tagged me in anything before. @JoshuaHaimViolin.

I'll need to click on the tab in order to see the post in full, but I'm frozen in place.

"Mom," I whisper.

"Hmmm?" She finishes turning over the potatoes and closes the oven again.

"Josh."

She whirls around to face me. "What? Where?"

"Here." I hold up my phone. "He tagged me." My voice is still quiet, as if it doesn't want to risk scaring the notification away.

"What did he say?"

"I don't know." My heart is rattling my rib cage. The phone is shaking in my hands.

"CeCe! Go look!"

But what if it's bad? What if a private declaration of being done with me wasn't enough? What if he's posting about our breakup to the app, just to make sure I get the message?

When I don't move, Mom grabs the phone from my hand and clicks on the post herself. I watch her expression carefully as she takes it in, whatever it is. But a slight uptick of the corner of her mouth is all I get. Wordlessly, she hands the phone back to me.

"What?" I demand. "Tell me."

"Just read it, CeCe." She's sort of smiling now.

Okay, *fine*.

I look at the post.

@JoshuaHaimViolin: Hi. I don't know much about this app, or social media in general, and I had to have my little sister, @GabbySingsXoxo, show me how to post this. (She also made me tag her, and asked me to ask you to follow her.) Anyway, I'm not good at this stuff, but someone I care a lot about is, so I'm giving it a try.

You may have seen the photos of @Hi_Im_CeCeRoss kissing someone recently. Well, that person was me.

I gasp. Look at Mom. She nods, full-on smiling now. Speechless, I go back to the post.

CeCe kept my identity secret, which I appreciate. But I've had some time to think. And then I watched her absolutely incredible speech. (Which you should do too, if you haven't already—you can find it <u>here</u>.) She was so brave, and inspiring, and I thought, "Maybe I can be brave too."

So. Yeah.

I don't know what else to say, except CeCe Ross is a really special person, and I'm glad to have her in my life. If she's still in my life, that is.

Oh, and if you're following me, it's probably because you like violins and classical music, so I'll try to post more of that stuff on here. With Gabby's, and hopefully CeCe's, help.

Okay. That's it. Bye.

The accompanying photograph is a selfie of Josh. It's backlit by the setting sun, so his face is a little out of focus. His eye line is all wrong—it's clear he's looking at his reflection on the screen, not at the little camera lens. But it's adorable.

And then I notice the background in the selfie. It's very familiar.

I thrust the phone at Mom, run to the front door, and throw it open. There he is, on my porch, phone in hand like he didn't know what to do with it after hitting the POST button.

"Hi," Josh says sheepishly, his cheeks pink. "Did I do it right?"

With a yelp of joy, I jump into his arms. He drops the phone, sending it clattering to the porch floor, and holds me tight against him with those strong, violin-playing arms.

"I'm sorry," I say into his chest.

"No, I'm sorr—" he begins, but I cut him off.

"Stop. It was all me. You did nothing wrong." I lower myself back to the ground and gaze up at him, taking his hands in mine. "Well, except the framing of that selfie—was that your first selfie ever?"

"No," he says, mock-indignantly, then laughs. "Close, though."

I smirk. "Don't worry. I'll teach you a few tricks."

"Hey, don't get too excited; it's not like I'm going to be posting all the time now. That selfie was a one-time-only occurrence."

"I see." I nod sagely. "So you're saying you did it for me."

"I did." He says it without even a hint of hesitation or uncertainty. He searches my eyes. "I care about you, CeCe. A lot."

We're close, standing here on the porch hand in hand, but I

lean in just a little closer, on my tiptoes. "I care about you too."

"You do?" He leans closer still.

"Very, very much." My gaze is trapped in his. It's only now, in this moment, that I'm realizing how much I'd been holding back from him, like I'd been wearing too-small, tightly laced boots our entire time together. But now that he knows everything, the laces have been loosened, the boots kicked off. I can stretch and wiggle my toes. It feels incredible. And now we can really *run*.

"Well then, okay," Josh says.

"Okay what?" I ask. Our mouths are so, so close now, our breath mingling, our voices mere whispers.

"Okay, maybe I'll let you show me a *few* selfie-taking tips. If it's that important to you." He allows his lips to lightly graze mine. They're soft, and warm, and smiling. But he's waiting for me to take the next step, and I don't—not just yet.

"Deal," I say. "But don't worry, they can be just for us."

He pulls back the slightest bit at that, to get a better look at me. His brows are raised high.

"What?" I blink innocently. "You don't have to post *everything*, you know."

Josh laughs. "I think I've heard that somewhere."

I can't hold off anymore. I grab his shirt, pull him to me, and kiss him. Properly this time, with no secrets, no one watching, and not a single care about what anyone else thinks.

"So there's this thing," I murmur when we eventually come up for air.

"Thing?" he echoes, his forehead touching mine.

"Yeah. This prom thing. It's on Friday."

"Ah. A *prom* thing."

"The tickets were on sale last week, but I didn't buy any because . . . well, you know."

Josh nods, and squeezes my hand as if to prove to us both that we're here, together. I squeeze back.

"It's too late to buy them now, but the GSA planned the whole thing, and Silvie and Jasmine are working the door, so I'm pretty sure I have an in."

"You and your connections." Josh rolls his eyes teasingly, and I pinch him on the arm.

"Do you want to go with me?" I whisper.

"Yes," he says without missing a beat.

"People's eyes will be on us," I warn him. "And pictures will probably end up online."

"I know."

"And you still want to go?"

"For you?" he says. "I'm all in."

My lips tug into a giant grin, and the rest of my body follows, rocking up onto my toes to kiss him again.

Delicious, delirious minutes later, our mouths part, but our hands are still linked. I turn to open the screen door. "Come on in," I say, nodding inside. "We're making dinner."

And Josh follows.

@Hi_Im_CeCeRoss: World, meet my boyfriend, Josh. Josh, meet my world. 🖤

#prom #love

CHAPTER 27

"Wait, is this . . . ?" Josh stops dead in his tracks and gapes around in wide-eyed wonder as we enter my school's gym. "Are we in the freaking *Vienna Musikverein?*" He stares at me, uncomprehending.

"Oh my god, I forgot to tell you!" I laugh. "The prom theme is An Evening at the Symphony. Inspired by . . . well, *you.*"

I do a slow twirl, admiring the GSA's handiwork. We busted our butts all week to transform the sweaty gym into one of the most famous concert halls in the world. Some of our members voted for Radio City Music Hall or Walt Disney Concert Hall, since the general student population would be more likely to recognize those, at least by name. But those of us who pushed for the lesser-known but much more ornate Musikverein prevailed. And I'm so glad we did.

The gym walls are draped in gold-hued panels silkscreened to look like windowed tiers, gold statuettes guard the room's perimeter, faux chandeliers hang from the ceiling, and DJ Karima K has her table set up on the stage, under the silver pipes we hung to resemble an organ.

At first I wasn't sure if we totally pulled off the classy concert hall aesthetic, especially since the center of the gym is taken up by the dance floor and dinner tables, rather than rows of red seats. But Josh recognized it immediately, so I'm going to count that as a job well done.

"I can't believe you did this," he says, still stunned.

The ballad that was playing when we walked in transitions into a pop song with a strong beat, and I have to raise my voice so Josh can hear me. "The DJ even promised to play some symphony music during the dinner hour," I tell him. "What do you think?"

He shakes his head, amazed. "It's incredible."

"Yay." I grin.

We stand there gazing dopily at each other for a long moment. Josh looks super cute in his maroon slim-cut suit and skinny black tie. His hair is just as messy as ever. I'm wearing a short, black, lacy tutu dress, with black tights, red heels, and red lips. The shoes are from a new company I'm working with that makes gorgeous footwear out of recycled water bottles. And the dress reminded me of something Madonna would have worn back in the '80s—which I felt was the perfect vibe for a night of dancing. My hair is pushed back from my face with a black plastic headband, making it look even shorter than usual.

"Um, I didn't realize there would be *supermodels* here tonight," a familiar voice says, and I turn to see Silvie, hand in hand with Mia, both of them admiring Josh's and my outfits.

"Hello, you two should talk!" I say. Silvie and Mia look

amazing in their dresses. Silvie's hair is newly dyed all blue, and Mia's is done up into an intricate series of braids with silver strands woven through. "Hashtag beauty queens."

I notice Silvie and Josh eyeing each other shyly, and realize a half second too late that though they've followed each other on the app, they haven't met in real life yet.

Nerves flutter within me as I turn to Josh. "Josh, this is Silvie and Mia. Silvie and Mia, this is Josh."

They all shake hands, and, somehow, it's not nearly as weird as I would have thought. It feels . . . right. It occurs to me that we kind of *are* on that double date I thought would never happen.

"You like my dress?" I ask Silvie, gesturing to my tutu. "I found it at a thrift shop."

"I love it!" The lights of our makeshift ballroom dance in her eyes. "You *have* to let me photograph you in it for my book."

"Really?" I didn't expect that.

"For sure."

"Okay." I smile, touched that she'd want me in the book, after everything that's happened. Guess we really have come a long way. "Cool."

Another fast song comes on, and Josh looks at me, then at Silvie and Mia. "So . . . anyone else dying to get on that dance floor?"

"*Definitely,*" Mia says. With a quick wave, she and Silvie dance over to where Jasmine and her boyfriend, Peter and his boyfriend, and the rest of the GSA are already jumping up and down to the pulse of the song.

Josh takes my hands and steps closer to me, leaning down for a long kiss. "Ready to be dazzled by your boyfriend's epic dance moves?" he says over the music.

"Always," I tell him.

Hand in hand, we make our way through the throngs of my classmates all dressed up in suits and dresses and jumpsuits, and that one guy in a kilt, and find an open spot on the dance floor. Josh immediately starts moving with the music in that joyous, uninhibited way of his—his exaggerated wiggles and kicks are the complete opposite of the understated step touch of many of the other kids around us.

I'm aware there are people watching us, their curiosity pulsing in time with their dance steps. But without hesitation, I join Josh, leaping and jumping and waving my hands high above my head. It's so much fun.

As the up-tempo music fades into a slower song, Josh does one more particularly goofy spin, and then seamlessly pulls me in close. As we sway together, his heartbeat pounding against my cheek, it hits me, with all the certainty in the world, from my headband down to the heels that I kicked off halfway through that last song: I'm in love with him.

For the next several hours, Josh and I laugh and kiss and dance our hearts out. And we even take some selfies too.

But I only post a few of them. Most, I save just for us.

@Hi_Im_CeCeRoss: I did it!!! I got the #tattoo I've wanted FOREVER. I drew it myself and had the tattoo artist trace my sketch. And I went to get it done alone—it was scary, but it felt right to do it that way, because this tattoo is for no one but ME.

I hope you like it, but it's okay if you don't. Because I LOVE IT. 😃

#rainbow #ink #pride #definebi

ACKNOWLEDGMENTS

This book has more bits of me, Jess, sprinkled into the narrative than anything I've published before, and that feels right, considering it's a story about influencers—people who put themselves out there for the world to see every day. This stuff isn't easy, and I am in awe of all of you!

Thank you to every single person at Scholastic—in particular Aimee Friedman, David Levithan, and Olivia Valcarce, but also many, many others!—for believing I could do justice to this story and for your invaluable help along the way. Lots of gratitude as well to Jessica Reyman for your super-smart insights. And a huge thank-you to my agent, Kate McKean, for, you know, everything.

As always, hugs and thanks to my mom, Susan Miller; my friend/extra set of eyes Amy Ewing; everyone in my life who's lent an ear during the ebbs and flows of my publishing journey; and each bookseller, educator, and librarian who has ever recommended one of my books.

This is the first novel I wrote since becoming a parent, and it would have been literally impossible without the help and support of my partner, Paul Bausch, and our daughter's daycare providers. I also have to give a shout-out to the baristas of Brooklyn—especially the ones at Muse Cafe, Edie Jo's, and Brooklyn Perk—for your endless supply of oat-milk lattes.

And to my kiddo, Markéta, to whom this book is dedicated—keep shouting, girl. The world is listening.

ABOUT THE AUTHOR

JESSICA VERDI is the author of *And She Was, What You Left Behind, The Summer I Wasn't Me*, and *My Life After Now*, and co-author of *I'm Not a Girl*. She is a graduate of the New School's MFA in Writing for Children program and lives in New York with her family. Follow Jess on Twitter and Instagram at @jessverdi.